I0739985

THE CARPENTER'S MOONS

A Tale From Beyond The Mirror Of Eternal Blissfullessness

DAVID JAMES HOLLAMBY

Copyright © 2016 by David James Hollamby.

All rights reserved. This book or any portion thereof
may not be reproduced or used in any manner whatsoever
without the express written permission of the publisher
except for the use of brief quotations in a book review.

The Author and Publisher can be contacted via email –

thecarpentersmoons@gmail.com

This book is a work of fiction. Names, characters, places, and incidents either are the
products of the author's imagination or are used fictitiously. Any resemblance to actual
persons, living or dead, businesses, companies, events or locales is entirely coincidental.

First Printed in 2016

ISBN: 978-0-9980755-0-1

Cover design and illustration by Sara and David Hollamby

For My Wonderful Wife.
You Are My Inspiration.

PROLOGUE

Join me if you will as we peek into a little known world where flattery and suspicion are equally prevalent yet frequently misplaced. A world that runs on its own prehistoric steam yet shares more similarities with ours than The Masters of The 2nd Floor of Space Ideology would care to fathom. This, my friends, is the most wondrous of worlds… The Wholeverse.

In this world you are just as likely to see an over confident, yet unpretentious Montar (think horse) blatantly cheat at a game of Farmer, Scientist, Smuggler (just to avoid clearing up after Ruby & Johnny's annual Siesta Soiree) as you are to gaze longingly into The Mirror of Eternal Blissfullessness and see a faint glimmer and skewed reflection of your own world.

Now where were we? Oh yes that's right, the annual Siesta Soiree! Wait I hear you cry… or perhaps faintly wonder… it sounded like you just referred to a horse-type creature that seemed rather human in my estimation! You would be right my friends. Right indeed! Probably in fact more right than Chester would care to admit. Fear not my friends. For Chester, Ruby and Johnny were and are; and probably will be (much to Johnny's chagrin) inexplicably linked by the business and home they all share.

To picture Chester you have to let your mind wander and dwell upon The Cliffs of Calamity while also leaving it open to the possibilities of the mundane being delightful. As we haven't yet explored the aforementioned Cliffs I will instead provide a cruder yet hopefully splendid image for one and all to muster! I'm sure you can picture a horse. Great! Now how about a Shire horse? Think bigger and broader. Now add in an ego… color him brown with a cream mane and add some hair towards the hoofs… a deep voice… a penchant for self-righteousness… and oh, did I mention… picture this horse standing upright and more often than not dressed in shorts and a sleeveless top.

Ruby and Johnny you might consequently picture as quite boring by comparison. Far from the truth that would be however. Much akin to human beings from your world, they both lead very interesting lives. In the midst of one of Ruby's more morally ambiguous missions their paths would intersect. Equally enamored and lost for words Johnny was taken aback by her brashness. They first met when 'The Peculiar' (Ruby's Interstellar jet; as ordinary as it is exquisite) needed a tune up. Having failed to meet three separate deadlines, Ruby decided to go down to the shop herself and have a stern talking to with this laid back workman. Following a tall tale of wild excuses and wilder lies, Ruby suggested Johnny should buy her a drink to make up for the delays.

Johnny has never been honest enough to share that he'd finished up the work in barely any time at all since there was really nothing much wrong with the craft. Instead he'd chosen to remark that she was just so striking in both personality and looks that he'd found a drive and determination he hadn't previously realized he possessed… at the same time Ruby has still not been honest enough to share that not only was this incredibly obvious… but more importantly, the bill even now, remains unpaid!

How these three came to own The Carpenter's Moons and how they still live together is a story of intrigue and eccentricity; running the gamut from wild excursions on wondrous planets to the regular dramas and dangers of Interstellar Pub ownership!

MONTARS OF MASS DESTRUCTION

To his patrons Chester is more than just the bar-keep at the fabled 'Carpenter's Moons'. He is also the fella you don't mess with at closing time. The friend that you never quite feel comfortable commenting upon their vanity… after all, how accurate can a reflection in the bottom of a glass really be?

Chester, you see, has the remnants of his ancestor's memories flowing through his blood. It is a gift his kind is generally grateful for, but it is not without its drawbacks. Waiting in line for the latest Missile Force sequel while having the compulsion to pat down every individual is one thing… tackling an unlucky young lady for an over-zealous sneeze is quite another! He was however, glad for that 'incident'… or as the paper called it – 'Sneezey Business'.

Montars are a magnificently intriguing race. Most have heard of their legend yet few truly understand their legacy. To human beings they would probably all look quite alike… then again, if you were to meet a Montar I very highly doubt you would be spending time comparing and contrasting facial features between one and the next. There is no denying their similarities to horses from your world. Standard colors and variations are present; black, grey, brown, white, purple etc.[1] Generally speaking they stand around 8 feet tall. If you're wondering how appearance differs between males and females, let me offer German Shepherds as a base. To the untrained eye it might be hard to tell the difference, but there is most certainly a distinct femininity to a female Montar. Yes, it is also true they stand on what you might refer to as their hind legs… their arms and chests both naturally and incredibly muscular… yep, no need for gym membership here!

Education is an interesting concept when your first Passing[2] in class involves acquainting yourself with the weight of an assortment of weapons. Now don't get me wrong, every Montar is supervised at all times… trips to the local Emergency Room are far from frequent. In fact I am obligated to note they are so rare the Nursery in question no longer has the Emergency Room on speed-dial. Play time is strictly regulated and observed and all soldiers will graduate with the necessary training to fully jump-start their inherited ancestor's memories. I must apologize… since a certain exposé that I won't mention… and a

---

[1] I kid… although there was once a purple Montar, he was most certainly not born that way. The Montar in question was an exceptionally gifted athlete… fame would quickly go to his head and following three consecutive MVM (Most Valuable Montar) awards, alcohol and addiction resulted in a hugely ill-advised full-body tattoo… purple was the color… flowers were the pattern… and regret was the feeling!

[2] A Passing is a measurement of time based on one complete revolution of whichever planet your unfortunate soul is lost upon.

specifically intrepid investigator's actions… the Press' freedom to comment on matters of this nature has been very closely monitored. Let's just say a certain student definitely did not swallow a certain 'toy'… and the teachers absolutely did not panic… and without a shadow of doubt, the student was in no way picked up and thrown a mighty distance just before screams of -

"Everyone get down! He's gonna blow!"

This would be completely unprofessional and clearly speak to the abilities of the Generals… sorry 'Teachers' at this Nursery… so again that didn't happen… just remember that… I mean don't remember it… you know what I mean.

It wasn't that Chester didn't enjoy his time at the Nursery. When every lesson massages an unspoken drive within you, it in fact feels quite natural. Imagine how hugely reassuring it is when all of your lessons feel familiar. It's a feeling much like déjà vu… at least I'm told. You see Chester hails from a race that are as unique as they are single-minded; the beneficiaries of an ability that came to be known as 'Intuition'. Memories are passed down through the generations like a mysterious wrapped present... you don't fully comprehend its contents but are reliably informed it will be sensational once you finally open it.

Now don't get me wrong… Chester isn't walking around suddenly feeling awkward and uncomfortable while remembering his Great Grandparents shenanigans that night underneath the Moons of Verisimilitude[3]! It's more like a muscle memory of sort. Imagine the techniques of a martial arts class feeling natural and flowing with ease during your very first lesson. Imagine anticipating a person's actions

---

[3] …On second thoughts, let's not elaborate on this night… I don't think anyone is really craving extra detail here!

before they occur. Intuition is truly heightened when eons of observed behavior are built into your subconscious. Oh and if you're wondering, Montars do make incredible lovers. He may not have to relive Great Gramps' shenanigans blow-by-blow but Chester has never been caught complaining about the inherent perks of lifetimes of trial and error! While we're at it, was that really where your mind went? If so I'm glad you've joined us! It appears you really do need to spend some time staring into The Mirror of Eternal Blissfullessness!

Although the skills Montars acquire can be mastered with relative simplicity, there is still a need for learning to take place… hence, the first goal of the Montar Training Planet (MTP)[4]. In order to be utilized effectively each skill essentially needs to be turned on. Your body may feel natural performing certain actions but those actions still need to be taught. A martial arts style only takes a few hundred Moments[5] to walk through and be mastered, but when you start to contemplate all of the distinct styles available … and then add on a complete study of all weapons as well, the time necessary for training becomes somewhat longer than you might first anticipate.

Call me forward if you will… call me daring perhaps… but I suggest there might be a question floating at the front of your mind right about now… regarding the terminology used by the Montars… specifically 'Nursery'. Well, I'm very glad that's where your mind was headed. If that question wasn't lingering, no worries… you'll now have the answer without even needing to think of the question! As it goes, 'Nursery' is actually quite accurate. Inheriting your ancestor's memories includes a wonderfully useful side-effect. Logically enough, a brain that

---

[4] Montars for some reason have an overwhelming love for acronyms… One of the Nursery's favorites is ACWIAFW - A Clean Weapon Is A Functional Weapon… otherwise known as the worst mnemonic ever.

[5] A Moment is relatively similar to a minute in your time but far less precise. Far more reflective of the flow and boundaries of a… 'moment' in time.

receives a multitude of memories from previous lifetimes develops at an almost alarming rate… alarming to your average Joe that is. Before their first Birthpassing, Montars are sufficiently articulate to be shipped off to the MTP. While a regular brain takes time to uncover the patterns necessary for comprehension, a Montar is born with these organically pre-loaded. Combined with their uniquely rapid growth, you're left with a set of students whose appearance and faculties greatly belie their minimal age.

The MTP is a relatively small planet. The Nursery itself is the only structure of note. An expansive property, it is large enough to house and train all of the Montar fledglings. Cabin after cabin housing ten Montars apiece fills the expansive base… Locating their assigned cabin is a learning exercise by itself!

"Two hundredth and first cabin on the right, sixteen rows down."

Outside the encampment an incredibly dangerous world awaits. How dangerous? Imagine jumping into a gator pit, wearing a suit made of veal… carrying a placard that says - 'Gators are slow, stupid and BTW, green is my least favorite color!'… in spite of being illogical, that would be a highly preferable option to venturing outside into the wild terrains where all manner of deadly and petulant beasts[6] lurk. The native dangers of the planet, does however provide a perfect setting for all manner of training exercises!

Chester would go on to Graduate as one of the Nursery's most successful soldiers… sorry… students. It wasn't without some hiccups

---

[6] Yes you did indeed read that correctly… they are beasts of the petulant variety! I'd say that's only fair… following the planet's colonization by the Montars, they rapidly became the primary targets for hunting practice!

though. Let me take you back to the first Passing of Quantas, a season on the MTP when all the leaves on the trees decide their time clinging on is over and depart their home. I should take some time to clarify here. If you're taking for granted that I'm just saying the leaves start to fall in a needlessly extravagant way; you are mistaken my friend. The leaves quite literally get up and go! You see the trees on the MTP are actually incubators for a fascinating race of beings that I'll have to elaborate on at some point; perhaps over a beer or two at the Carpenter's Moons. Suffice to say once they grow large enough, their cocoons fall to the floor, open and out walks a fledgling Ramdil[7], ready to take on the world!

Chester had become quite the Stallion amongst his peers. He was always first to finish the assault course; traversing snow-swept mountain ranges, fighting through the Serpent Waterfalls[8] and correctly naming all of the tag-lines to the first 10 Missile Force movies. It was a grueling camp yes, but they always included trivia. The Elders quite quickly discovered that although Montars make incredible soldiers they aren't the easiest to keep in line. After the inaugural class of Graduates went on to follow careers in film and stage, the Elders realized they needed to implement a new strategy. This is where the need for a second

----

[7] Oh, go on then… I'll share a little more now. Ramdils are born fully grown. Having exited their cocoon their growth from then on is only spiritual. The lack of energy expended on physical growth may well be the reason behind the development of their unchallenged spiritual prowess. It is said they have the ability to communicate with nature itself… but then again who could really argue with them?... you're very unlikely to be able to disprove a Ramdil's reading of a tree's emotions…

[8] Don't worry… they aren't as scary as they sound… as long as you get along 'swimmingly' with snakes! The only way to traverse the falls is by a path that runs partially behind the cascading water… students must maintain their balance and composure while a charming mix of water and snakes flow around their eagerly escaping legs!

goal for the MPT arose. Each Montar required taming. For some reason modern culture trivia seemed to mitigate the recruit's need for independence and alleviated their creative drives. 'Breaking in' a Montar proved exceedingly fruitful and ensured the Nursery only produced the most compliant of soldiers; fully committed to the fate 'destiny' had laid before them. Oh… before I forget… yes that is a Montar in Missile Force 5: Missile Party[9], jumping out of a Birthpassing cake.

"I hope you enjoyed your party! Now it's time for your presents!"

How these endless sequels keep getting green-lit I don't know…

However… back to Chester! On this first Passing of Quantas his need for independent thought had really started to present itself. One of his instructors had asked the soldiers… students, to tackle one of the aforementioned trees before the cocoons could reach the ground.

"Soldier; tackle that tree! I want to see roots!"
Chester began to run but faltered. "Why?"
"Excuse me Son! What did you say?"
"I asked why" Chester responded.
"It is not your place to question me. Do what your ancestors did! Do what feels natural, boy!"

---

[9] It may not have eclipsed the Box-office success of Missile Force 4: When Missiles Collide, or garnered critical praise in the way of the drama-driven original sequel - Missile Force 2: The Return of Missile Force did, but it does however stand out as the only entry in the series to have been translated into a live musical production. If you ever receive an offer for tickets I strongly advise you politely decline and hasten speedily to the nearest exit!

Chester had many desires but partaking in a conversation he didn't care to be in, especially one where his mind was already made up, was not one of them. So with that he walked off back to his barracks… ahem… dormitory.

This seed of disobedience would grow steadily within Chester's mind. Disobedience might be the wrong word though. It wasn't as though he went out of his way to break rules… he was just ready to follow his own path, not one forced upon him. There was no easy way to achieve this from within the Nursery so he did his best to play by the rules, biding his time while his independence grew exponentially.

Chester went on to Graduate with honors… but it is at this point that his path diverged quite radically from that of his peers…

SPACE BINGE

Ruby had intimidated the opposite sex as far back as she could remember. Johnny was indeed not the only one to be struck by her beauty. Her blond hair caught onlooker's attention while her eyes enraptured anyone whose glance was more than fleeting. She is by all accounts a veritable knock-out, a goddess walking amongst mortals; the reason many a man has walked head first into a wall. While her looks are daunting it is her personality that really makes her unique. Fearless in her self-belief and never one to baulk at a challenge, she finishes second to none.

Born into a successful family she blended in as much as The Blue Lagoons of Tranjuri[10]. Her parents owned the renowned 'Planet

---

[10] The Blue Lagoons of Tranjuri DO NOT blend in. By all accounts they are a splendid sight to behold. The aquatic life in the lagoons thrives by the light of Tranjuri's three suns. The combination of which has influenced their genetics in

Tours'. From humble beginnings they had grown their business to encompass a variety of galaxies and packages. For the not too flamboyant cost of the average worker's monthly wage, their client's could travel to the far reaches of the beyond and customize their experience in truly unique and diverse ways. I would be remiss if I didn't at this point also mention the early reports of "As many as 8 out of 10 clients never return", "Service so poor you'll beg for a Royal Blinding" and "The lunch service was mediocre at best", were in the main, wide of the mark. I can however attest to the lunch service. Mediocre at best is actually quite a compliment! After paying for the silence of a few and demoting a handful of perilously careless employees to cleaning assignments, the company has grown to be the leader in its field, boasting a fleet of Interstellar ships.

Ruby never did take to this life though. Maybe it was her need to be unique and create success for herself. Maybe it was the way strangers would judge her immediately from their pre-conceived notions… or maybe it was that in her early teenage Cycles[11] she'd been

---

such a way as to induce an almost hypnotic blue haze that radiates from their pores. As the lagoon unconscionably became a place for sightseers to dump their waste, a very bizarre effect emerged. The water amplified the blue haze to such a degree that to observe the spectacle with your bare eyes is to say goodbye to that sense once and for all! It should however be noted that as a happy result the lagoons are now quite immaculate. Tourists may only visit at the behest of The Royals of Tranjuri. By riding in specially designed Hovercraft the fortunate few will receive the sight of their lives without sustaining any lasting damage. As an aside the rumored 'Royal Blinding' punishment that involves setting a criminal down with their eyes closed and promising rescue if they can keep them closed until their captor returns has very much been phased out. The accompanying rumor that Princess Safiera punishes those who would spur her advances in this way can neither be confirmed nor denied by this author.

[11] A Cycle, quite literally is the time it takes for The Wholeverse to complete one revolution. Fortunately this time is roughly similar to a year and a quarter in your understanding… "Hang on, revolving around what?" Itself of course… well its center to be more precise. The Masters of The 2nd Floor of Space

told very politely but nonetheless very sternly that she should never talk of a particular client… who is still to this Passing unaccounted for[12]. Whatever cause you want to identify, it is an undeniable truth that Ruby was always destined to walk her own path.

At the tender age of fourteen Ruby packed up her bags and absconded with 'The Peculiar'. It was a well designed vessel meant for deep space travel for a small crew and a handful of passengers. Growing up with such easy access had meant piloting this vessel became second nature. Quite often a mother's call, "Have you seen Ruby?" would be met by a nonchalant father's reply, "Have you searched the local Systems yet?" When she left that Passing she wasn't quite sure where she was headed to. In reality she was only sure she needed to forge her own path.

Fortunately 'The Peculiar' was stocked with enough supplies to last Ruby a few months. Her parents, although at times irrational and focused on their business, cared greatly for Ruby and had arranged for these supplies… just in case their daughter should make the bold decision she did that Passing. With bountiful supplies Ruby had approached her first week of space travel with a significant amount of whimsy and carelessness. Setting the ship to automatic and binge watching episodes of 'Check Hazard'[13], while gorging on a few Passings

---

Ideology discovered this many generations ago… which is a story far too broad for a simple footnote… another Tale perhaps? It should go without saying that The Wholeverse greatly benefits from this method of time keeping; allowing everyone to relate to time in the same way… such a shame they didn't instigate the same train of thought for Passings!

[12] His disappearance was only identified when it was discovered the breathing apparatus utilized for demonstrations had gone missing… everyone involved made the rather wise but unethical decision not to continue that chain of thought to its shocking conclusion!

[13] An episodic show revolving around the renegade Check Hazard. 'Check' was a lonely man who lost his wife and vowed to avenge her murder by 'Ridding the universe of thieves, criminals, conmen and clowns'. The clowns turned out to

worth of candy was not the most promising of starts. It did indeed promote a bout of ineptitude that resulted in accidentally burning four entrées in a row.

After a sugar-induced nightmare woke Ruby from not only her sleep but her lethargy as well, she sat down to take stock of her leftover supplies. With only a few Passings remaining she would have to come up with a plan. This is not however her strong suit. Ruby is a lady of action! This she praises herself on a wildly frequent basis. Her first stop would be the closest port. She searched the nearby systems and found Beaconville was only a matter of Periods[14] away. Here she told herself she would begin to find her destiny.

Beaconville belied its title. It was not welcoming and definitely did not provide safe harbor to those seeking it. Ruby would have noticed this if only she'd possessed the patience to read further than - 'Beaconville - Port - Very Close / Close'. The full text did paint a fuller and more disturbing picture –

---

be quite literal, resulting in the series' lowest rated episode - "Clown, you stole my sole". The episode centered on a Clown who resorted to stealing shoes and selling them to pay for food. It was received poorly by its fan base but in reality was a remarkably shrewd observance of causality in the rising poverty crisis that had begun to cripple the Intergalactic Circus marketplace.

[14] A Period is a unit of time. Roughly equivalent to 2.36 of your world's hours… very roughly.

Beaconville - Port - Very Close / Close

AVOID at all costs. Criminal activity is categorized as CONSTANT. Land here only if CRITICAL to survival. Full body armor is NECESSARY. Travel in large groups only.

Dinner suggestion - Kalandri's[15] - Serves hot and cold breakfast fare all Passing, every Passing.

Thankfully for Ruby, concerns such as these didn't really bother her. Even though she had few Cycles to her name she'd found her way out of many scrapes before. As she stepped off 'The Peculiar' the full extent of her situation was nicely summed up by screams she heard coming from ahead.

"Oi! You! Where do you think you're going! Come back here with that… never mind… you aren't worth my time."

A shot followed and a loud screech as the beam from the yeller's weapon ripped through the sprinting criminal; dropping him to the ground. The tall creature then slowly meandered over to his fallen victim and picked up the item from his tightly clasped hand. Ruby could just about make it out. It appeared to be a portion of bread; no doubt hastily torn from a loaf.

"Grrr… this is no good now," the creature said as he threw it to the ground.

---

[15] The specials here are divine!

Without further ado the lifeless body was scooped up by a passing Automated Cleaning Vehicle (ACV)[16] and the incident was reduced to a mere memory. It was telling that the creature gazed in Ruby's direction but didn't bat an eyelid. This was going to be more of an 'adventure' than Ruby could have possibly imagined… in a place where fear had no home…

---

[16] The first iteration was designed to function without service for hundreds of Cycles. While perfectly ingenious it was quite a shame its inventor hadn't contemplated a way for the vehicle to clean itself. This particular vehicle was caked in so much dirt it ironically posed quite the health hazard.

THE BUFFOON & THE CARPENTER

An unassuming man by nature, Johnny is not the archetypal leading man but neither is he someone to be underestimated; the type to rise to the challenge when necessary without needing the validation inherent in displays of ego. Let's not however paint over the cracks… Johnny's lack of focus has always held him back in life.

Johnny's upbringing had been pleasant; his family as average as could be imagined… Their tendency to fade into the background did allow them the opportunity to occasionally surprise you with their unique talents… I guess in that manner they are quite similar to the Devil Hawks of Darlee[17]… that's probably overselling them… does

---

[17] With a cursory glance and the basest of grammatical comparisons, the famous Devil Hawks are indeed much like Johnny's family… as far as the potential to

juggling count as a unique talent? They weren't entirely uninteresting though…. for example, did you know Johnny's family own a moderately priced vessel capable of reaching half way through the system at speeds that could only be described as acceptable, bearable or perhaps even the ever pertinent so-so?

As a boy Johnny had always felt a certain disconnect with the world around him. Interplanetary travel, I assume, seems peculiar and fantastical to you and once upon a time it did so to me too. Interestingly enough Johnny also never quite felt comfortable with these notions; a stranger in foreign lands… an observer more than a player.

Most likely in a vain attempt to fit in, Johnny threw himself into the mechanics of Space travel. Helping out at his father's shop he was to learn what made these 'beasts' tick… I say beasts but generally it was more of your garden variety gently to feverishly used vessels he worked on. Maybe it was his lack of connection to the role or maybe it was the monotony of repairing and maintaining ships that were clearly closer to the scrap heap than the store but Johnny quickly became known as an underachiever, an also-ran or even a 'Hax Bajler'[18]!

---

surprise that is! In truth the Darlee Hawks couldn't be more different. Now before you accuse me of leading you astray, let me explain. The Hawks truly did surprise their prey; very literally. Nature had gifted them the ability to refract light with their feathers. I know, in reality once you understand these killer birds the simile really falls apart. As an added extra however, remember it is just their feathers that refract light… imagine if you will, how bizarre the sight of a torso-less beak and feet suddenly plummeting towards you would be!

[18] From the dead language of The Mire Folk. While an exact translation isn't possible I'd ask you to imagine a town where straw huts are constructed with a fierce tenacity; ensuring they survive even the strongest of storms. Amongst them there is one hut that is so haphazardly built it requires constant maintenance. Further imagine each storm leaves the remnants of that hut scattered across the entirety of the town. Now finally imagine walking up to the owner of that hut for the umpteenth time, say the first thing that comes to your mind! YES! Hax Bajler is exactly what you would say!

Johnny is a creature of habit that's for sure. At the end of each Passing he would head straight over to an establishment that would later become known as 'The Carpenter's Moons'. When he began to frequent the Public House, it was unnamed and a long stretch from the welcoming, talking point of the Keliptar System[19] it is now.

The Carpenter's Moons is built upon the smallest of Andros' Moons. Before you ask the answer is seven. Seven moons cycle around the planet Andros. They vary in size, from roughly a quarter of the size of Andros to the quaint backyard of a moon on which 'C Moons'[20] resides. At this point I would hope your adventurous mind is drifting to the origin of this watering hole's name. You might presume that Andros was given its name in commemoration of the famous carpenter Andros III[21]. That would make a lot of sense… unfortunately sadly that is not the case. Andros, rather embarrassingly is named after a Bashtak. Think Orangutan but smaller, far less playful and with a complex history of casual racism and gung-ho politics. For most in the assorted galaxies the Bashtaks are clearly not a race to be celebrated. Prince Trado's skewed

---

[19] The Keliptar System is a galaxy in your terminology. It houses twelve planets, including Andros and Tranjuri. FYI - Meteor showers are a frequent spectacle for those living on Keliptar's planets. It's sad to say but many take these amazing light-shows for granted. I personally still find them to be fantastic, but most inhabitants barely notice them anymore. Take rain for example… I'm sure you likely don't marvel every time water falls from the sky… a desert dweller however would, I'm sure, have a fundamentally different perspective.

[20] A nickname that had briefly taken off before Chester threatened to bar anyone he overheard referring to his treasured business in such a way! Unbeknownst to Chester the term is still widely used out of reach of his prying ears!

[21] Andros III was a truly great man and would forever be remembered as 'The Carpenter'. He spent a large part of his life building mansions on an abandoned planet before giving them away for free to orphans. He felt there was a poetic nature to this act of kindness that made him feel at peace. Naming the planet after Andros III would have been a mighty fine choice.

perspective however doesn't see the Bashtaks in this light. Then again he is also known for being the only person ever to remain with his eyesight intact after a 'Royal Blinding'!

Prince Trado is, to put it bluntly, a spoilt brat. The firstborn of seven, he is the only remaining 'child' to still live at 'home[22]'. Even by official records he has been branded a 'Lost Cause[23]'. In a misplaced but valiant attempt to spare others from the indignity of having to tolerate his presence, The King & Queen bestowed upon him naming rights to one of the planets of their system. In exchange for this privilege he limits communication with those outside of the family to no longer than five Moments. As it turns out this is more than long enough to get into trouble (just ask Princess Safeira[24]!) To Prince Trado the Bashtaks are a marvelous race that is merely misunderstood.

The most famous of Bashtaks has always been Andros. In his haste to forward the prominence of his species he built a wall encircling their homeland. As is true in life, poorly constructed plans… and walls… seal their own fate. Within a mere matter of Cycles his people began to grow hungry, angry and turn against him. His ineptitude would

---

[22] 'Home' in this context being the sprawling mansions collectively owned by the Royals. Trado has his own room, in his own mansion, upon his own land, which is loosely connected to the assortment of property owned by the Royal Family of the Keliptar System.

[23] See 'Official Naming Terminology - Royals from A - Z, Edition 3', Page 24.

[24] Once upon a time Prince Trado had propositioned Princess Safeira within his allotted five Moments. It is fair to say that commenting upon a person's flesh and questioning if all of said flesh is as smooth, is not the most appropriate of chat-up lines. Trado's failings were annoyingly always coming to his rescue. Having succeeded in offending the Princess his punishment was camouflaged behind a twisted sense of humor. The Princess asked him to close his eyes before dropping him off next to The Blue Lagoons; promising that she would be right back after slipping into something a little more comfortable. Returning three nights later she found Trado lying provocatively with a grin on his face and his eyes still clamped shut. Prince Trado is a punishment it seems everyone will have to endure, whether they like it or not!

also be his people's savior. The poorly built structure was so brittle it began to disintegrate shortly after completion. Andros' final address to his people fell flat. What I mean is quite literally the remnants of his wall fell atop his podium mid-speech.

His final words quite wonderfully were -

"You, me and all of us. Together we will rise. Our current crisis is temporary and is no hardship in exchange for the expulsion of those who would challenge our way of life! Stand with me now and these walls with forever protect us!"

Irony truly is a beautiful thing! Without talking ill of the deceased I do believe you will agree his fate was sealed by his own actions.

Thus we arrive back to the naming of Andros. For eternity officially remembering one hell of a buffoon!

Johnny and Chester always begrudged the truth behind Andros' naming. With this mindset they set out to right such "a travesty... an unbearable travesty!" With the most indignant of motivations 'The Carpenter's Moons' was to gain its name. A superficial victory yes, but the pair would agree... with the right branding and enough time... they might just be able to convince everyone the planet was really affectionately named for the late, great 'Carpenter', Andros III.

It was an average night when Johnny first entered the pub that would become The Carpenter's Moons. A lone drunk Bashtak could be seen underneath a table in the corner of the room. His derogatory mutterings carried quietly but egregiously across the evening air. The noise in the room emanated from the opposite side, where three friends were loudly cheering as they played what seemed to be a very raucous game. In front of him Johnny spotted the bar and walked up to what appeared to be a Montar. He remembered thinking to himself it seemed odd. Maybe it was for security he pondered.

"What can I get for ya," the Montar asked.

"Hmmm… what's good?" Johnny inquisitively responded.

"What's good?! If you want 'good' go to a store. I only serve refined drinks fit for Kings here."

Johnny wasn't expecting such a defensive response. He made a mental note that this Montar took a hearty amount of pride in the pub and therefore his earlier guess of security didn't quite fit. It also occurred to him that unless he was hugely mistaken this Montar was quite clearly delusional about his surroundings.

"Sorry. What do you recommend?"

"We have the standard labels but if you're after something a little different I'd suggest my Homebrew[25]."

"Sure, I'll go for a glass of that."

The Montar gave him a stern look.

"Chalice I mean… a chalice of that would be nice. I'm Johnny by the way."

"Chester. Glad you stopped by."

---

[25] As you can tell, this Montar is pretty deluded as to the level of his skills. His Homebrew is a result of mixing whatever is left in empty glasses at the end of the night with grapes imported from Tranjuri. This concoction then marinates in a barrel for a couple of Cycles until it is deemed 'ready'. In fairness it is unquestionably hard to limit yourself to a single Chalice of this Homebrew. If there was ever an exact definition of 'more luck than logic' this would be it.

The two shared stories as they started to get to know each other and a rapport was built that would flourish as the two became close friends. After a few drinks the noise emanating from one side of the room had now evolved from raucous to rapturous.

"What's going on with those guys?" Johnny asked with a slightly worried look.

"No need to get scared Son, they're just playing," Chester responded with a rather patronizing but faintly reassuring tone.

"Hey... another round over here," one of the group shouted over while gesturing his hand in a circular motion above the table.

Chester shot over a look that combined with his stature and bulk was enough to keep the majority of customers in line.

"I'll come and get 'em though Sir... and in your own time... no rush."

The group in question had been playing Farmer, Scientist, Smuggler[26] for the majority of the night. After a few rounds the game

---

[26] This game truly needs to be seen to experience the full range of emotions it provokes. Essentially each player chooses to be a Farmer, a Scientist or a Smuggler. From here they are tasked to battle with the use of their imagination... within reasonable boundaries... until a clear winner is unanimously agreed upon. For example the Farmer may choose to cross-breed two animals and send the resulting offspring to fight for him. The Scientist meanwhile might develop a powerful weapon to extinguish his two competitors... while The Smuggler may simply smuggle a Devil Hawk to surprise them both! At its heart it really is a charming game; calling upon a great deal of imagination, patience and understanding! As you can imagine however, over a couple of drinks, unanimously agreeing upon anything becomes very contentious and invariably descends into aggressive demonstrations of how the theoretical battles would play out. For a complete set of rules please reference a copy of 'Top 10 Games to Incite a Riot: Complete Rules &

had descended into a furiously competitive battle which was edging ever closer to all out mayhem.

The largest of the group was a green being; tusks rising from his mouth, curling upwards and back towards his forehead. While not horrifying in nature I would hazard a guess you would not class him as attractive. His clothes dirty and tattered, Johnny could tell this male had been hard at work somewhere; most likely for a prolonged period. Dirt had caked itself into the ridges of his skin; adding to his intimidating appearance. To his left was a typical Zimplaxion. In a world where species are as diverse as the endless galaxies, a Zimplaxion is a vanilla bean minus the notoriety of a pleasant taste. Zimplaxions are very similar to the look and feel of your human beings. Over endless eons beings from all manner of galaxies have spread out across the far reaches of The Wholeverse[27]. With such a range of diversity the Zimplaxions are nearly always seen as bland and uninteresting[28]. Finally there was a

---

Suggested Defenses". Make sure to purchase the latest edition though. It comes complete with a price guide for local alibis!

[27] The 'Wholeverse' is a unique term coined by moi! It represents the entirety of this wonderful world I'm sharing with you. The completeness of one's world is of course a matter of perception. It is for this reason I have never shared the term with any of its inhabitants. I dare not risk the inevitable confusion or alarm that would follow. I quite happily entrust its use with you though… please be gentle!

[28] It is worth noting an interesting novelty that has arisen in the law as a result of this very fact. In order to obtain a marriage license where both members of the couple are Zimplaxions, the female has to undertake a series of rigorous mental sobriety and agility examinations. If she should pass these tests she may then marry her fellow Zimplaxion. This was soon amended after the first female Zimplaxion successfully sued the morning after matrimony. She had successfully argued the pre-marital tests were not stringent enough… it being incomprehensible that a sane female would elect to spend the rest of their life with a Zimplaxion! A Waiver of Rights of Recrimination was subsequently incorporated into the regulations. Remember that next time you tense up at the thought of asking someone for their number… it could be far, far worse!

Kartill jumping up and down on the table, flailing her arms about wildly for attention.

Kartill's you see are generally no larger than a greedy rat. While you have the size of a rat in your mind, pick up your metaphorical mind pen and draw the outline of a Koala Bear. Smudge in the cuteness and replace it with a coy foxiness. Now think aquamarine. The image you have should be pretty close to a Kartill. If not please restart at step one. Did I lose you at 'coy foxiness' perhaps? Don't worry I'll wait for you. I have faith… OK, have you got the image now? Good. When thinking about the Kartill you should also bare a few factors in mind. Due to their size their voices are also considerably faint and hard to hear when drowned out in a raucous argument. Their strength however much belies their diminutive size; a quirk of nature indeed but a decidedly humorous one in situations like these. After a heavy session of drinking, once the intoxication fully kicks in, it is relatively easy to forget just how strong a Kartill can be. That is exactly the situation we find this Kartill's two friends in.

As Chester prepared a round of drinks, the group's game had well and truly boiled over. The Kartill's patience had finally run out. Sprinting across the table she grabbed the green creature by the tusks and hurled him across the room. Fortunately Chester could tell where this had been heading and ducked as the Gorat flew past him, smashing against the wall and slumping down in a stupor. Chester's look was unimpressed but unsurprised.

"Whoa. Is the show included within the admission price?" Johnny quizzed.

"You wanna be part of the show?" Chester swiftly responded.

Johnny had grown a sense of misplaced confidence after a few too many drinks. He walked over to the Zimplaxion. "I guess she wins then," he said pointing towards the Kartill in a patronizing manner.

The Zimplaxion immediately knew his Kartill friend would react in a protective manner and jumped up; standing in the way. Ironically in her rage the Kartill threw him aside in order to attack Johnny.

In the midst of all of this Chester had anticipated the escalation and was approaching their table. He caught the Zimplaxion mid-air and placed him gently back down.

"Enough," he demanded in a powerful yet hushed tone.

Johnny was more relieved to hear Chester than he would admit that or any night. The Kartill had climbed to his chest and with her arms around his neck was pushing out with her legs. Luckily upon hearing the command to stop, she immediately dropped to the floor. Looking around she whistled to the Zimplaxion. After a few seconds it was clear her Gorat friend was still unconscious and would not be joining them without assistance. She pottered over to the corner, grabbed him by the tusk and began dragging him out; followed sharply by the remaining member of the trio.

"See you tomorrow," Chester called out after them with a well-mannered wave.

That would be remembered as the first of many occasions Chester would save Johnny's Razcan[29].

____

[29] Similar in taste and texture to bacon but considerably more delicious. For your own safety please do note that until recently the sale and consumption of this meat was illegal. Shortly after its initial discovery, chefs began to realize the

highly addictive nature of the meat. A number of customers had gorged themselves to death and thus the law intervened. Now what follows is purely conjecture… rumor has it that after a well-known fast food restaurateur caught an equally well known politician in bed with his wife he had agreed to stay quiet on condition of the legalization of Razcan. By reducing the proportion of Razcan in their burgers to less than 5%, the restaurateur was able to ensure his customers would come back every Passing without eating themselves to death. What a novel if not menacingly deceptive turn of events!

THE SHRINE OF THE FIRST

The Shrine of The First is the holiest of places for all Montar kind. Located on the Montar Home World (MHW), civilization was built around this landmark as a constant reminder to each and every Montar of their roots. The Shrine itself was long ago encased within a thick transparent compound that surrounds its perimeter and reaches higher into the sky than eyes can follow.

Shortly before their first Birthpassing, every Montar is taken to The Shrine. A pulpit was long ago erected directly facing the fabled monument. During the 'Blessing of the Descendants' a Montar Elder anoints the fledgling Montar in the presence of The First's Everlasting Gaze. The ceremony itself is a sight to behold. It is customary for Montars passing by to stop and bow their heads for the duration of the ceremony. Having witnessed a handful of these blessings I can share that a great peace sweeps over one's soul when encountering a display of such respect; a time honored tradition of reverence for their oldest ancestor.

I will however add that the gravitas of the Moment is somewhat overshadowed by its unfortunate placement. You see, being the center of civilization means this area is a hive of activity. The main stores in the city are all housed nearby. It is not unheard of to reserve an entire Passing for shopping. I'll proffer you an example. Imagine if you will a romantic meal has worked very effectively as an aphrodisiac. Like a Fupple[30] you're not prepared sufficiently and a horrible realization has dawned upon you that you are out of… well… you know… so you seductively ask your date to relax and enjoy a drink while you very briefly get some supplies. I dare say you probably understand that this by itself is a near impossible task as it is… let alone the next challenge. Having to stop and bow your head every two Moments or so while the next Montar in line is blessed is a major burden when attempting to be swift! It is also terribly off-putting when you're in the mood but surrounded by hundreds of Montars; a town intermittently frozen in time without any care for a man on a mission! You only need to return to a sleeping but clearly agitated partner once to realize… there is no such thing as a quick trip to the stores surrounding The Shrine![31]

The Council of Elders has for generations provided the rules by which all… scratch that… nearly all Montars live by. Their Sanctum is an elaborate building overlooking The Shrine. If you can, imagine a Cathedral, but in the place of pillars stand great statues of the original

---

[30] An endearing way to point out someone's stupidity for a fairly obvious mistake. E.g. "You forgot protection… you Fupple". In reality a far stronger term would most likely be used!

[31] As it turned out 'agitated' was a grave understatement. The bed was slept in by only one of us that trip.

eight Elders of The Council. The official reasoning being the Elders should be seen as carrying the sanctity of the species upon their shoulders[32].

The history of The Council of the Elders can be traced back to the birth of the First's offspring; a time when the Montar's revered 'Intuition' would first present itself. At an early age it became clear the First's child was different. Solomon developed at a spectacular pace; displaying cognitive skills beyond his Cycles and quickly mastering his father's talents. As a species the Montars had been exceptionally gifted but these developments quickly brought attention to the family.

Following the birth of The First's grandchild, the future of the Montars would irrevocably change course. Solomon Junior's 'Intuition' grew to surpass that of his forebears; mastering two generations of talent with relative simplicity. The questions that were previously raised of Solomon escalated into a fully fledged investigation into the entire family.

After a few cycles it was discovered The First was truly unique. The smartest Montar minds deduced a genetic abnormality enabled The First's memories to meld with his genes; enabling his learned abilities to be passed from generation to generation. At the time this was seen as wild conjecture by many. Eight Montars envisioned great possibility however and established The Council of Elders. They foresaw the exponential possibilities that the First's lineage could produce and wanted to ensure this was capitalized upon for the prosperity of Montars everywhere. At first The Council were no more than eight lunatics screaming to be heard. I'm reliably informed for a time they were indeed

---

[32] The unofficial reasoning is somewhat more accurate. Montars alone are egotistical… when it comes to Montar Elders you might as well be invisible. The conversation is certainly not going to revolve around you… or even necessitate your presence!

locked up. Preaching that The First and his children are the only ones who should be permitted to breed and that all other male Montars should be prohibited from procreating will quite rightly lead to a loss of your civil liberties!

During the rise of Solomon III, public opinion began to greatly sway. The combination of four generations of mastered skills stood him head and shoulders above the rest of his race. His Intuition was even more impressive. His father, grandfather and great-grandfather all passed on their memories of actions and reactions they had witnessed throughout their lifetimes. This presented itself in the subconscious mind of Solomon III in such an astounding manner that he could predict what people would do before it had even entered their minds. Learning to harness this he began to understand how to adapt his actions to facilitate the reaction he wanted. While Solomon III used his Intuition for (mostly) altruistic purposes, his rise to prominence captured the imagination of his race, who no longer laughed at the Elder's plans. The unrelenting passage of time had bestowed credibility upon their proclamation of divinity. With the Montars accepting them as eight prophets, The Council of Elders gratefully accepted their place as both saviors and rulers of their people.

What followed was a truly bleak time in the Montars history… unless you're looking from the Elders perspective that is! The Elders diabolical strategy was given the go-ahead; allowing only Solomon and his male heirs to reproduce. Over the Cycles, many great Montar families died out; leaving only Solomon's lineage to thrive.

Having overseen the rise of a terrifically powerful species, The Council turned their minds to how to use this power. To understand where their minds turned, you have to remember the mindset of the Elders. Their egos drive them and are responsible for their strengths but also their weaknesses. When your ancestors are responsible for creating one of the most powerful races in The Wholeverse, it's not hard to imagine how the power might start going to your head… and my gosh how it went to their heads! What do you get the Elder who already has a monstrous amount of power? More power of course! Furthermore when you've already been known to regulate the very gift of life, there's probably not much you can't get away with. So The Council in its infinite wisdom decided they should start to profit personally. They had after all been the 'saviors' of the Montars. This is how the Montar Tax was born. Every person or company that employed a Montar would also have to pay a 5% tax to The Council of Elders. I'm sure it goes without saying but at the rate Montars had evolved they were a highly sought after commodity. As a result The Council became hideously rich.

Let's skip forward another hundred Cycles or so. The disgusting and inconceivable sums of money flowing into The Council were still not enough for them. Depending on the ebbs and flows of various markets their income would fluctuate. Dare you imagine how hard it must be for any of the eight Elders to fall out of the Top 1000 Wealthiest list?[33] They needed a way to ensure a more reliable and stable source of income. Thus they met, as so rarely they needed to at this point in time, to decide their next steps.

"I call to order this meeting of The Council. For too long we have been at the mercy of the many galaxies we trade with. This cannot go on. To continue to thrive we must seek to take back control of the demand for our product!" The Master Elder began. "Who has the genius to save this Council from the bleak Passings ahead?"

---

[33] The list is published annually and dare I say garners far more interest from society than is healthy. Daxter Tiphophaleeze recently earned his place at the top by virtue of some of the most sensationally successful inventions to hit The Wholeverse for many Cycles. What makes him inherently more interesting is his apparent penchant for philanthropy!

"I do. I have fallen asleep many nights foreseeing these times that have befallen us" shared the Elder of Jomine. "When pondering these matters the answer did light up a dream of mine. There is one thing certain throughout all galaxies and all times. Crime will forever be plentiful and war even more bountiful than that. Our soldiers are unrivaled in combat and their Intuition is our most enviable and marketable trait. The Soldier of Fortune revenue stream has seen double digit growth as far back as I can recall. We would be selfish to overlook these facts. It is clear to me we should commit solely to the supply of soldiers."

"What a wonderful thought my fellow Elder. Let us vote. All in favor say Aye," the Master Elder declared.

Before you ask, no, I didn't shorten or paraphrase that in any way. The meeting was indeed that succinct. The Elders had vacations to get back to you see! The vote was unanimous and just like that the future of an entire race had once again been decided within a matter of Moments. The plan itself was implemented by manner of a Decree from the Master Elder and within a mere cycle The Montar Training Planet had been established.

The decree itself was hastily scribbled upon a napkin[34] -

---

[34] The used napkin was taken from an exquisite bar at The Falls of Tranjuri; a five star resort for only the wealthiest of individuals. Its customers are guaranteed serenity and complete anonymity. 'What happens at The Falls stays at The Falls."

By Decree of the Master Elder

1. Find abandoned planet; must be cheap but spacious.

2. Set up a Nursery to train soldiers and minimize independence.

3. Following their blessing at The Shrine send every newborn Montar to the Nursery.

4. Remind me to get a new pen, this one is runni

Upon receipt, the Master Elder's secretary pressed ahead with these instructions… and also sent a whole new box of pens.

THE MONOPOLIZATION OF BEACONVILLE

As Ruby made her way through Beaconville, all manner of squeals, yells and cries filled the early evening. At one time this had been a port that reached out with open arms and hugged all who chose to land upon it. Open front stores welcomed passersby who were greeted by a warm smile and a warmth and integrity lost in modern times. The marketplace was set out like you'd imagine a typical town from one of your old Westerns. Single story buildings ran either side of the main thoroughfare allowing those who landed to easily observe their options. Unfortunately time had not been kind to Beaconville. Jarko "Rapture' Rapturin had seen to that. When he first purchased land at the end of the strip, the town had welcomed him as they did any newcomer. His motives however, much like the sullied sands of The Dunes of Yandel[35], were not at all pure!

---

[35] The Dunes of Yandel are one of the true wonders of The Wholeverse. Rather than the color of sand you have come to expect they are instead a marvelous mixture of various shades and tints. After a storm many arrive to gaze upon the newly created patterns of color emblazoned on the dunes. It is said that every

When he descended upon Beaconville, the male known as Jarko, or Rapture to those who feared him, was quite frightening to the uninitiated observer. As a Gampo this came naturally to him. They are as a species, probably best described with a shudder. Dark red scales cover their bodies and provide significant protection from all but the most vicious of scuffles. Most prominent however are their wings; folded back when relaxed they rise half of their height further into the air and end in a thick spike. Like the rest of their body the scales of their wings can be used for protection as well as to enable flight. Jarko's appearance fortunately provided a warning to those who would be careless enough to encounter him.

Neon signs hung outside the once busy stores and pointed newcomers towards 'Rapture's Landing'[36]. This was the splendidly apt title that Jarko had decided upon for what would soon become the only establishment in the port. Initial designs called for a centrally located Bar surrounded by plenty of space for expansion. The building was about half the size of the port itself. As soon as the enormity of the building was experienced, the surrounding store owners were quick to share their concerns amongst themselves. These concerns would prove to be

---

being can find their destiny amongst the dunes if only they open their minds wide enough to interpret the message. As pilgrims descend upon The Dunes however, the beauty takes on a rather less-appealing complexion. The chance to see one's future is such a great draw that thousands gather their supplies and set out every which way on their own personal journeys. With the heat broken temporarily after a storm, many fail to anticipate how quickly the temperature will rise once again. Not long after departure this dawns upon the now quite lost individuals, who generally resort to dumping their belongings in a shallow attempt to mitigate their exhaustion. Thus the beauty is temporarily but severely sullied. The Dunes it seems do have a wicked sense of humor. Rapidly enough the next storm draws in to repeat the process; ensuring the remains of various discarded supplies and bodies are covered over to once again unveil this natural wonder for all to see.

[36] Otherwise known as 'The Black Hole'. A nickname it wholeheartedly deserved!

accurate as they were transformed, far too briskly, into a horrifying reality.

Shortly after opening, the Bar gained a reputation for leniency towards the shadier dealings commonplace in The Wholeverse. Jarko had long ago earned notoriety amongst the underbelly of society which only amplified the call for the sleaziest of criminals to whet their appetites in Beaconville. As the average visitor to the port became far less wholesome so did the rest of the town.

Having drawn the specific clientele he required to the port, Jarko wasted no time in enacting the second part of his plan. Each of the stores, with their dwindling takings, would soon bow down to Jarko's will. The first to fall was 'Scrumptious Sensations'[37]. While not surprising, it was none-the-less alarming for the town to witness. Jarko had built a 'restaurant' around the main bar which catered to the significantly lower expectations of Beaconville's newest visitors. 'Sensations' closed within only a handful of Passings. The success of this strategy encouraged Jarko to press ahead and before you could blink, Rapture's Landing had become a marketplace that could provide anything a traveler should need… only at a far higher markup and a far lower quality. Most items purchased would fail within a matter of Moments and would inevitably lead to complaints. This potential issue was quickly resolved by the slightest name dropping of the markets infamous owner. Rapture was not to be trifled with and most in The Wholeverse had either witnessed or been warned about this. With its monopolization complete, the decay of Beaconville was exponential. It's only visitors were either demented enough to have nothing to lose or were innocently unaware. The latter were generally lost to this Black Hole of a port.

… I believe this is where we left the young and oblivious Ruby. As she walked closer to town the garish lights of Rapture's Landing

---

[37] One of the greatest losses from this sad tale. Scrumptious Sensations truly did live up to its name. A quite marvelous place to dine; their desserts could make a mouth water from ten paces!

tackled her senses and reflected in the pools of water that filled the many pot-holes scattered throughout the street. Her first experience of this planet had not instilled any great measure of hope. There was a notable eeriness arising from wild screams that echoed around the abandoned buildings. Fortunately fear of the unknown had never been an issue for Ruby… living to regret inaction however was the concern that constantly plagued her mind. As it goes, this had actually served her pretty well… she never did fear a challenge… which is worth mentioning resulted in a sizeable financial burden to her parents!

Upon entering Rapture's Landing, she was drawn towards the Bar that stood before her. She still hadn't quite figured out what her next steps would be, but if she was to branch out by herself she felt strongly this was the place to start. She sat on a stool and addressed a Pefrin[38] working behind the Bar who seemed almost hypnotically entranced by the blood stains he was attempting to wipe away.

"Any idea if there's work to be found around here?"

"The only work available has been taken," the Pefrin cautioned back.

"How about smugglers then… they always need help," Ruby rather carelessly added.

"Don't say that," he whispered back. "You don't want to encourage that kind of attention."

The Pefrin was right but unfortunately, or fortunately… depending upon your view of destiny and its causality, it was too late already. A menacing Gorat had started to not only approach the bar but more worryingly, Ruby.

"I hear ya looking for smugglers little girl. You think that's wise do ya?"

---

[38] An unassuming race known for their incessant need to define their lives in terms of subservience to a master. Tall and thin, their head is the widest part of their body which consequently leads to another of their strongest traits… clumsiness! Should you ever dare order a round when served by a Pefrin I strongly advise you collect the drinks yourself!

"Of course I do," Ruby retorted; not understanding the danger that had arisen.

The Gorat laughed sharply and briefly before tightening his muscles in such a menacing way that Ruby regretted her initial fortitude.

"Well I don't think it's wise child. I think it's very unwise. It's been quite some time since I've tasted Zimplaxion meat." He turned his eyes toward the Pefrin. "How quickly could you serve up a bowl of Zimplaxion stew?"

Ruby's brain moved to flight or fight.

"I am not meek. I am not timid. I am strong and not afraid!" She said trying to convince herself as much as anybody else.
"We shall see about that little one," the Gorat almost chanted as he raised a fist and moved to smash it down.

Ruby had prepared herself for the mess she had courted and quickly moved out of the way; narrowly avoiding the Gorat's arm as it smashed down on her stool. The Gorat was enraged and swung wildly again, this time missing Ruby's head as she ducked. The two misses had filled Ruby with a false sense of capability that resulted in the Gorat's next swing knocking her across the Bar and atop a nearby table. This was met with a devilish smirk as the Gorat lumbered quickly towards her.
A loud thud silenced any noise left in the room as Ruby looked up to see the kneeling creature that had dropped from the second floor and landed squarely between the two combatants. As the creature rose, its wings retracted back to their resting positions and its intimidating height was apparent for all to see. The room took an audible breath in as the creature surveyed the scene. Ruby's foe had already retreated by the time Jarko turned to her.

"You must have some kind of death wish. By now you can see everyone here knows who I am. They're probably wondering how much time is left before you never wonder anything again."

Ruby couldn't muster any words but made sure the look she shot back was one of somewhat plausible confidence. Her aggressor once again surveyed the bar and began walking over to a table in a dark corner where patrons knew they shouldn't sit. His back was turned to Ruby as his voice carried.

"Follow me child if you should wish to survive the Passing."

Ruby was brave but she wasn't stupid. She clambered off the table and followed him over. The darkly lit corner also seemed to restrict the sound… or maybe Ruby's heart was just beating louder… loud enough that she could hear it trying to escape her chest.

"Clearly you don't know where you are. Clearly you don't know who I am. If these two are true then I'm sure you don't know who you are. From what I witnessed however, there is more to you than meets the eye. You will work for me now until you pay off your debt."

Ruby passed back an unconvinced look which unbeknownst to her was actually her saving grace. For Jarko's shrewd mind had seen potential in this sassy Zimplaxion whose nature presented a stark contrast to her appearance. Where Jarko saw potential he also saw opportunity and it was for this reason that Ruby's life was spared.

"Once your debt has been paid I will permit you to leave but not before then," Jarko added without a shred of honesty in his voice.

With this, the first step on Ruby's path had been taken. Over the next ten Cycles under Jarko's tutelage, Ruby would develop some exceedingly useful skills… as well a few that were… shall we say… morally ambiguous. The initial assignments she received were mundane even if they were accompanied by a significant amount of danger. The instructions were simple enough; lay on the ground as if dead to attract would-be thieves dismounting their ships. With the thief approaching, another of Jarko's minions would abscond with the ship. This had become an exceedingly successful scheme. It did however rely upon Ruby identifying the safest opportunity to escape. This hadn't always played out as Ruby intended. On occasions when she did get caught the potential that Jarko had foreseen paid off in full. More often than not, Ruby was able to talk herself out of trouble. Where her charm alone was not enough she was able to rely upon her newly honed expertise in the art of hand to hand combat. Spending her teenage Cycles living amongst some of the most dangerous criminals in any of the galaxies near or far, the need for survival had demanded she learn how to efficiently protect herself. This was certainly true for Ruby but I wouldn't recommend this path… and I'm sure Ruby would agree!

Proving to be a valuable asset, Jarko had elevated Ruby's assignments to beyond Beaconville and eventually without the need for accompaniment. While he'd begun to trust her abilities he never fully trusted Ruby. Long ago he had given her a necklace once owned by the Queen of Brantillis[39]. He'd explained the nature of the Necklace[40] and warned that if the need ever arose for him to use its power he would only use it once… Ruby knew what he meant by this and towed the line accordingly. For ten Cycles she would learn from the thieves, criminals, and miscreants that surrounded her… until one Passing… when the opportunity she had patiently waited for, finally presented itself to her. The opportunity for escape!

---

[39] The King of Brantillis was hideously untrusting. Accordingly he'd requested a necklace be made which would ensure its wearer would always feel compelled to return when its owner commanded it. The King however was as weak as he was untrusting. Upon learning the true nature of the Necklace the Queen swiftly executed her husband. She did however continue to wear the Necklace for many Cycles after, as it had not only lost its power over her but as it goes was a truly beautiful accompaniment to all manner of gowns!

[40] The Necklace is really quite fetching; its silver chains embracing a large seafoam-colored gem. The opaque gem, itself mounted on silver, somehow refracts light in the most perplexing of ways.

FROM THE MAILROOM TO THE MASSAGE PARLOR

In the Cycles following his Graduation Chester tried his hands at a variety of different vocations. His time at the Nursery provided more than enough motivation to cement an unquenchable desire to seek out a future of his own; not one assigned by virtue of his race.

Chester's first foray into the world of full time employment was in a mailroom. To label this as a brief encounter would be complimentary at best. Chester has always had a shockingly high opinion of himself, even for a Montar. During his induction at the Planet Tour's Mailroom it didn't take much time before it was obvious Chester would likely not make the grade.

"OK. So the incoming mail is delivered to us every morning for sorting," Ridel[41] explained, pointing to the box marked 'Incoming'.

"Why is it marked Incoming?' Chester questioned.

"… because it's mail that is coming in rather than going out…" Ridel responded with a puzzled look and clenched eyebrows.

Chester too looked puzzled. "Wouldn't it be easier if there was a box for each person rather than all of the mail being lumped together?"

"Well… that's really our job… that's what we are going to do…"

"That seems inefficient to me," Chester added, clearly not fully understanding the entire point of a mailroom.

Later that Passing Ridel received a call to assist with some general handyman work… a few Cycles earlier his job description had been expanded following company-wide lay-offs. As Planet Tours grew so did their initial poor reviews. After one vessel returned with an inebriated Captain, a large supply of Crotoxin[42] and 10 suitcases (minus their owners) the company needed to take drastic action to ensure its survival. Fortunately for Planet Tours' owners[43], with just the simplest of

---

[41] Ridel is a charming Zimplaxion. He'd worked in the Mailroom for more Cycles than I care to recall and had become truly comfortable in the role. Training new staff was however the least favorite of his duties as it cut squarely into his mid-morning napping time!

[42] A drug with significant medicinal properties that was capable of simultaneously providing an extremely mellowing effect. In a great twist of fate it was originally a legally prescribed painkiller. Heralded as a wonder drug it cured many serious afflictions. All too quickly the criminal world saw an opportunity for profit. A number of crooked politicians received sizeable donations that resulted in the criminalization of Crotoxin. It's not a gamble I'm willing to take by naming the party responsible but amongst these pages you will find the name of the crime lord responsible for this travesty… ahem…cough, cough (Rapture) cough… dreadfully sorry folks I must be coming down with a cold. The drug's medicinal benefits would be all but forgotten... there was however a terrific rise in the number of extremely poor yet mellow citizens who as it goes were also incredibly healthy!

[43] Mr. and Mrs. Flare. A remarkable couple whose success is both unearned and bewildering!

investigations they were able to cut their expenses by nearly 95%. Don't worry, I know what you're thinking… was that a typo? You meant 5% right? Nope… it was indeed 95%.

The first glaring inconsistency Mrs. Flare found was a small handful of employees who were seemingly accounting for half of the payroll and were most certainly names she didn't recognize. So sloppy was this deceit that she quite quickly figured out the names were in fact characters from her husband's favorite show, Check Hazard. While addressing the issue with Mr. Flare the response she received would greatly endanger the couple's marital bliss! It is however wise, when attempting to make a point, not to be equally guilty yourself! For many Cycles, Mr. Flare had been aware of his wife's various schemes. The most revered of which was to refund non-existent customers money to her own personal account.

With their unscrupulous natures the two were ideally suited to each other. They were not without some level of decency however. It had become clear that without major change their company would fail and then how would they support themselves and their daughter, Ruby? Their lavish lifestyle was clearly most important to them but they did have a soft spot for their daughter. This was likely the reason they overlooked Ruby's frequent and expensive joy rides.

I'm sorry, I digress once again. I must take this opportunity to complement you on sticking with me! I have been known to stray off topic once in awhile... which I guess I'm exemplifying right now… anyway! Ridel had received a call to assist with moving some boxes.

"Let's go Chester; we've been called into action!"

"Nice! Where's the attack coming from? How many are there? What are they armed with?" Chester excitedly replied, failing to repress Cycles of training.

"What? Have you been smoking Crotoxin or something? We have boxes to move."

"Boxes… they're hiding in boxes? Cunning! We should scope them out before trying to move them though. You have more bravery than I would've guessed!" Chester continued, making somewhat of a Hax Bajler out of himself.

"Look Chester… there is no attack… there are no enemies… we just need to move some boxes."

Chester's shoulders slumped down; his inner child on display for all to see. "Fine…"

It was just his second Passing on the job when a typically over-zealous Chester crashed not one, but two of Planet Tours' most expensive vessels. In fairness his actions would however lead to the capture of one of The Keliptar System's most wanted criminals[44]. Chester was in the middle of a perfectly mundane stationary sorting assignment when he spotted something that set his mind racing. In the hangar bay that lay before him, Chester could see a host of passengers boarding one of the ships. One passenger however stood out as anomaly. Maybe it was the choice of attire. A dark robe; hood pulled up to obstruct their face. Maybe it was the trail of toilet paper embarrassingly trailing from his shoe… or even simply the bizarre way 'The Fixer' had been carrying himself.

Chester let his observations whirl around in his mind for a Moment or two until he was sure he'd correctly deciphered the message his Intuition had been screaming. By this time the ship door had already started closing. Inhibitions discarded, he sprang into action and commandeered the closest ship he could find.

The ship and its full complement of passengers were steadily approaching the hangar doors, leaving Chester no choice but to take an action of last resort. Steering directly into the hull of the escaping ship, there was a terrific smash as the two vessels collapsed to the ground. You'll be happy to know all on board survived. Less happy however were Mr. and Mrs. Flare who would end up having to pay each of the passengers a sizeable sum to keep them from suing or publicizing the

---

[44] The Fixer, as he is affectionately known by the underworld had made it to number 4 on The Wholeverse's Most Wanted list. His crimes include murder, drug trafficking and non-payment of taxes owed. Shamefully enough it was the latter that resulted in his escalation to number 4. Previously he was lying outside the top 100! I'll let you draw your own conclusions from these facts!

incident. Oddly enough this even included 'The Fixer' who was sentenced to 400 Cycles for his crimes. He lived the high life while incarcerated as a result of this significant payout... until he was paroled only 3 Cycles later. It had occurred to him you see, that with his new found wealth he could pay off the tax debt he'd accumulated. This was viewed as turning over a new leaf and The Fixer was promptly released. Sadly yet hugely unsurprisingly to most, The Fixer returned to a life of crime and is now very proud of his elevated status at number 3 on the Most Wanted list... yes... he went back to not paying his taxes... but let's not dwell on that... his other crimes are surely far worse.

Sadly, but not surprisingly, Chester was fired. For some reason the immense cost to the organization didn't seem to outweigh the successful capture of a famous criminal. Chester wasn't heartbroken though. It was fairly obvious he wasn't built for the mailroom and as it goes the mailroom wasn't built for him either. In the matter of a mere Passing and a half Chester had managed to break three chairs, two desks and most importantly, one novelty mug![45]

Chester decided he needed to try something very different. Sadly for him his resume didn't provide much scope for choice. The Nursery wasn't viewed particularly favorably by most... in fact, with the peculiarity of a Montar seeking employment outside of the Soldiering (yes that is a word thank you!) realm, it occurred to Chester that he should refrain from mentioning it at all. His brief time at Planet Tours had provided a source of inspiration. He'd overheard a few flamboyantly dressed passengers discussing 'The Falls of Tranjuri'. Although he was a little turned off by some of the tales of debauchery[46], he was nonetheless eager to see the views they had described.

---

[45] The mug in question was Ridel's favorite. A souvenir from his second trip to see Missile Force 5: Missile Party: The Musical Extravaganza. He'd been lucky enough to meet the cast after the show and consequently the mug was awarded a bizarrely special place in his heart... and no... I didn't chuckle as I wrote that... seriously though... please do NOT go and see the show... you'll only be encouraging them further!

[46] You have a 'game' in your world involving a bowl and sets of keys...

'The Falls of Tranjuri' are famous for their opulence. The Hotel itself is constructed at the precipice of the magnificent waterfalls that stand as a monument to Tranjuri's beauty. The Hotel is built upon a mass of land that juts out from the top of the main waterfall and is surrounded by turbulent rapids on all sides. Boats ferry the hotel's guests a short journey from the shore at their beck and call. Every room has a wonderful view of the water cascading below. Over the horizon you can see the blue haze rising from The Lagoons. It is the ideal place to witness the phenomenon without suffering any lasting effects. Although there are only twenty guest rooms available, the amenities are endless. Luxury spas and restaurants cater to the most expensive of tastes. Should you wish for Bashtak for breakfast; this can be arranged. If you fancy your chances against a Kartill, in the hotel's state-of-the-art hunting grounds, this can also be arranged. The services at The Falls, you see, are not the most ethical but command a high price and attract only the wealthiest and most sordid of clientele.

Chester would find, even with his notably bleak resume, that the hiring manager at The Falls of Tranjuri was only too eager to interview him. For a trained Montar his Intuition really should have made it apparent there was an inherent risk in this… he was however too wrapped up in the idea of coalescing with the 'Upper 1%'. This life, he thought, would be as far away from being a soldier as he could imagine. The first question during his interview would prove to be a particularly blunt introduction to the hotel's staff.

"We've been looking to add security to our establishment for quite some time. The unique nature of this establishment actually demands it. We hadn't previously contemplated the Tax we would owe your Council but neither had we contemplated hiring a Montar… in truth your skills would make you more than qualified for the position… when would you be able to start?"

For the first time, Chester saw how stereotypes would limit the opportunities available for him to pursue. He broke away from the path he was destined for to get away from a future like this… sure it wasn't leading a squadron into war but Montars were certainly hired for security… albeit only for the richest of businesses. Money however wasn't what Chester sought. That old headline - "Sneezey Business' flashed before his eyes. His strengths were very much his weaknesses in his eyes. He didn't enjoy how his mind would constantly wander and scream at him to be wary of specific individuals. That Passing he'd just wanted to see a movie but had yet again unintentionally profiled everyone around him. An innocent sneeze later[47] and he'd been ushered away from the building. This had proved the last straw for Chester. That Passing he swore to himself he would follow a path of his own choosing and not the one he'd been bred for.

Having been silent for almost an entire Moment the manager felt a prompt was necessary.

"Are you using your Intuition right now? How many fingers am I holding up?" he asked holding his hand behind his back.
"I'm sorry… and it actually doesn't work like that… I was thinking more along the lines of masseuse?" Chester queried almost comically.
"Hmmm… we might have a position open. Could you start this afternoon?"
"Sure!" Chester responded with a cautious confidence.

At this point Chester would have been wise to listen to the unspoken feelings he felt in his gut. While Chester's mind was wandering, the manager's had joined him. The Montar before him

---

[47] It is a great shame that Chester wasn't allowed to stick around to see the movie… not least because that 'innocent' girl would go on to sneeze over almost everyone in the audience. Turns out she'd caught a nasty virus that would send everyone in that showing to hospital later that Passing. Chester's Intuition it seems was even more advanced than he could anticipate… don't worry; I know what you're thinking! "But wouldn't he have caught the virus as well"… yes that may be true but at least he would have seen his 'mistake' was not an overreaction and maybe that would have spared him a whole lot of bother.

presented some previously unthought-of opportunities. Montars are famous for their superior fighting skills and would most certainly command a magnificent bid by some wealthy but short-sighted resident of the hotel. The chance to track and kill a Montar in the confined safety of the hotel's hunting ground was to be the most enviable of secrets for the privileged few that Passing.

If Chester was not so caught up in the excitement of his newly found employment he would have quite easily been able to guess the devious plan that was being executed around him. Unfortunately for him, the Call of the Masseuse was too strong. While you may wonder how on Andros' Red Ocean[48], a creature the size of a Montar could deliver anywhere near the required delicacy a sensual massage requires, I would ask you to suspend your disbelief for just a Moment or two. It is within the same logic that I previously explained Montars make incredible lovers that we find they similarly make wonderful masseuses. A Montar is singularly adept at anticipating exactly where the most tension is held without the need for guidance or concern. It is in fact one of their greatest tools in order to set the mood… Chester would quite readily admit how often he employed this tactic… Johnny meanwhile would attempt to recreate this feat many times without even the most marginal iota of success[49].

---

[48] OK… which would you like? The truth or the legend? What? Both? Oh, OK. The red tint seen in the Oceans surrounding the Bashtak continent is rather mundanely due to the almost constant eruptions from a collection of underwater volcanoes… see, who wants to hear the truth when legends are always so much more interesting! Now for the latter… legend has it that Andros III or 'The Carpenter', as you may recall he was otherwise known, spent an endless afterlife cursing his Bashtak namesake. Having observed the terrible actions of the Bashtakian Andros, he used his formidable spirit powers to sully any waters unlucky enough to touch upon the Bashtak continent!

[49] Johnny's masseuse skills… well lack thereof… were actually to blame for the end of his first serious relationship… Tabatha had construed from the pain she was subjected to, that Johnny had fallen out of love with her but just couldn't tell her. Tabatha went on to pen an oddly insightful self-help book for males entitled 'The 69 Steps to Sharing Your Innermost Thoughts with Your Loved One: An Illustrated Guide'. The follow up video release became the most

Sadly for Chester his first masseur client would also be his last. 'The Falls' received many bids that Passing, with a particular resident even going as far as to offer their first-born if the hotel accepted their bid. The resident in question had been trying to find a way to offload his worthless child for many Cycles with no success. The child in question will be, I believe, someone you will remember (I have my fingers crossed). Any guesses? He has six brothers and sisters… need a bigger hint? He lives at home with his parents… OK, last hint… he survived an encounter with Princess Safeira unscathed! You've got it… I hope… Prince Trado!

The Hotelier was not to be fooled by this. He accepted the King's bid but only on the strict condition the Prince was not included! After a contract was signed and the remittance transferred, The King of The Keliptar System was ready to fight a mighty Montar!

Later that Passing, Chester began his first… and last ever professional massage. His client, unbeknownst to him was actually a maid at the hotel. She remained silent throughout, not wanting to give her true identity away. With the maid relaxed on his table, Chester began kneading the deep knots in her back muscles. The maid was actually very much enjoying the sensation but unfortunately for her, it was exceedingly short-lived. The Hotel Manager had callously arranged for a special concoction of smelling salts to be placed in the room. After only a few Moments of sensual healing, the aroma found its way into Chester's system and with a gasp he fell to the floor.

Upon waking, Chester's previously clouded mind suddenly made sense of the earlier events of the Passing and it became all too apparent what had transpired. Looking around he could see he'd awoken in the hotel's hunting grounds. Made to look most convincingly like a jungle, exotic birds of the most vibrant of colors flew from tree to tree. The transparent roof of the hunting grounds amplified the temperature inside to a dizzying degree. Despite the conditions he found himself in,

---

widely viewed self-help film of all time… many would however complain that the title was highly misleading.

he felt an assured confidence. For reasons he couldn't fathom Montars were quite often underestimated. Their heritage and their abilities were no secret. Chester could only surmise therefore, the wealthiest among us are also the most insecure; yearning for constant reassurance.

Although his reasoning was solid, there comes a time when even an impartial and unbiased man such as me has to say Chester's ego could be too much. It was times like this when his self-assured nature would swing straight into overdrive. The logical reader, as I am undoubtedly certain you are, will have already guessed how this incident played out. It was incredibly short without the need for violence, just the smallest sprinkle of intimidation combined with a drop of arrogance. Chester's mind had already played out the scenario without needing to break a sweat. He'd heard The King of The Keliptar System was staying at the hotel earlier that Passing. With this knowledge the rest was simple. He knew the King's reputation well enough to understand he would pay anything for this opportunity… his Intuition enabling him to deduce the weapon the King would choose; the approach to hunting he would adopt and even the most likely path he would decide to pursue. Chester's thought process may be obvious for a keen Montar expert, such as I, but for the King and the Hotelier this was far from clear.

Having seen the King's path in his mind's eye, Chester headed straight for the opportune position. A beautifully large Noctrim[50] stood

---

[50] Noctrims truly are splendid trees. In terms of scope, you should compare them to a standard four storey building I'd suggest. Now for their appearance I'll need to ask you to imagine twisting a towel until you can twist no more. If you've never done this before and have just returned from a real life experiment, I tip my hat in your direction! The towel you've seen, takes on a tight, corkscrew like, form. The trunk of a Noctrim is very much like this, only far wider! Chester could comfortably lie down and not be seen from the opposite side of a Noctrim. As for the branches, therein lies a Noctrim's true magic. Much like its trunks, branches compete and wrap themselves around each other… although very rarely can you observe this peculiarity without climbing up into its upper echelons. The Noctrim you see is nearly always covered in leaves. Not particularly fanciful or dissimilar in shape to your world's average variety, they are however most resplendent with their shades of scarlet and teal.

beside a stream that was rather more trickling than gushing. The branches of the enormous tree provided shelter from detection as well as the ever escalating heat. It was here that Chester would wait a handful of Moments for his Hunter to appear. The stream created a perfect warning system. Bracing his back to the tree, Chester waited patiently until ripples began echoing through the current. He watched intently as the King crept conspicuously by him… it seemed the biggest difficulty for the skilled Montar would be to avoid breaking out in a fit of laughter!

It came as a huge surprise to the King when Chester silently crept up from behind; lifting him by the belt.

"I presume it's me you're hunting?" Chester asked in the most rhetorical tone possible.

The King tried to bring his lips to deliver a response but lacked the will or courage to do so. With Chester's ego on full display he walked back towards the hotel; the King still being held aloft by his belt.

On arrival at the front desk Chester most politely asked to speak to the Owner of the Hotel. The concierge took note of the now barely conscious King and calmly but quickly picked up the phone to call for the Owner. Within the quickest of Moments the Owner arrived and looked as dumbfounded as could be as Chester dropped the King to the ground.

"So we have ourselves a situation here I'm sure you'll agree," Chester said with pure force. "I'm fairly sure the world at large doesn't know what goes on here. I wonder how they'll feel when they find out."

The Owner and The King knew this would present major issues for both of them. With a nod, a wink and a handshake a deal was arranged that left everyone relieved. Chester left that Passing with even more confidence than before and a bank account positively bursting at the seams… and I'm sure you can guess where a portion of that money went…

CROPS, FINANCIAL INDUSTRIES & FROZEN YOGHURT STALLS

The ten Cycles spent under Jarko's control would create many mixed emotions for Ruby. Given the opportunity she certainly wouldn't have chosen to follow the path forced upon her. It did however provide an escape when Ruby was desperate to break free from the life she'd been born into. Let's pick up three Cycles in, at the point Ruby had been permitted to travel away from Beaconville.

The opportunity to leave Beaconville almost brought Ruby to tears. The Gorat she would be traveling with however meant maintaining her calm facade was crucial. It would only be for a short trip and an accompanied one at that, but it was worth it, she thought to herself. If nothing else it was an opportunity to dream of escape without the constant gaze of Jarko's lackeys.

The Gorat in question was the same charming being Ruby had encountered upon entering Rapture's Landing for the first time. Heethal had warmed up somewhat in the preceding three Cycles… and by warmed up I mean he no longer attempted to strangle Ruby every time he saw her. Even though Gorats are almost identical for the main part, Heethal always appeared particularly ugly to Ruby. His skin she'd often joked to herself, sagged in such a way that she presumed it too was trying to escape.

Upon hearing that he was to be assigned as Ruby's mentor and guard, Heethal would generally have reacted wildly. As the wish had been delivered directly from Jarko he managed to suppress the anger that boiled inside. For the first few Passings, Heethal's instructions to Ruby were communicated only by way of a series of glances and gesticulations. On one of their earlier missions Ruby was nearly killed. The irritable Gorat was supposedly providing back-up as Ruby approached what she presumed was an unmanned vehicle. The owner of said vehicle happened to be returning at just the right time and jumped Ruby from behind. In his bloody-mindedness Heethal refused to warn his young mentee.

There is one thing that should most definitely be remembered about Jarko[51]… he hates waste. Ruby herself was unimportant to him but the potential she represented was not. Having learned of the near-miss, Jarko made sure Heethal understood the consequences of his actions.

"Do you think you are so important to me that you can apply my instructions with such reckless abandon?" Jarko fumed. "For the sake of clarity you are not. Look around you. I have ten more like you to call upon at my very whim. This is not a warning. You should be aware by now I have zero tolerance for disobedience. Instead I will give you ten Cycles to live. Enjoy that time as it ticks inevitably down. Or if you so wish I can instead end you right now."

Heethal remained quiet but his look was enough to convey his forced gratitude.

---

[51] Another interesting anecdote regarding Jarko is his favorite color is red. As the most common color of blood throughout the many species of The Wholeverse, he'd grown a rather disconcerting passion for it.

Following this confrontation, Ruby and Heethal's relationship steadily improved. Words were used sporadically and after awhile one might even say frequently. After three Cycles of forced cooperation the two were working well together and would sometimes even talk about subjects outside of work. Escape was frequently Ruby's favorite talking point but occasionally she would participate in some of Heethal's more mundane banter[52].

One of the perks of this first mission outside of Beaconville was the ship they would be using. Ruby had called upon her most charming of tones in discussing the benefits with Jarko. Having single-handedly flown The Peculiar for a large portion of her life she convincingly argued she would be able to escape even the most hostile of attacks. Jarko had agreed with this logic but had made sure to palm Ruby's Necklace; leaving no doubt surrounding the punishment that would befall her for betraying him.

Upon entering The Peculiar a flood of memories filled Ruby's mind. Her old life contradicted her new one; the memories feeling familiar yet distant. The fourteen-cycle-old girl perhaps a friend she used to know rather than an earlier version of her current self. Although this clash of old and new was unsettling, the recollection that followed would be a happy surprise for Ruby. It dawned upon her that when she left the ship three Cycles ago a small quantity of supplies still remained. Heethal looked on as the suddenly fourteen-cycle-old again Ruby sprinted by him, nearly knocking him to the ground.

"What's the rush girl?" Heethal snorted.

Having located the box; Ruby's remaining supplies prompted a smile Heethal hadn't previously seen.

---

[52] The toxic sounds of 'The Painful Graves' were often offered by Heethal as an appropriate talking point. A band comprised purely of Gorats; to call anything they have produced 'music' is complimentary by anyone's standards. One of their 'classic' albums - 'Dying to Survive', has often been used as a rather effective method of euthanasia. Those that elect this method, it should be noted, are what you would probably refer to as 'gluttons for punishment'.

"What happened to your face? Are you in pain? What's in the box? Is it medical supplies?" The confused Gorat questioned.

"What?" the older and bolder Ruby shot back. "It's the last of my food!"

That night Ruby and Heethal would partake in a Space Binge the likes of which have only been surpassed by Ruby herself.

The Peculiar is a modest ship. The main cabin providing just enough room to move about in without feeling restricted. Tastefully designed, it was originally intended as a service ship. After the Flare's fleet expanded, The Peculiar became a luxury the family used for their private trips. Over the Cycles it served as a sanctuary for Ruby and as such had taken on the appearance of a young teenager's bedroom. Posters were scattered around and for all Heethal could see, not a single one of them featured 'The Painful Graves'.

The aim of this Mission on early inspection had seemed simple enough. They were to travel to the 'Land of the Bashtaks' and collect a valuable trinket that was said to belong to the late Andros. By the time the pair arrived at 'Planet Bashtak'[53] their food comas had been replaced with a sensation somewhat akin to the shock of a hangover on an empty stomach. As they stumbled off the Peculiar, the remnants of a rather poorly built wall could be seen trailing off into the horizon.

"Where do we start? Do you know where we're supposed to find this Chief?" Ruby asked as she looked over to the Gorat who was still attempting to balance himself.

The mission may have been clear but the details were not. Jarko had instructed them to first find the Chief. He should be within the 'Old Wall' Jarko had offered. Without the knowledge that you and I share,

---

[53] Planet Bashtak was coined by Andros during the development of 'The Wall' with a view to inspire his people. It was completely unofficial and went unrecognized by all. The Bashtak continent is in fact located on the planet Andros.

Ruby and Heethal had taken this as appropriately specific enough. Somewhat from a preconception that a wall couldn't cover that large of an area[54] and somewhat because as we all know, arguing with 'Rapture' is not something you do!

"I guess we just start making our way in-wards. There's gotta be someone around we can ask," Ruby noted with as much positivity as she could possibly muster.

It wasn't much of a plan, but it was something and something Ruby had always told herself was better than nothing. Climbing over the fallen wall they noticed how barren the land appeared. Where grass has previously flourished, there was nothing but dirt. The occasional tree scattered the horizon in front of them. They too were a testament to the death that had embraced this land. Buckling at the trunks, their leafless forms appeared as ghosts roaming the wilderness.

Although the wall had not stood for long the message it communicated to surrounding nations had been received loud and clear. The Bashtaks had relied heavily upon the goodwill and free trade arrangements agreed upon with its surrounding nations long ago. This was a fact that Andros, in his infinite wisdom, had not contemplated. The rest of the planet treated The Bashtaks much like an annoying cousin[55]. Ideally you would prefer not to associate with them but

---

[54] If anyone should ever try to convince you that building a wall to separate entire countries is a matter of common sense or plausible in any shape or form you should laugh at the mere suggestion... and if they should ever run for any manner of office you should most definitely not vote for them... you should however, also not share where you heard that advice. Thank you!

[55] Comically enough even the Bashtaks were rarely able to tolerate one another. Imagine if you will, experiencing a severe bout of claustrophobia... now add into the mix that 'friend' you can't stand to be with for more than five Moments at a time. The two of you trapped both desperate to escape. This was the fate that befell the Bashtaks... self-imposed I'll give you that... but it's not unheard of for a portion of a nation to get so wrapped up in one demagogue's rhetoric that they will follow him to the precipice of absurdity.

inevitably failing to do so will end up causing far more grief. After the wall fell, the Bashtaks soon realized it had been seen as a blessing to the other nations; the result they had secretly desired... with the added bonus of none of the associated guilt!

Without Andros or a wall to stand in their way, a subset of Bashtaks, which in fairness tended towards the younger more liberal minded amongst them, chose to depart their Homeland and assimilate with the world around them. A fair portion of the remaining population stubbornly followed Andros' beliefs long after his death. Refusing to accept any assistance from the outside world they created their own metaphorical borders. Crops, Financial Industries and Frozen Yoghurt stalls fell just as the wall had before them[56]. With the dissenting voices now long departed for freer continents, the stubborn Bashtak mentality was free to thrive. As time passed, this self-imposed solitude led to a growing hostility and distrust of the world around them... which, funnily enough Jarko had failed to warn Ruby and Heethal about.

When they finally did encounter a Bashtak the full extent of this races' hostility was beautifully illustrated when a number of shots narrowly missed the pair's heads.

"What are you doing here?" The curiously loud Bashtak screamed towards them.

The question, it seemed, didn't require an answer; another round of shots ringing off and fortunately missing once again.

"We're looking for the Chief!' Ruby screamed back, trying to ensure she was heard before any more shots were fired.

This Bashtak appeared smaller than most but seemingly supplemented his size with an extra serving of distrust. His orange, unkempt fur provided a perfect accompaniment to his prickly personality.

---

[56] For the record this is the saddest part of the whole affair in my estimation. Younger generations will sadly never experience the caliber of technicians that were once so prevalent in the Bashtak culture... Frozen Yoghurt will truly never be the same...

"What do you want from the Chief?" He shouted back while firing off another round. This time the shots hit the ground a more comfortable distance in front of the pair.

Ruby, somewhat carelessly, took this as a positive sign and stepped forward. "He has something we'd like to buy."

Another series of shots made their way once again closer to Ruby's feet.

"We DON"T trade with the outside world!" The Bashtak yelled.
"Not even the relic?" Ruby nervously queried.

At this point I feel it's only fair to mention to you as the reader, another key fact Jarko had failed to share. The Relic was indeed once owned by the late Andros. Rumors had emerged of its existence around The Wholeverse and rather more interestingly the power it possessed. Whether true or not, it was told that he[57] who should hold the Relic could instill great fear in those who heard him[58] talk. The Bashtaks never chose to believe this to be true… most likely due to the implication they had fallen under its spell themselves. If these two had come for it though… others may follow. It was for this reason alone that Ruby and Heethal survived. With their attacker offering to walk them to The Chief, they began to anticipate what they could only presume would be an even more threatening Bashtak.

When they arrived at the Chief's hut the pair were surprised by his appearance. Unlike the first Bashtak this creature was not at all disheveled. His fur groomed immaculately, he was unarmed and appeared quite calm as they stepped towards him.

"I expect you're looking for The Relic," he posited in a delightfully relaxed tone.
"Yes. But how…" Ruby began to answer as he interrupted.

---

[57] or she.
[58] or her.

"No one dares comes to Bashtak territory without necessity my dear. Come with me."

As he turned and started to walk, The Chief ushered them to follow him into his hut. It seemed to be fairly well constructed; not so much small as quaint. A bed nestled in one corner, the rest of the room taken up with all manner of trinkets stacked haphazardly on the floor around them.

With the other Bashtak not invited to join, the three were now alone and free to talk.

"You are either incredibly bold or perhaps incredibly stupid to come here looking for The Relic. Do you truly have nothing to live for?" The Chief quizzed them.

"Yes. I only have seven Cycles left," an uninhibited Heethal explained.

"While I have a debt, which will likely never be paid off, I also need to figure out how to have his punishment lifted," Ruby added, motioning towards Heethal.

Heethal was surprised to hear this. The pair were considerably closer than they had been, but it had never occurred to him she felt responsible for his punishment.

The Chief gave a telling nod and continued. "So this reckless mission of yours isn't yours at all. At whose pleasure do you serve?"

"Jarko… you may know him by his other name…" Ruby started before being interrupted by The Chief.

"Rapture… yes I know of him. I'm not surprised he is seeking The Relic. Those who have power are always preoccupied with a thirst for more," The Chief explained.

After these brief Moments it became clear The Chief was not at all the Bashtak they had prepared themselves for. Unlike the Bashtak they had just met, The Chief's demeanor was very collected and almost mellow. Not quite enough to suggest he was experiencing the effects of

Crotoxin, but it was strange nonetheless. The mania of his hut was in direct contrast to the way in which he carried himself. He didn't seem at all threatening… in fact he seemed quite friendly.

I suppose you're starting to wonder what the Chief's story is. Well… let me fill in some of the blanks, so you may return to resting that weary mind of yours. The Chief was one of the more liberal minded of the Bashtaks. While others had left when the walls fell, he'd remained. As a Bashtak himself, he had nothing to fear from his kind and could live in peace. Living in solitude however wasn't his goal. He pitied those around him who had become stubborn and fearful, but he hadn't given up on them. He'd been unable to make his compatriots see sense when Andros had risen to power. His sense of guilt was somewhat amplified by the time it had taken him to attempt to bring order to the madness.

Andros' rise to prominence had been deceptive in its speed… and plausibility! The more open-minded of the Bashtaks, The Chief included, had speculated early on that Andros was no more than a flash in the pan. It was rare that Andros' words wouldn't upset at least one subset or another. The Chief and his peers had taken it for granted that others would see through this and regularly laughed at the lunacy they witnessed. As time passed and Andros gathered support, a great divide split the Bashtaks in two. By this time it was too late to intervene. The Chief carried a considerable amount of guilt over this, which was apparently the reason he felt compelled to assist Ruby.

"Before I discuss this any further I need to know how you feel about Jarko…. and I need you to be honest," the Chief asked as his tone became deeply serious.

"He is our Master. We are here to obtain the item he wishes for," Heethal responded, never being sure who may be listening.

"I ask you again. I need to know how you feel about Jarko. There is no ear that can penetrate this hut. No words will escape from my door. Tell me how you truly feel," The Chief stressed; a sincerity convincingly appearing on his face.

Ruby still had a level of courage Jarko hadn't been able to whittle down. "Jarko is not my friend, he is my captor. He doesn't care for Heethal or I… he cares only for the treasures we can deliver. I have no doubt once my relevance has passed, he will end my life. I am his prisoner and I spend each and every Passing hoping to find a way to escape him."

Heethal was once again taken aback by Ruby's boldness. The fear that had forced him to learn to tolerate her, similarly warned him of the repercussions that would surely follow. The Chief could see this as he absorbed Ruby's words and Heethal's look of dread.

"Fear not my friends. You are safe in my presence. I had to be sure of where your hearts lay."

The Chief then began explaining the truth of The Relic. As the rise and fall of Andros became commonplace to share with children at bedtime, the stories became wilder and less accurate. A skewed version of the truth you might witness upon gazing into The Mirror of Eternal Blissfullessness! The Relic was perhaps the greatest of the half-truths that would appear in these fantastical fables; Bashtak's telling of its power to promote fear in anyone who its bearer should wish to address. It was indeed true that Andros had worn the crown during his rise to power… but the fall of the Bashtak civilization could not be blamed upon this Relic. It was purely at the hands of Andros that blame should fall. It was however a rather convenient flame of 'truth' the Bashtaks would choose to stoke! What a wonderful excuse they had collectively and individually rationalized. Surely no responsibility can be leveled at them when a great magic had been at play; taking control of their innermost fears. As you can see this was a rather dismal attempt at ignoring their culpability. It was their dormant fears that had been captivated by Andros' guidance. The Relic was no more than a novelty; an item Andros' ego so rightly and richly deserved.

"You may have The Relic without cost. However, be sure not to share the truth as you now know it. Ensure the falsities of its power remain and in time the Relic will do to Jarko what it once did to Andros," The Chief concluded.

It did indeed take some time, but The Chief's premonition would come to pass....

THE LEGEND OF THE DUNES

When Chester first consulted his bank balance, he couldn't quite believe it. He definitely hadn't earned the vast sums now present, but he most certainly felt he deserved it. Although he was no closer to understanding what it was he wanted from life, this money would allow him to take a far simpler journey to the destination he sought.

Maybe it was his ego that stood in his way, maybe instead it was the fact he was trying to create a destiny when one had already been chosen for him… or maybe it was the vast possibilities that suddenly present themselves when you have more money than a Spitturn in Spreezle[59]… whatever reason was truly to blame, Chester just couldn't decide what he should do next.

---

[59] I'm glad you met me down here in this most fascinating of Footnotes! First I must advise that Spreezle holds a double meaning for those on Tranjuri. The first and… well…. most pleasant, is the season in which temperatures start to rise. The second, less pleasant meaning is with regards to the Spitturns. Imagine if a bear and a fox could procreate. Reference the size of a kangaroo and then add in some greed and a disregard for life and you'll have yourself a Spitturn.

So, as many beings with more money than sense do, Chester decided to go on a wild spending spree… and when traveling through The Keliptar System where else would you head but directly to the Mall of Indascia[60], where the stores range from the hideously to the heinously expensive. The cost of parking alone is so prohibitive only the richest of rich have deep enough pockets to do more than just window shop. In honesty, although Chester I'm sure wouldn't admit it, this was probably the main draw for him. Having recently been on the receiving end of the whims of the super wealthy, he had a yearning to turn the tables. As with most dreams that arise through impulse rather than evolve over time, he would find no answers, only more questions.

Chester spent an entire Passing spending frivolously from shop to shop; looking for the most expensive items without regard for his needs or wants. By the end of the Passing he'd accumulated an entire wardrobe of unnecessary garments, more jewelry than he could wear in a lifetime and a shocking amount of guilt. He stopped for a second, sipping on his exotic smoothie that had allegedly been "sourced from the juices of the most luscious fruits in existence before being liquidized over the course of several Passings." Suddenly the waste became all too

---

Spreezle is a perfectly absurd and dare I say dastardly practice that rose in popularity amongst the Spitturns. A terrible virus had been finding its way around The Wholeverse… its origin could be traced back to a movie theatre where a terrifically unhygienic young lady had been inconsiderate enough to infect her fellow audience members. Older Spitturns, it turned out, were particularly susceptible to this virus… subsequently the majority of them were wiped out and an entire generation's savings suddenly made its way down to the next branch of the family tree. Bizarrely the sons and daughters of the deceased found both comfort and prosperity in their grief! Many of you, hopefully, would see this as a tragic event. The Spitturns rather oddly saw this as an opportunity. To commemorate the anniversary, they re-release the virus each Cycle and following the completion of probate, rejoice at their inheritance. See! I told you it was fascinating!

[60] Officially voted 'Least Cramped Mall' 100 Cycles in a row… it also received the awards for 'Most Likely to Bankrupt its Customers', 'Most Arrogant Owners' and 'Tidiest Restrooms'.

apparent to him. He was no closer to identifying which direction his life should take and had managed to squander a large chunk of his windfall.

It was clear Chester needed some sort of guidance. His actions since leaving the Nursery were having the exact opposite effect he had hoped for. So far he'd done a mighty fine job of proving the Elders right. He could imagine them smiling and laughing when they heard of his failings.

"That's why we are Elders boy! We know you better than yourself! You are what we made you and nothing more!"

It's odd how a hypothetical conversation can inspire you. Particularly so in this instance, when the Elders, in reality, were still not even aware of the danger this renegade posed to their best laid plans... at this point they weren't even aware of his existence! We should be thankful at least, for the wakeup call this Passingdream[61] gave Chester. Very quickly and most suddenly he reconnected with his desire to find his own unique path... sure he'd been distracted and lost his way... but at least he'd realized before it was too late. Perhaps all he needed was a little help to point him in the right direction... almost as if The Wholeverse had been listening to his inner monologue; Chester heard a call from behind him.

"Sir, sir... you've forgotten your genuine Ceremonial Mire Folk Headdress!"[62]

Chester sighed as the full extent of his shopping frenzy dawned upon him. "...thank you... you wouldn't happen to know what I should be doing with my life would you?"

---

[61] Similar to daydreams in your world. Chester would quite often Passingdream about telling the Elders their fortunes. Given he'd never met or even seen them, his dreams heavily relied upon imagination. His obsession with breaking away from their influence no doubt drove to this therapeutic fascination.

[62] A hugely unnecessary purchase but oddly one of the few items that Chester would go on to wear quite frequently. Side note - The item was reduced by 60%! Bargain!

"Shopping sir?" The shop assistant suggested. He could see this was not the answer Chester had been looking for. As part of the staff at the Mall of Indascia, the assistant was contractually compelled to leave every customer with a smile[63]. Finding a different answer he tried again. "Why don't you look into 'The Dunes' sir?"

"…The Dunes?" Chester queried with an increasingly intrigued look filling his face.

"Yes, The Dunes of Yandel sir. Many search for answers there. It's said if you search long enough your fate will reveal itself to you."

Having asked for a sign, Chester gladly accepted this suggestion. Even if it had been delivered by an employee known for only telling customers what they wanted to hear!

When Chester landed at The Dunes of Yandel it was clear a storm had recently passed through. The Dunes were positively bustling with activity. A hotel stood out as the only building within sight. The 'Fate of the Dunes' prospers greatly from its prime location; tourists from all over renting rooms before setting off on their own personal journeys into The Dunes of Yandel. As students of the art of capitalism, the owners had shrewdly realized there was a fortune to be made and quickly expanded to two thousand rooms.

The premise was simple and appeared innocent enough… in order to allow their customers to obtain the most from their experience, the owners wouldn't require guests to stipulate how long they intended to stay at the hotel. Instead their rooms would be held for as long as they needed them. The beauty of this plan relied upon their guests' obsession with finding clues to their futures... ending up hopelessly lost in the dunes, they would never find escape and consequently never return to close out their accounts! After thirty Passings the hotel would assume the worst and collect their takings. This plan had become so profitable that rooms would often be cleaned and rented out to the next customer. On the sporadic occasions a customer actually made it back, the owners would claim the room had needed to be cleaned while taking the opportunity to return the customer's belongings. A little known fact is

---

[63] Another major reason the rich were drawn to this Mall… especially the men!

the often fully booked 'Fate of the Dunes' very rarely has more than a hundred or so of their beds being slept in!

As Chester made his way through the lobby his attention was drawn to a number of statues dotted around the room. The marble sculptures were almost life-size and depicted a variety of races staring into the distance; each with a look of pure wonder. Chester presumed this was supposed to represent the magic that awaited guests in The Dunes… but in reality it looked a little more akin to a bizarre tourist attraction… he could even see a Zimplaxion in the corner attempting to climb one while his friend captured the occasion for prosperity!

"Do you have any rooms available?" Chester asked as he arrived at the front desk.

"Of course Sir… for the benefit of our guests we will hold your room for as long as you need." The receptionist replied and then restarted after seeing the Montar standing before him, "…I'm sorry… here I am presuming you're here to walk The Dunes. I didn't even stop to think."

Chester interjected sternly, displeased at once again being stereotyped by his race. "I'm here for The Dunes thank you. Your typical package will be just fine!"

"Not a problem sir. I hope you enjoy your stay," replied the receptionist, not wanting to prolong the awkwardness.

With that, Chester proceeded to his room. The views from his balcony couldn't be faulted. In fairness it is a fool's errand to attempt to locate a single room with a bad view at 'Fates'. With nothing but dunes surrounding the hotel on all sides, each view is guaranteed to be wondrous… unless you don't like endless dunes of color that is. Even when littered with tourists it is truly a sight to behold. If that isn't your thing though, each room is outfitted with complimentary Pay Per View channels and unlimited room service… the rooms being fully utilized at the hotel are undoubtedly a reflection of these amenities. The very offer of unlimited room service speaks perfectly to how rarely guests actually use their rooms! As it is, this cost can be covered by just one of the many guests lost to The Dunes!

Looking out that Passing, Chester could see many had already fallen to the heat; blindly following their need for spiritual guidance. He could set out now but another storm was sure to roll in soon. Besides, he wanted to start his journey with The Dunes unblemished. He didn't want to clamor through hundreds of 'tourists'. As soon as the next storm began to die down he would set off. Chester was pretty sure others would not be so brave without first receiving the all clear from the hotel.

So there he was, a Montar impatiently waiting for nature. The hotel was still pretty quiet, other guests not being so patient; setting off even with another storm imminent. The wait allowed Chester to test the hotel's amenities; an exercise so many others never made the time for. First up was a Razcan burger. Chester had never eaten a burger with quite such a wonderful taste before. He found it oddly moreish as well. So much in fact, that even his second and third Razcan burger didn't seem to quench a newly acquired thirst for this delicacy. Upon calling for his fourth helping Chester was surprised to be turned down.

"Sir, I apologize but for your own health we are going to have to cut you off. If you call back tomorrow we would be delighted to assist you."

Placated but a little disturbed Chester decided to turn his attention to the PPV channels. Much to his excitement he found the first fifteen Missile Force movies lined up and ready for his viewing pleasure. Fortunately this discovery distracted him from searching deeper into the hotel's rather more 'debaucherous' offerings. Had Chester made it to these sections the likelihood is the hotel would once again be cutting him off for his own health and safety!

It was roughly half way through 'Missile Force 7: There are No Missiles in The Afterlife!'[64], that Chester heard the unmistakable sound

---

[64] One of the least successful of the series, this sequel followed the tale of Dirk Killinger who had been killed in the previous installment. Many found this elaboration completely unnecessary… and they would be quite correct. The opening scene involved a close up shot of Dirk; the audience being treated to

of a thunderclap. He rushed over to his balcony to find that the wind had started gathering speed. The Balcony Protector™ slid down into place allowing a beautiful, unrestricted view. The storm would last a while, allowing Chester to finish his film. Following its fascinating conclusion, Chester returned to the balcony to observe the climax of this latest storm.

Looking out from his balcony, Chester could see as far as the hotel's lights would carry. The horizon was dark, only the howl of the wind and crack of thunder letting him know the storm was still very much alive. Out of the darkness a lightning strike lit up the sky, giving Chester a brief view of The Dunes surrounding him. Although sand had started to cover the various bodies and trash scattered around, they were nonetheless still eerily evident. Chester continued to stare off into the storm for many Moments, noticing The Dunes looking purer with each lightning strike. As the winds started to lessen he prepared to set off. If this was to be the event that decided his fate he wanted to fully commit. He selected the largest bottle of HydrateFive[65] from the mini-bar. This was all he needed. He did not intend to return without experiencing a vision… and that my friend is precisely the kind of thinking that results in so many lost souls never returning!

Chester made his way down to the front lobby, the noise from the storm audibly fading away. He poked his head out of the front door. The wind was still blowing but it was not enough to scare him off. In the distance the sun has started to rise from beyond the horizon. The Dunes

---

his inner monologue while the camera slowly panned out over the course of fifteen Moments!

[65] HydrateFive has for sometime been the first choice for extreme athletes throughout The Wholeverse. Its popularity is largely due to a set of commercials that included hypnotic suggestions designed to induce consumers to purchase HydrateFive in immense quantities. Although the commercials would later be ruled to have broken several marketing laws, it was too late. The suggestion had been planted and consumers to this Passing continue to purchase HydrateFive. Even the Judge responsible for the ruling can't quit; frequently feeling a sharp twinge of shame as he looks down at the bottle of HydrateFive that somehow miraculously finds its way to him!

stretched out before him; an unquestionable beauty. The endless peaks and troughs perfectly complemented by the vibrant masterpieces now blessing their surfaces. Once again brilliant colors intermingled in the most delightful ways, dancing before his eyes. The hotel around him was dead, no one else brave enough to head out into the post-storm dunes quite yet. Chester took a deep breath and convinced himself his destiny lay before him… and with that he stepped out into the morning sand.

Chester felt a renewed sense of purpose as he left the hotel behind him; the compulsion to turn around and confirm its location not once entering his mind. Looking around, the magic of The Dunes screamed to him. The sun was nearly completely up and the wind almost non-existent. All around him were swirls of color. He couldn't make out any organized patterns or messages, it all appeared completely random. The eclectic nature of the sands was truly breathtaking. He could easily see how with enough imagination you could interpret any view into the message you sought. He somehow felt special though. When he found something he was sure it would be too clear to demand interpretation. The pamphlet in his room had expanded on the mythology of The Dunes -

---

The Legend of The Dunes

It is said for those who believe, The Dunes hold the answer. To understand their majesty every person must experience it themselves. There will be no mistaking when you uncover the stretch of sands that contain your destiny.

Some say they can feel the truth without even opening their eyes. Others can feel from somewhere deep within their souls; the pattern was meant just for them… and then there are the truly blessed. If you are lucky to be in this special minority, the sands themselves are said to hear your call and unveil the secrets hidden within your future.

The pamphlet had convinced Chester his decision to undertake this journey had been the right one. He had however questioned the credibility of a pamphlet wedged between 'Ride the Dune Buggies - Includes lap dance, lunch and photo (sorry, no substitutions)' and 'Midnight Dunes Massage - Experience the intimate touch of more than just The Dunes!' The potentially sordid true nature of this hotel wasn't going to stand in his way… besides… he could always experience those two excursions upon his return!

Chester's mind raced as he travelled further into the maze of dunes. He'd been so preoccupied he hadn't even realized a whole Passing had been and gone when the sun began to rise again. Passingdreams kept his mind busy as the Moments ran past him. He was so distracted he almost missed a spark in the distance. It lit up the horizon but wasn't obvious enough to generate a complete thought in Chester's mind. Fortunately it re-appeared, this time a more noticeable shimmer in a dune up ahead. Its prominence caught Chester's attention this time. Running full-pace towards it, his legs alone weren't enough to thrust his body forward with the same desire as his mind. He cast all his inhibitions aside; dropping to all fours and galloping onwards; his speed finally matching his expectations[66].

Chester abruptly stopped as he reached the dune he'd been drawn to. The sight before him was almost impossible to describe… but given you're reading so diligently I will do my best! The wind from the storm was no longer howling or moaning… it wasn't even whispering yet before him Chester could see the sands shifting and adjusting. At first it appeared completely random. His mind shocked and scrambling to put together the simplest of coherent thoughts. He tried his best to

---

[66] You will very rarely see a Montar running on all fours. If you should so happen to glance upon the sight I would strongly suggest you deny, deny, deny! Long ago the Elders had observed how others perceived such a spectacle. From being viewed as equals, if not superiors, witnesses would adapt to treat Montars as lesser-beings after seeing them run in this way. "Any being that fails to walk upright surely can't be intellectually astute." I trust this reaction sounds bizarre to you but I hope you'll find some comfort in the similarities between the shortcomings of our two worlds.

interpret something but nothing was there. Suddenly he felt a sense of calm and serenity wash over him. He'd hoped to find a pattern in the sand but couldn't have foreseen anything like this. That feeling grew exponentially as his mind came to understand the truth. This experience was meant specifically for him.

The sands seemed to understand the peace that had descended upon Chester; forming clearer and more coherent patterns. His eyes widened as he witnessed the first message appear before his eyes. Slowly at first, Chester saw what appeared to be a leg, then another; the colors of the sand jostling for position, screaming to be heard. An image was definitely forming now; it was clearly the outline of a being; standing upright, broad and maybe even menacing. The outline complete, grains of sand shuffled; a multitude of colors adding further detail to distinguish the figure.

"A Montar!" Chester exclaimed "but which Montar... an Elder?"

If The Dunes could have shaken their heads at this point they would have. There was no mistaking the representation. The sands blasted out in frustration, grains catching Chester in the face. He shook them away as another image started to appear. It was just a face, the detail manifesting ever quicker. There was no confusion this time.

Chester gasped. "It's me! You've drawn me."

The sand shimmered as much in agreement as relief.

"Thank you! I knew I'd find the answers here. I could feel it. I've become so lost. What should I do?"

The whole of the Dune pulsed as the image disappeared. Ripples resonated throughout the sands. Images started to form once again, but this time the canvas was much larger. The images were no longer still; sands constantly fluctuating, displaying moving pictures for Chester. A system of planets appeared and focused in on one in particular. Seven moons were sketched out, one visibly smaller than the rest.

"...balls? Are they balls? No, no… food… maybe some kind of… food? Meatballs?" A rather stumped Chester offered unconvincingly. "No, that's silly… it's balls isn't it… a game? You want me to play a game? A career? You want me to play sport professionally!?"

It was planets and moons… very clearly planets and moons!

The sand blasted out once again. A bemused Chester understood this message at least and concentrated harder. The same images appeared again, this time slower and larger, compensating for Chester's confusion.

"…Planets?" Chester offered, his voice trying to exude a sense of respect and innocence.

The sand shimmered again.

"OK! So they must be moons… seven of them! The smallest is the one you are focusing on… Andros is the only planet I know with seven moons."

The sands shimmered again, this time with a renewed optimism.

The canvas shook itself free as it prepared for the next illusion. The sands sped up as they reformed into a building surrounded by fields.

"A building! And fields… somewhere on the smallest moon?"

The sands shimmered continuously this time, awaiting an elaboration.

"OK… you want me to find that building and destroy it?"

The Dune's patience was wearing thin. It interrupted Chester's flow and once again sand particles met his face. He'd started to look very sheepish.

Images quickly flashed before Chester's eyes in quick succession now. The depiction of his face, a stack of cash and the building again.

"Me, money, building… you want me to go there and steal money? That's not who I am. Surely that's not my future?"

Enough was enough. For a final time the sand blasted Chester. Something new started to take shape… it was a letter… it was an 'N'… then another… an 'O'… and an exclamation mark.

"NO!" Chester read, feeling ashamed.

More letters in quick succession followed…
'H'... 'A'... 'X'...
'B'... 'A'... 'J'... 'L'... 'E'... 'R'...

"Hax Bajler" Chester muttered, not wanting to bring too much attention to his failings. "…seems harsh…" he added almost incoherently.

The sands reassembled one final time. Chester waited for them to come to a complete stop before hazarding his guess. This time there was no interpretation necessary. He simply read the words clearly spelt out before him.

"Buy the only building on that moon!"

The sands shimmered and returned to a dormant rest.

"What next? What do I do after that?" Chester asked. The question fell on metaphorical dead ears. He wouldn't see anything further in The Dunes.

So that is the story of how Chester identified the path his life would take. Not the most flattering representation of Chester's abilities I'm sure you'll agree... it's probably helpful though in understanding why playing fair isn't his best angle of attack during Farmer, Scientist, Smuggler!

Chester went on to buy the land and property at a remarkably fair price… which was incredibly fortunate given his travels had greatly depreciated his reserves.

As the owner of a Public House, Chester would begin to find a peace that had eluded him for so long…

FAKE BEARDS, RIDICULOUS HATS & TRENCH COATS

In reality Ruby hadn't really put much faith in the promise of The Relic bringing about Jarko's demise. She did however make sure never to share the truth of its nature. There was no sense after all in ruining the chance that it may help her escape.

In honesty, Jarko hadn't seemed particularly interested when Ruby and Heethal returned safely with The Relic in hand. Ruby had often wondered if Jarko was trying to hide his perceived value of the piece by acting with the utmost nonchalance. That being said she did also speculate that Jarko knew the truth and instead hoped Ruby and Heethal would meet an untimely demise at the hands of the Bashtaks.

If The Masters of The 2nd Floor of Space Ideology would allow you to condense the next seven Cycles into a Moment or so, Jarko's fall from 'grace' would be all too obvious to see. The Masters by their very nature are inherently restrictive with the elements of Space and Time. The mysteries surrounding the Masters, their true purpose and even the apparent lack of a 2nd Floor in the Space Ideology building, are deliberately kept under the most stringent of confidentiality protocols. For order and balance to remain in The Wholeverse, Space and Time are not to be trifled with. It is for this very reason that anomalies of The Wholeverse like The Dunes of Yandel, keep the Masters very busy indeed. Establishing the rules is someone else's business… investigating when they are broken, or even bent, however, is very much their business… but you didn't hear that from me… In actual fact you didn't hear that at all! If you were to repeat any of this you would regret it… believe me… don't think for one Moment they wouldn't break their own rules to protect the Sanctity of Continuance[67]!

That being said… and without the assistance of condensed time, I will do my best to articulate the rise and fall of Jarko. The very best place to begin is behind closed doors.

In the beginning, Jarko was for all intents and purposes a very insecure being. As you've probably surmised, those who met him were very much unaware of this… anyone who dared cross him had most likely recently also taken out an expensive insurance policy[68]. If only they had seen him when he was alone they wouldn't have been quite so worried. As we've all heard many times, power is fleeting at best. Those who possess it are so scared of losing it they're constantly trying to gain more. This was very much the case with Jarko.

His first foray into the criminal world was actually quite by accident; at a time when he found himself between jobs. Jarko's previous roles involved working for minimum pay and were far from inspiring. At

---

[67] The Sanctity of Continuance is the most basic tenet of The Wholeverse. When meddling with Space and Time it is crucial to preserve the natural flow as was intended. The Masters found they may interact with Space and Time but only after very careful consideration. Without this The Sanctity would be irreparably damaged. Fortunately The Masters had learned this lesson very quickly with the first and only mistake recorded in their secret journals. That one mistake revolved around a very famous legend… The Mirror of Eternal Blissfullessness… that is however most definitely a story for another time…
[68] Have you ever tried purchasing a policy that didn't exclude an 'Act of Rapture'? Exactly! Expensive is a grand understatement!

one point in fact he had been a staggeringly unsuccessful street singer[69]. Back then he was far from intimidating. A prerequisite of intimidation is being memorable and that my friends, he most certainly was not. After ending another Passing making precious little money he made his way to a dive bar that had become his second home. A darkly lit corner awaited him; offering the opportunity to drown his sorrows in peace.

Later that night, more than a few drinks in, a case of mistaken identity would change his life dramatically. This dive bar you see was also frequented by an alarmingly high number of smugglers. One smuggler in particular was due to deliver a package that night… an unforeseen sequence of events meant he arrived that night knowing he'd need to excuse the absence of the aforementioned package. Making his way to the bar; he asked the server where Toorif could be found.

Now it could have been the server's frustration at being treated like a concierge… maybe it was the poorly lit room, or perhaps even the jaunty hat Jarko was wearing that night. One thing's for certain though… it was not Toorif that the smuggler ended up addressing that night… it was instead a terrifically inebriated Jarko; hat tipped down over his eyes, almost asleep. As it would turn out, the smuggler had never actually met Toorif[70].

"Excuse me sir. I'm here to deliver the package," the smuggler hesitantly whispered towards Jarko.

---

[69] I'm sure you're simply dying to know that it was Bluegrass Funk... or at least it was supposed to be… I'm not sure anyone stayed long enough to hear more than half a Moment at the most!

[70] Unlike Jarko, Toorif was an experienced criminal. Famous for never being caught, his success came as a result of his expertise in eluding detection. His skill was so highly advanced his profile on The Wholeverse's Most Wanted list was notably missing a photo. Even the description was underwhelming - 'Skilled at evading detection. Height – Unknown. Race – Unknown. Distinguishing features - Excels at avoiding capture… rumors suggest he has a great sense of humor'.

Jarko remained still, not knowing how to respond. He figured the stranger would realize his mistake and walk away. Jarko's silence however only amplified the smugglers anxiety.

"… I was meant to deliver the package… but I haven't got it. I'm sorry, it's a long story but I'll get it. I promise. Please, just give me a little more time."

Jarko remained seated, now wishing he'd spoken up. His opportunity had passed. The stranger before him was clearly wrapped up in some kind of criminal enterprise. He'd heard enough that if Jarko admitted he wasn't whoever this stranger thought he was, it could lead to trouble. He decided to play with his drink instead.

The smuggler was unnerved by the lack of response and continued speaking to break the uncomfortable silence. "OK… OK… you can have all of the money I have as well… just please don't hurt my family."

The smuggler riffled through his pockets and planted a large amount of cash in front of Jarko's glass.

"There, that's all I have. Let me go now and I'll collect the package for you."

Jarko didn't dare speak. Lifting his arm slowly he motioned for the stranger to leave. With that, Jarko was once again alone. He let out a sigh of relief, his mind retracing the interaction. The pile of cash before him cried out to be counted and Jarko could not resist. It was more than he'd made that entire Cycle… and for what… a Moment's silence?

Jarko would dwell upon that night for the next few Passings. Quickly enough the dots were connected and Jarko began to understand the principles of intimidation. Without saying a single word he'd convinced a complete stranger that there would be consequences for displeasing him.

Jarko wasn't completely delusional… just mostly! He realized it was not all his doing. Whoever he was mistaken for must have been incredibly intimidating… but even with that in mind he'd somehow managed to sustain that existing level of fear. Unlike this unknown menace, Jarko was not known by anyone at all. He wouldn't have to change his reputation; he could just create a fresh persona… a remarketing of his brand if you will. It worked for HyrdrateFive after all![71]

We can trace the birth of Rapture back to that very Passing. Fed up with being an unknown and making very little money he threw himself wholeheartedly into this new life. The old Jarko would be forgotten, leaving Rapture to take his place. His first challenge would be to propagate the Legend of Rapture.

Anyone who saw him during this time would have been highly bemused by his appearance. His idea, you see, was to disguise himself[72] and then travel around town; sharing stories of the "truly terrifying Rapture" and warning of his imminent arrival. It should make you chuckle to hear that many of the famous Rapture anecdotes were made up by the man himself[73]! Jarko went from market, to dive bar and back; lies and subterfuge being left in his wake. He was quite shocked at how

---

[71] Prior to HyrdrateFive's successful re-branding the company were actually on the brink of collapse. Not surprising really when their product went by the name 'Hydragnificence'… imagine having to ask for that at your local store!

[72] Disguise is in reality hugely flattering. He stood out like a sore thumb but at least he didn't look like himself. Think fake beards, ridiculous hats and trench coats. To his advantage the stories would actually travel around town far quicker because of this. Anyone who shared his story would end up referring to the lunacy that had befallen one of Rapture's victims.

[73] One of his most famous tales from that time involved a punishment he called 'Rapturing'. This was the fate forced upon anyone who dared question Rapture's authority. The unlucky soul would be taken into deep space, given the opportunity to beg forgiveness and then be abruptly kicked out. It was said suffocating to death would be your atonement for non-compliance… your body succumbing to Rapture's rule!

well this ruse worked. One specific Passing he knew it was time to take his plan to the next level. As he was walking through the market he could see a child in the distance running wildly towards him. The approaching child started screaming.

"Run! Everyone run! Rapture is coming! Rapture is coming!"

His strategy was finally paying off!

Jarko spent the rest of the Passing psyching himself up in the mirror. "You can do it. Everyone is scared of you now. All of you have to do is live up to the legend!"

That evening he went back to the dive bar where he'd originally met the smuggler. This time however he didn't head over to the darkened corner; neither did he have a disguise to hide beneath. Instead he headed straight to the bar and asked the server for a drink.

"Do you think these people know?" Rapture questioned.

"Know? I don't follow. What do you mean?" The server responded.

"Do you think they know I'm here? Do you think they realize they are drinking here because I allow it? Do you think they understand just how lucky they are that I allow them to live? Do you? Do YOU know who I am?" Rapture continued with a surprisingly convincing glare.

The server looked confused; he wasn't accustomed to begin spoken to in such a manner. Then the stories that had been circulating flooded into his mind and a rather more terrified demeanor came forth.

"Are you Rapture? Sir…" He stuttered back.

At this point the persona was taking on a life of its own. Rapture nodded and turned around to address the bar.

"Silence" he shouted, loud enough to break the commotion. The whole bar turned to meet his gaze. "I'm sure you've all heard of me. Things are about to change. Those who care to survive will comply. Those who don't will be Raptured! I am the only truth you know. Your every breath is a gift from me. I am the fear you've been dreading… I am Rapture!"

The room was frozen still. The rumors had worked; no one dared to speak.

"This bar is now mine. Anyone who would like to thrive in this new world should seek me out. I will not carry you… but for a price you may find shelter in my shadow."

With that, Rapture's rise became exponential. The fear instilled by his infamous legend was enough to convince all to tow the line. The fearful many sought out his protection; following his orders to spread word of his legend to all manner of galaxies near and far. It wasn't long before he was feared by all; accumulating businesses and wealth by intimidation alone.

As tales of his infamy grew so did his insecurities. Having deceived so many, he was constantly worried his luck would finally run out. In times of solitude he found no solace. The opportunity to drop his façade was quickly overpowered by his torment; personal demons toiling, festering and plotting his demise.

It was this fear of his true nature being uncovered that led him to seek out The Relic. Jarko had heard the rumor many times; an item that would instill fear and compliance in all those he wished to control… it would be the perfect way for him to maintain power without having to live with the fear that had become his most hated best friend.

When Ruby handed The Relic over to Rapture he was indeed quite unimpressed. Jarko however was completely overwhelmed; finally obtaining the item he most desired. He went back to his room and tried on the crown. His whole body relaxed as he let out the largest sigh of relief. Unfortunately for Jarko, The Relic would indeed be his downfall. Unaware the legend of its power was wholly fictional, Jarko would come to rely on it completely. His insecurities may have been a burden to carry but they also served as a constant reminder to stay in character; to never let those around him see who he truly was. Submitting to The Relic allowed the concerns that protected his legacy for so long to evaporate… and with that the demise of his reign was sure to follow.

At first the confidence boost ensured his persona remained. As the Cycles passed his complacency allowed cracks to appear within his deceit. No longer feeling it necessary to frequently remind the world of his legend, more menacing criminals unafraid to follow through on their promises began to rise. With his surrender to The Relic complete he relied on its 'power' to instill fear in any challengers to his throne. What followed was a series of embarrassing retreats; his influence fading fast. With too much time passed before him, Jarko had forgotten the self-taught art of intimidation.

In the first couple of Cycles, Ruby started to notice Jarko becoming warmer towards her… well, not warmer but less threatening let's say. Gradually over time she also noticed those who used to fear him began to start taking liberties… a Passing late on a payment here… negotiating on delivery dates there… by the time she witnessed Rapture's flunkies courting arguments, it was clear something had changed. Whispers were rife with speculation but the legends surrounding Rapture helped him maintain his stranglehold on power.

After ten long Cycles, the countdown on Heethal's life was over and Ruby's tenure at Jarko's side was about to come to a most abrupt end. Jarko was aware of his failing power and needed to find a way to scare his followers back into orderly obedience… which of course led him to a most absurd and clumsy attempt to retain his power… commanding Ruby to take Heethal's life! Death had always proved a marvelous motivator… taking a life however was not on his wish list… which is how he arrived at the idea for Ruby to take one for him!

Heethal's punishment was as a result of his treatment of Ruby after all. Appropriately poetic, Jarko had thought to himself.

By the time Jarko decided to pursue his plan, Ruby was almost ready to take a stand… hearing the order to take Heethal's life officially tipped the scales. There was a line in Ruby's mind… during those ten Cycles there were undoubtedly some missions Ruby would rather forget… but she never crossed an ethical line she'd painted from the Moment she met Jarko. That line was sacred to her. As a young girl she'd been intimidated by Rapture, escape seemingly implausible. In spite of this her morality kept her safe and warm. While she didn't dare risk her life unnecessarily, she was always confident that if an order ever came that her moral compass strongly opposed, she'd sooner confront Rapture than live to regret her actions and the consequential guilt that would follow. Fortune had somehow always allowed her to avoid any of these ethical ambiguities… until now… murdering her friend was most definitely crossing the line!

Sat at Jarko's private table, Ruby's face had taken on a fabulously red tone. With her hands trembling ever so slightly she gave voice to her feelings.

"No Jarko. That's it. I've served you ten Cycles too long. I should have stood up to you the first Passing I met you. People may fear your wrath but at least they've never seen you as irrational… asking me to kill Heethal shows how truly lost and desperate you've become!"

Jarko was shocked by Ruby's outburst. His fixation on maintaining power had ironically made him oblivious to his slow fall from grace. Threats were all he had left.

"Don't be stupid Ruby. If you don't do as I wish you will die too!"

Ruby had gone too far to turn back now; her mind blocking out any negativity. "I dare you to try! You don't command anyone brave enough to take me on… and I've known for some time you wouldn't dirty your own hands!"

The adrenaline was coursing through her veins. She didn't even pause to consider the consequences as she turned and walked away from Jarko. All she knew was she'd finally done what she'd been dreaming of for so many Cycles. That was enough; that was all she could focus on.

Unfortunately this confidence ensured she forgot one very important fact… a fact she was reminded of each Passing… which is probably why it hadn't occurred to her… as is always the way… when we see things so often we effectively become blind to them. The glamorous Necklace Ruby had grown so fond of; the one Jarko had gifted her so many Cycles ago. In all her time serving Jarko, Ruby had never failed him; thus the summoning power of the Necklace had never been called on. While Ruby had forgotten its real purpose, Jarko had very much depended on it; keeping anything that reminded him of his authority readily at the front of his mind.

Ruby managed to make it into orbit before Jarko called upon the Necklace's power. If he couldn't rely upon Heethal's death to force his followers into submission, humiliating Ruby would have to do instead.

Ruby was still flying high, literally and metaphorically, when the Necklace received the command. Ruby was suddenly facing a bizarre conflict in her mind. While she was driven to continue to fly away she found herself turning The Peculiar back towards Beaconville. Her mind screamed to force her body to listen but the cry fell upon deaf ears. Trying harder and harder to refuse the Necklace's power, Ruby began to panic as she struggled to regain control of her body. Amid the panic she finally remembered the Necklace adorning her neck… she cursed her forgetful mind as the panic lessened. Ten Cycles of on the job training set in as she regained her sense of composure. She reminded herself of the confidence that instigated this chain of events… the confrontation she was headed for couldn't be avoided. She needed to finish this once and for all… it was time to put her game face on.

Stepping into the bar at 'Rapture's Landing' there was a crowd awaiting Ruby's entrance. Jarko had warned of the imminent show; his audience suddenly nervous and questioning whether their view of his depleting power had been misplaced.

"Well, well, well, Ruby… how sweet of you to join us all."

"You know I don't have a choice Jarko," she replied, deliberately enunciating his given name.

Jarko laughed before continuing, "Exactly," he screamed. "That is exactly the point. You don't have a choice! You are a slave to MY wishes… you will serve me until I can no longer tolerate your presence!"

While Ruby had forgotten the Necklace's power, Jarko had failed to fully understand its limits… summoning a wearer was quite a trick… but that was the extent of its hold on Ruby's will. The Necklace held no power to force her compliance. Having successfully returned to Jarko, Ruby was free to once again act of her own accord… and I don't mind telling you Ruby was more than aware of this! The scene was set, she'd come this far… it was time to cash her chips in, time to make a scene!

Ruby stared down the now enraged Jarko and walked very deliberately over to the bar. She grabbed a glass and downed the entirety of its contents. Smashing the glass back on the bar, shards flew in all manner of directions before she moved back to face up to Jarko once again.

Jarko was doing his best to keep up the masterful façade that had for so long been his comfort blanket; his mind struggling to determine what his next move should be. The crowd around him wasn't used to seeing Rapture confronted in this way and had become acutely aware of the enormity of the scene playing out before them.

Ruby meanwhile sensed Jarko was flustered and braced herself as she pushed against his chest with both hands, sending him flying to the ground; Cycles of hollow intimidation disintegrating for all to see. His secret unmasked; 'The Great Showman' revealed as having no power greater than the mere enchantment of his words.

The shock from all those around her was electric; various vocal iterations of awe underlining the collapse of Jarko. Ruby didn't waste a Moment; pouncing on her opportunity.

"Everyone, listen to me," she said, vocalizing her passion. Turning back to Jarko she continued. "You once told me I would work for you until my debt was settled. Well here I am. My debt is paid… in full!"

A downed Rapture attempted to regain some control. Sitting up, he brushed himself off in the most nonchalant fashion he could muster and looked up. "Ruby… I fear you are forgetting your place."

"I have forgotten nothing," she seethed back.

Jarko was once again stunned; his mind scrambling to maintain the illusion of control. "Ruby… last chance… bite your tongue," he warned.

"That's just it Jarko. There never was a need for a last chance with Rapture. We all know the legends; we've seen how you work… but not anymore. You hold no power over us any longer; you command no fear. I may be the one standing before you but my actions speak for all of us," Ruby almost chanted as she braced her foot against Jarko's chest. "Tonight your reign comes to an end. The world will see you now for who you really are." She continued, now looking around the bar. "Friends… you have no need to be here… leave this lonely old man to cower in his solitude."

With a final rush of adrenaline Ruby kicked forward; Jarko's back once again meeting the solid floor.

It felt like a whole Moment before anything happened. Ruby was regretting her words but then from behind her she heard footsteps. It was Heethal. He was walking towards the door. One by one the rest of the bar stood up and left.

Ruby looked once more towards Jarko. "I only wish I'd done this sooner. If you dare follow me you will regret it." Ruby concluded, her confidence flowing naturally.

With fear no longer present she reached behind her neck. Unclasping the Necklace, she held it in her hands for a final time before dropping it to the floor.

"You can keep this as a reminder of the only real power you ever possessed!"

With that Ruby slowly made her way to the exit, never looking back. She was finally rid of Jarko and had become quite the legend herself…

A SHELTER FOR THE SOUL AND A RATHER CONVENIENT SOURCE OF ALCOHOL

When Chester purchased the land on the smallest moon of Andros it came as quite a shock to his realtor Simone Slazenger[74]. The previous owner had died some twenty Cycles earlier and although it was in a significant state of disrepair the land had plenty of potential. On all sides of the property, fields stretched as far as the eye could see. Right in the middle stood a two storey building. A two bedroom apartment made up the top floor while the ground floor contained a fully functional Pub. Fortunately for Simone, Chester could see past the cobwebs that polluted the interior and the 'jungles' that had previously been fields. Little was she to know this Montar was following spiritual guidance.

It's incredibly fortunate that Chester had been prompted to make this purchase... and I say that for one simple reason... without his

---

[74] Simone Slazenger: Professional Realtor & Part-time Orthodontist.

experience at The Dunes to spur him on, Chester would have given up Moments after entering the building for the first time. Even though he was tempted… VERY tempted indeed, he didn't quit.

Over the course of a number of Passings, Chester restored the premises; driven by a new sense of belonging he cleaned like his life depended on it[75]. When it came to the Pub, Chester found little work was needed. After the cobwebs and Cycles of dirt and grime were removed a quaint Pub in the style of your world's small town English Pubs remained. A rustic wooden bar catches the eye while a wood-burning fireplace stands as the centerpiece of the room. It would become much more than his home; a place for him to be himself, the Montar he had chosen to be.

So let's talk about the fact that this wasn't yet The Carpenter's Moons. Chester as we have discussed, wanted to be his own Montar. Not the Montar of the Elders design. In spite of this he wasn't oblivious to their wishes. Understanding his newly found vocation probably wouldn't be met kindly by the Elders, he decided to keep his Pub low-key; word-of-mouth driving its success. He also kind of liked the fact it had no name. In his mind it meant only the worthiest of customers would visit[76].

As it goes, word-of-mouth really did drive the Pub's success… if by success you mean a handful of patrons stopping in each Passing. The Moon's orbit just happened to place it right in the path of a high number of 'Dark Routes'[77] traversed by the underbelly of society. This

---

[75] An interesting FYI here. Chester's life literally did depend on it. Although he hadn't been told, the dirt had accumulated to such a degree that it was toxic to those who were exposed for long periods… we can blame Ms. Slazenger for omitting that detail… one could speculate that's what happens when you don't sign up for the 'Combo Package' that includes Orthodontic services!

[76] At this point I'd ask you to cast your mind back to Johnny and Chester's first meeting… the worthiest of customers were clearly not attracted… or perhaps they were indeed the worthiest customers a Pub with no name could hope to attract!

[77] Dark Routes are often used to evade detection. Essentially they are routes through the System used primarily by the criminal underworld. Authorities

didn't seem to bother Chester. In actual fact it made his life easier. A quiet bar let him lead a less stressful life. With only a few people to monitor, his Intuition would remain fairly under control. It was in larger crowds his mind would head strongly into overdrive. Imagine being dumped into the corner of a pitch black room full of rat traps and being forced to find your way out! That's roughly how Chester felt when surrounded by a large number of people. Every step, look or movement would result in his Intuition sharply poking him in the side; forcing him to take notice and overreact at any number of harmless gesticulations. So yes, definitely… his quiet Pub came as quite the relief! A shelter for his soul and a rather convenient source of alcohol!

It continued this way for a while. Chester was happy with his peaceful existence and the Pub was making enough to stay in business. In fairness this was more to do with the money left behind by patrons rather than actual takings… as you've probably already gathered, the Pub was quite often home to an assortment of brawls, skirmishes and general shenanigans. It is a truly bold being that risks antagonizing a Montar. Invariably Chester just walking slowly but confidently over to the imminent ruckus of the night resulted in its participants running hastily towards the exit, leaving their possessions behind. When it became obvious their owners wouldn't be returning… well… can you really blame Chester for profiting from the scenario? It's not like it was intention from the outset!

After meeting Johnny, the path of both the Chester and the Pub would begin to shift. I'm sure you'll remember we've previously discussed how the Pub came to be known as The Carpenter's Moons[78]. It was an evening like any other. Johnny had finished work at his father's

---

generally chose to avoid these routes for their own safety. As a result it became known that only the most fearless weren't afraid of the Dark!

[78] If you don't I suggest you swiftly rummage back to the earlier chapters of this glorious Tale… oh come on! You need me to tell you which Chapter as well? Unbelievable! Fair enough… it was 'The Buffoon & The Carpenter'… but don't say I never give you anything!

shop for the Passing and had taken refuge at The Carpenter's Moons. As always, he spent the first couple of drinks moaning about work[79]. With a comfortable level of inebriation achieved, the logic behind the naming of The Carpenter's Moons was unveiled…

"Yes! YES! I love it! So now we have the name, this place might finally start attracting some regulars… The Carpenter's Moons… isn't that a name you can hear everyone talking about? You'll be the most famous Montar in the System!" Johnny said, not holding back his excitement.

"Wait. That's not what I want. There's a reason I've kept this Pub low-key. Naming it is one thing but I don't want to be in the spotlight myself," Chester responded, clearly worried by the direction Johnny was headed.

Johnny was surprised by this response. The adrenaline had mixed marvelously with his intoxication and Chester's downbeat reply had slammed on the brakes.

"But why… this is such a great idea! This place has so much potential. Why wouldn't you want to be associated with that?" Johnny offered, trying his best to keep the momentum going.

"Johnny. I think a lot of you… and I think you're great for a Zimplaxion… truly one in a million… but I have to ask… how stupid are you? Don't you know anything about my kind? Chester replied in the sincerest tone he could find.

With that Chester felt compelled to bring Johnny up to speed. He started by explaining his inherited Intuition and how crowds caused his mind to run into overdrive. After several attempts to articulate this in a way Johnny could grasp he then moved on to the Montar Training Planet; the training he and all Montars are subjected to.

---

[79] This Passing in particular had involved arriving a hundred Moments or so late for work, nicely followed by an extra long lunch…. I'm sure your heart positively bleeds for him!

"There really is no choice for my kind… we're born and bred for war. It's as simple as that. If the Elders found out about me…" Chester continued.

A question sprang to Johnny's mind and he couldn't help but interrupt. "But even if you do manage to remain unnoticed… what about the rest of the Montars?"

Chester fell silent. He had no answer to this question. He'd been so wrapped up in himself it hadn't occurred to him there was a whole race who most likely had the same desires as him but didn't have the same drive to break out. Johnny's innocent question had forced Chester into some serious introspection.

Johnny continued, not realizing the full impact this conversation was having. "I mean… you could encourage others to follow… once they understand they have a choice…"

"The Elders definitely wouldn't like that. It would cause anarchy…" Chester responded sullenly.

The topic would remain at the front of Chester's mind for the next few Passings. He wasn't ready to speak out against the Elders and risk everything he'd worked for but his mind had broadened beyond his own existence. He decided he would dip a toe into the waters of controversy and agreed to establish the Pub as 'The Carpenter's Moons'… if it courted the attention of the Elders then he'd have to deal with that but for the time being he'd successfully postponed any further need to question the meaning of his own existence!

As a reward for both helping create the name and forcing Chester to think outside his limitations of self, Johnny was given a 2.5% ownership stake in the Pub. It was a token as much as anything but Chester felt compelled to thank Johnny for his input. Besides… at that point the overheads negated any revenues the Pub could produce. Chester obviously wasn't including the abandoned loot he collected from time to time in the Pub's revenues… he was Johnny's friend after all…

not a charitable organization[80]. 2.5% might not seem much… well…
actually it really isn't much… especially when you consider Johnny's Mrs.
would go on to be a far larger stakeholder…

---

[80] He had interestingly enough tried unsuccessfully to claim the associated tax
credits!

'A MONTAR'S CHILDHOOD - A TALE OF GUNS, GRENADES & GREED'

The Council of Elders is responsible for many unjust practices. One in particular provides a magnificent example of their obvious hypocrisies. As with most rules the Elders enforce, the unique version they live by, is notoriously different. The Elders you see are sadly the only living descendants of the original Montar race. When the law against procreation was passed there was an alarming clause regarding Council Members... namely it didn't apply to them! Before approval the validity of this exception had fortunately been questioned. The reason for its inclusion, it was argued, was to ensure the noble lineage of the Elders would remain throughout the ages. Unfortunately no one dare argue with an Elder, so the law was approved as submitted. Upon the death of an Elder their title would pass to their eldest child... thus the Elders stranglehold on their race was destined to continue indefinitely.

This Council of eight Elders was perhaps the most flimsical of its iterations. Meetings were far more frequent than had been the case for hundreds of Cycles… they were however also far less productive. The MTP had become so efficient there really was precious little for them to discuss. After one notably short meeting[81], the Master Elder decided The Council needed to make better use of their time together. Accordingly he catered in an eight course meal and a complimentary all night bar. Shockingly enough The Council unanimously voted to continue meeting on a regular basis[82].

I should probably mention the one meeting in recent memory that involved anything of significant substance. After Monica Barbo's shocking expose revealed to the world the extreme lengths the MTP went to in perfecting its Montar soldiers, The Council really had no choice but to designate some time for meaningful conversation. The article in question - 'A Montar's Childhood - A Tale of Guns, Grenades & Greed', was widely read within the first Passing of its publication. It would however only be available for that solitary Passing. The boundless supply of money accessible by The Council was soon to become readily apparent. A bribe you see is only as good as it's monetary value… in this case, where the bribe was equivalent to the GDP[83] of many small planets, it would be terrifically convincing. Any and every record of the article was promptly eradicated. Furthermore, any reference to the

---

[81] The meeting involved a trivial Economic update entitled - 'Money's Rolling In: Happy Times'. The presentation descended into a quick question and answer session… i.e. do we need to worry, yes or no? Times were good so the answer was a resounding no.

[82] In case you're wondering, my favorite was the Missile Force themed party… excuse me, Missile Force themed meeting. Each Council member dressed as their favorite character and spent the entire night doing their best impersonations… which truthfully were pretty awful… but it was honestly quite the spectacle!

[83] Gross Drama Productions… not to be confused with Gross Domestic Product. Creative productions, both theatre and cinema had become so popular it was decided a planet's economic value would be more accurately represented by its creative output.

article's contents was strictly regulated; violators being prosecuted in both civil and criminal courts. Fancy receiving a life or death sentence for referencing the facts of that article? Yeah, me neither! Having resolved the issue, the relaxed, playful meetings would return for a few Cycles…

Just as Chester had predicted, it wasn't long before news of The Carpenter's Moons reached The Council of Elders. Now don't get me wrong… 'The Carpenter's Moons' is a truly magnificent title… I mean Pub name… but that by itself wasn't enough to gain the interest of the Elders[84]. A Montar owning a Pub however, that was definitely a development to wake them from their slumber!

It's fair to say The Council had taken their eyes off their metaphorical balls… really? You're going to chuckle at that? So be it! Anyway, in partying more than addressing issues affecting Montar-kind, it had escaped their notice that Chester had been experimenting with lifestyle choices that didn't befit a Graduate of the MTP. In reality they had been warned about this multiple times. At least three memos had been passed to The Council. Apparently these memos made delightful drinks coasters and consequently remained unread and unnoticed.

A Montar choosing to own a Pub was news that spread from one Montar to the next faster than a Zimplaxion wedding[85]! The first matter on the agenda was therefore none other than Chester himself.

The Council members were sat around a luxuriously ornate table; golden chalices and dinnerware positively glistening before them. The Master Elder was placed at the head of the table; sat upon a chair as exquisite as it was uncomfortable[86]. The Elders were all appropriately dressed in their elegant but garish robes[87].

---

[84] Unless it was willing to host Council Meetings… then it would most definitely be worthy of their attention.

[85] Zimplaxion weddings are known for being devastatingly quick! The male daren't risk the female changing their mind!

[86] To maintain his elevated position in The Council, the Master felt it always more important to look good than feel good!

[87] The Elders are required to dress in their robes during all official activities. Loosely fitting, the soft (and expensive) white material hangs delicately against

"I call this meeting to order! Order please! Elders! You must sit down now. We will get to the cocktails in good time. First, as you are all aware, we have some work to see to," the Master Elder began, trying his utmost to control the unruly Elders before him. "In talking to each of you it is clear you have heard about the Montar known as Chester. I shall presume you all have the sense to understand the monumental risk his actions present. I have already personally observed great excitement among our kind. We cannot tolerate Montars believing their lives have value beyond the options we place before them. If we are not careful, this renegade will inspire a whole generation to 'follow their dreams'. Our strategy requires one hundred percent compliance. Without that it will surely fall apart. Who here wishes to live like our lesser privileged ancestors? Falling revenues is unacceptable… but no income at all is the fate that should worry us. That is the fear that needs to spur this Council on to greatness!"

The Elders were shocked as they turned to each other in terror. Not only was this a fate they dare not speak of… it also meant the chances of a Cocktail Party had just plummeted drastically!

"How do we solve this problem? The ultimate punishment is the only option that remains. Chester must pay with his life!" The Master Elder blasted with overwhelming authority.

The table erupted with applause of mindless compliance and reckless abandon. One Elder however had a more logical yet equally manipulative plan.

"Master Elder, may I suggest a different approach?" The Elder of Eshua queried.

---

the skin. They would be rather fetching if only the Elders weren't so obsessed with making money! Upon seeing the pure white robes for the first time, the Master Elder had been hit with a flash of inspiration. Soon enough HydrateFive became The Council's official sponsor; their logo emblazoned in huge letters across the back of the robes and in smaller, more modest type at the upper left of the chest area.

His comment was met by a silent nod from the Master Elder; a sign to proceed but with caution.

The Eshuan Elder continued, "Chester's death, I believe, will not solve our problems. Rather it will exponentially aggravate them. He will become a martyr to the masses. From his ashes hope will rise and bedlam will ensue. The virtue of his cause will be amplified in a way his life was incapable of. What's more, it will call into question the credibility and morality of this Council." He could see the Master was becoming agitated by his words. He felt it best to reach his point quickly before being silenced and ousted. "There is a way to solve this problem while maintaining our noble stewardship of Montars throughout the universe. We must persuade Chester to return to a career in keeping with his rich heritage. His brothers and sisters will then truly understand the destiny we create is the only one that exists for them."

The Elders were now listening intently; expressions morphing from skeptical to aspirational. There was a shared feeling of divinity rising amongst The Council that was most likely inspired by serious discussion returning to their usually playful gatherings.

The Elder of Eshua chose his words carefully. "Convincing Chester will not be easy. We must entrust this task to a skilled third party. If he knows of our involvement he will undoubtedly reject the idea and will instead be compelled to journey deeper into his disobedience. Furthermore he must believe this revelation is of his own discovery. That is the only way it will thrive within his consciousness and ensure he follows our guidance."

The Master's demeanor was now far softer, but he was clearly yet to be convinced. "Elder, exactly how do you suggest we achieve this?"

Fortunately the outspoken Elder had already contemplated this. "Chester's training will actually do most of the work for us. All we need to do is present the perfect opportunity for Chester's Intuition to commandeer his mind. He will inevitably become a savior to all of those around him. A single act of heroism should spark his innate desire to protect others and fully utilize his gifts. This and I believe only this, will not only bring Chester back home but will also preserve our future."

"I trust you have spoken your peace now Elder," the Master Elder began. "Elders… we have borne witness to the two options that lay before us. Having listened intently to the Elder from Eshua I have concluded that his is the path we should follow. This is a Council of Eight however. We decide together or not at all. Elders, do you follow where we both shall lead?"

The Elders surrounding the table murmured incoherently between themselves for just a Moment. Their resounding chorus followed, "YES, we do."

"Then it is done," the Master Elder concluded. "Elder of Eshua… it was from your mind that this path was forged. It will be by your hands one is chosen who will usher the lost Montar back to the destiny we worked so diligently to create for him."

The meeting concluded; Chester had unintentionally become a central figure in the famous War of the Montars… a conflict that would be studied for hundreds of Cycles to come. He didn't know it yet but Chester would soon initiate a chain of events that promised to decide the fate and freedom of The Montars once and for all…

FINDING LOVE IN THE TWILIGHT

That final Passing on Beaconville, Ruby waved goodbye to Heethal, not knowing if their paths would ever cross again. From an almost deadly introduction, they had discovered a mutual respect for each other. Heethal was in fact one of the main proponents of Ruby's legend. Having resigned himself to an inevitable execution at Jarko's hands, his fate was now as open as a Ramdil Cocoon in Qantas. On Ruby's departure he promised to one Passing repay his debt, a word he'd detested for so many Cycles; the very articulation of his servitude under Rapture. The word carried new meaning for him. It was a matter of pride, a tattoo he proudly displayed. Ruby had set him free and he hoped he would one Passing be in a position to repay her.

In the Cycles that followed Ruby's emancipation from Jarko, she would never be found wanting for work. Standing up to the infamous Rapture had gained her notoriety throughout The Wholeverse. Free to finally captain The Peculiar on whatever mission her heart or whim should choose; she was finally living the life she'd left home for. Flying from one Planet to another she found her reputation did indeed precede her.

Offers came thick and fast. Sometimes thicker than fast and sometimes faster than thick… but always Ruby discovered she had the luxury of hand picking which assignment to select. The payment was obviously a great motivator but before too long she had accumulated enough wealth to pursue somewhat nobler causes. Whether it be rescuing Trado[88] for the hefty sum of a Prince's ransom or freeing captives from a Bashtak encampment, there was always a significant demand for her unique services.

Ruby's legend was proliferated across The Wholeverse to such an extent it even reached the inward looking minds on the Montar Home World. One mind in particular; that of the Elder of Eshua; was quite fascinated by the stories of Ruby's travels. As it goes fascinated doesn't even begin to describe his mood. It had been a fair number of Passings since his plan for Chester had been approved. So far he hadn't been able to find anyone he could entrust the task too. At one point he thought he was very close but the candidate turned out to be a wonderfully gifted actor who thought she was auditioning for a role in the latest Missile Force movie. Accordingly he explained the mix up and gently let her down. He did however make sure to ask for an autographed headshot… her potential was clear and… well… she was amazingly striking as well![89]

It's more than fair to say therefore that upon hearing of Ruby's expertise the Elder was desperate to locate her. If the rumors were true she would be perfect for this crucial mission… and of course it would keep The Council off his back. Disappointing The Council is one thing… but to disappoint them with respect to a task created and championed by oneself… the consequences didn't bear thinking about!

---

[88] The Prince had somehow managed to lose himself in the Jungles of Shradell. By all accounts his intentions were to "uncover the true nature of… nature". Unfortunately for the Prince and the King (who would be forced to fund the rescue mission), nature and its inhabitants had instead 'uncovered' him!

[89] The actor in question was the beautiful Diana Tulip. As it goes she went on to star in Missile Force 14: The School Cycles.

The Eshuan Elder contacted the Master Elder's secretary with the utmost haste. She was given two tasks that Passing. First and most importantly was to make contact with this 'Ruby' and request a meeting. To attract her attention, compensation was to be no obstacle; her attendance alone would be rewarded with enough cash to run The Peculiar for a few Cycles. The second task was to arrange for his office to be renovated. The golden window frames had been slightly smeared by Montar fingerprints[90]. In his estimation the entire office therefore needed to be torn down and replaced.

Ruby was intrigued by the request to meet that came directly from a Montar Elder. She knew very little of the Montar race, save the unique division of their wealth and the unfavorable rumors that pulsed throughout The Wholeverse. There was no harm in meeting with the Elder, especially given the handsome sum that was being offered without having to exert any effort at all.

When The Peculiar landed in Eshua the sun had been up for some time and the heat of the Passing was taking hold. The glorious greenery of its abundant forests set Eshua apart from the other territories on the MHW. While the sun was out, Ruby was sure the rain would soon follow. The magnificence of the botanical world around her was reason enough to inspire this journey.

As she made her way through town to the Elders office, Montars surrounded her on all sides. Eshua was relatively remote and

---

[90] Fingerprints? From fingers? On a horse like creature? Maybe this has been bugging you… what good would hooves be? How could Chester have been tending bar with hooves for hands? Surely that would be a recipe for disaster! Please remember, although Montars are similar to horses they are also quite different. At the end of their strong arms you will indeed find equally strong but chubby and relatively short fingers. A Montar's knuckles are pronounced, protruding from their hands and increasing their already not insignificant bulk. There is however beauty to be found in the design of what might otherwise appear quite unwieldy. When a Montar seeks to initiate hand to hand combat or perhaps even partake in an all too rare gallop, they are endowed with the ability to lock their fingers into tight fists and create what you might very well liken to hooves.

tailored for locals, not tourists. Ruby's presence was somewhat of a novelty and as a result the Montars of Eshua halted their respective tasks to stare at the outsider. Ruby was struck by a unique trait all of those around her appeared to share. They were by her estimations all fairly senior[91]. She couldn't see a single Montar that she would label as young or even middle aged.

When she arrived at the office she was greeted by the Elder of Eshua himself. "Welcome my dear. I am so happy you accepted my invitation. Please do take a seat."

The newly renovated office was beyond opulent; the Elders desk appeared to have been sculpted from a large piece of marble. His wall nearly entirely filled with photo frames; a flamboyant self-portrait taking center stage. Ruby almost felt rude as she took a seat in the exotic chair that appeared to be made of pure gold.

"I hope you had an opportunity to observe the beauty of my territory," he continued.

"Partially yes… just while making my way down to your office really," Ruby responded.

"Well that is a shame. I shall have to call for someone to take you on a tour before you leave. I asked you here for a reason though, so I must be respectful of your time. If I may… how much do you know of my race?"

Ruby went on to bashfully admit her knowledge was mostly restricted to the tales commonly shared by smugglers and travelers. The Elder wasn't surprised and was perhaps even pleased. It served his purpose nicely to have a fresher canvas to paint 'The Montar Story' on. Now I'm sure you will have already guessed the facts as he presented them were ever so slightly skewed by perspective and bias… there was

---

[91] An interesting point to mention here is the difficulty many find in guessing a Montar's age. While they mature over time as all beings do, they are fortunate the effects do not readily display themselves in their appearance. An old Montar in reality would probably appear to a layman to be middle-aged at most.

however always an element of truth in everything he shared with Ruby that Passing. His assertion of a Montar's retirement was exceptionally interesting I hope you'll agree…

"So you see, after every Montar has served dutifully at the behest of their Council they are awaited and welcomed as Kings and Queens back on the MHW. In their retirements they want for nothing. Accommodation and sustenance is provided at no cost to our noble kin. They are free to enjoy the sunsets of their lives in pure bliss," the Elder explained, his words met by a certain level of skepticism. "You may have noticed a large number of couples as you walked through town today. We find after many Cycles serving their people, a Montar's focus turns towards finding love in their Twilight Cycles. It's always such a delight to see Montars finding companionship. The other seven Elders and I swore off this gift so we may serve our higher calling[92]."

"Where are the children then? I didn't see any," Ruby interrupted, still not fully buying into this tale.

"A masterful observation my friend… we owe a great deal of gratitude to our Montar Veterans. They give themselves fully for the benefit of all. Not only do they spend their retirement Cycles at no personal cost but we also nurture their offspring. In this way they can be assured of the brightest possible future for their descendants while enjoying their remaining Cycles without the associated stress," the Elder explained.

"And that's where the Nursery on the MTP comes into play?" Ruby suggested.

---

[92] It would be remiss of me not to at least attempt to correct this statement. While it may be true the Elders never settle down or marry, the whole truth is rather more telling. The Elders are really quite obsessed with their legacies. Without an heir to pass their title on to, the inherited privilege is defaulted upon and becomes the prize for a Council sweepstake! This obviously only encourages the Elders to sew their seeds with reckless abandon! Of course their Council roles are sadly far too important for them to dedicate time to parenting… and how convenient it is that when close to death they suddenly start to show an interest in their forgotten offspring!

"Yes… exactly! We spent many Cycles perfecting our schooling system. If we succeed in teaching our Montar children to reach their potential we have truly served our purpose and our people. In my humble opinion, I believe that goal has wholeheartedly been achieved," he added.

Now I trust you are seeing through The Eshuan Elder's words. I would ask you to remember that Ruby was not privy to all of the facts as you are. This was her first real interaction with a Montar and from those she'd observed in the territory they all appeared happy and free. There really was no reason to disbelieve what she was being told. Perhaps it was the way of their culture. She was sure she would have heard at least some level of complaint or dissent if the Montars didn't approve of the leadership of their Elders… what's more the Montars were in reality all following along with the lives they were handed… but as we have seen throughout both of our histories… just because a race is treated in a certain way doesn't mean they deserve it… nor do they have a 'choice' in the truest sense of the word!

Having won Ruby over with his colorful interpretation… and the promise of considerable riches for her assistance, the Elder went on to explain how they wished to 'rescue' Chester and the strict requirements that needed to be met.

"Chester must make the decision to return home of his own free will. We don't wish to force him into this decision. His life is his own to live. After much discussion however, we believe the world around him has placed an undue burden upon his soul. Under the right circumstances we are sure he will remember the wondrous feeling he experienced as a student following his destiny… and will once again cherish the gift our race is blessed with."

Ruby listened intently and was persuaded by the Elder's deceptively innocent motives. She didn't have to force this Montar in a direction he didn't innately want to follow. Quite the opposite, she was being warned not to push ideas into his head.

"OK… what do you mean by the right circumstances though?" Ruby queried.

"That's where your expertise will come into play. The gifts that all Montars receive are meant to be fully utilized. We only feel complete when we've reached our full potential. It is for this reason that we are so sure Chester will remember his true calling," the Elder shared; the purity in his voice was evident but not necessarily definitive. "We need you to create a situation where Chester can fully exercise his Intuition and combat skills. The danger only has to be as real as he believes it to be. If you've never seen a Montar in battle it will be hard for me to articulate but please understand there is very rarely any danger a Montar can't handle. His subconscious mind will take control when risk presents itself. He will rise as a hero and the call to return home will undoubtedly sooth his soul".

With that Ruby was officially hired. She received a tour as promised and relished the opportunity to see the forests of Eshua through a local's eyes. It also allowed her the chance to speak with an average Montar who had nothing but nice things to say about the Elders. Unfortunately for Ruby this would only convince her further of the innocence of the assignment she'd just accepted...

WHAT WAS ONCE MEANT TO BE, IS NO LONGER

The Space Ideology building is a grand building indeed. Although it houses many floors that explore the endless wonders of The Wholeverse, its outside appearance is quite misleading and is very much the reason tourists flock to the SI Headquarters. Originally just a standard tower block, Executives at HQ decided they needed to ensure the importance of their work would be received and understood by all. As a result the ground floor was turned into a marvelous museum for kids and adults alike. The results of their investigations became the subject of interactive exhibitions for all to enjoy[93]. This proved to be so

---

[93] The most popular may well be the family-friendly 'Wonders of Invisibility'. The technology had been adapted after Cycles of study into the Devil Hawks of Darlee. The attraction is relatively simple in execution, consisting of a stage and a block of seating for audience members. Every 10 Moments a new show commences where volunteers are asked to join the presenter on stage and try on an uninspiring apron… with the flick of a switch, not only the apron but

successful they decided to renovate the exterior of the building in keeping with this image. The main vocal point being a fantastic rainbow waterfall that cascades diagonally up from the building's moat, all the way to the highest floor, over the top and then back down behind… I know! I wanted to see it when I first heard about it as well!

Space Ideologists are not only revered but in the eyes of many, have actually supplanted mainstream religion. The main tenets of SI are very similar to standard religious principles; respect one another, everyone is created equal and with true dedication a special sense of divinity can be found. In the case of Space Ideologists, these principles are achieved by furthering the collective understanding of the mysteries of The Wholeverse. As a result the relentlessly updated 'Guidelines for a Good Life' are published twice every Cycle[94]. While many see the Guidelines as 'preachy', the experiments carried out throughout The Wholeverse undoubtedly push the limits of science. It is for this reason they receive funding and special acknowledgment of their importance from the 'Union of The Many'[95].

It is fascinating to see so many travelers stop and stare at the SI building. For many it represents an endless thirst for knowledge; a belief that through invention and discovery the lives of the collective whole will attain greater meaning… which coincidentally enough is their official mantra!

There is much they are famous for but it's their secrets that provide their greatest purpose and significance. Many discoveries have been made regarding Space and Time that will never see the light of

---

everything behind it becomes transparent! It's very humorous to see kid's torso-less limbs jumping around on stage. Well worth the price of admission alone I'd say!

[94] Guidelines included such 'winners' as - 'In order to co-exist we should all seek to harmonize and focus on our similarities rather than our differences'. Some were marginally less relevant but still useful, 'Thou shalt not eat Razcan'.

[95] The UoTM is sanctioned by nearly all Systems; a governing body of sorts. In trying to serve all of The Wholeverse they invariably end up achieving precious little. They do however throw a spectacular fundraiser every Cycle.

Passing; endless funds protecting The Wholeverse in ways that can't possibly be comprehended by those outside The 2nd Floor.

The 2nd Floor is in fact so confidential that even the highest of high at Space Ideology aren't privy to its business. The 2nd Floor itself can't be accessed by a lift or stairs. It is to all who work at SI HQ a complete mystery; a legend or myth that could just as easily be a work of total fiction… only compounded by the confusing absence of an access point to The 2nd Floor anywhere in the building!

For a number of significant and genuine reasons I will avoid sharing the details of how I came to learn the secrets of The 2nd Floor. Suffice to say if there was a way to share that information without serious consequences I would… probably.

Those on The 2nd Floor are immensely passionate about their work. In reality, working on The 2nd Floor is far more than a job; it is a way of life. The strictest protocols effectively result in a personal or social life being impractical and nigh-on impossible. Aside from necessary expeditions around The Wholeverse, those who work on The 2nd Floor live and remain on The 2nd Floor. With such focus there is little room for relationships any greater than casual friendships. That isn't to say there is no room at all though. Accordingly, I'd like to introduce you to Jerome.

At the time of his recruitment Jerome was one of the foremost Zimplaxion scientists[96]. His interview was like any other, save when he questioned what his role would be and why they chose him. These questions would continually be met with non-answers; "would you prefer not to work at Space Ideology?[97]", "we sought you out for a reason" and "look! Over there! Did you see that?" Shortly after the interview he received a formal offer which was accompanied by a confidentiality agreement. Failure to adhere to the terms contained

---

[96] Jerome is most famous for his crucial research into Razcan that uncovered its highly addictive properties.

[97] To be clear, everyone wants to work for Space Ideology. It is the highest of callings for scientists… and they offer a killer benefits package!

therein would result in total loss of his freedom. The offer still didn't identify exactly what he would be doing. His interest was however peaked by one particular sentence in bold -

---

strictly forbidden. This includes all life forms in all social situations.

Upon acceptance of these terms you will receive unrestricted 'Master' access to the secrets of Space and Time.

Please remember to bring two identical passport photos on your first Passing. Lunch will be provided but you may wish to bring a dessert of your choosing.

The promise of unrestricted access proved too much of a draw for Jerome. He'd heard the rumors of a 2nd Floor and this was surely what he'd been headhunted for. Returning the contracts he started the very next Passing[98].

The other significant item to mention about Jerome is he was lucky enough to find love with another Master. Constantly working and living together it wasn't long before they became very close; their romance producing a son, James. Sadly Jerome's luck rapidly turned to misfortune. During a complicated delivery Jerome would have to say goodbye to his wife just as he welcomed his son. The child was to be his salvation; reminding him every Passing of the woman he loved dearly… the same child would however also end up keeping him very busy. Imagine trying to care for a child when your every waking moment is spent working!

Until their first major discovery The 2nd Floor was purely aspirational. They had hoped to uncover the great secrets of The

---

[98] He brought a Chocolate Fudge cake if you're interested. He did however forget the two passport photos!

Wholeverse but were falling extremely short. Their biggest discovery up to that point had been identifying a series of planets whose orbits could predict the future[99]. The discovery of The Sanctity of Continuance was a turning point for the Masters; finally blessing them with a legitimate reason for the existence of The 2nd Floor. With the knowledge of this crucial rule of Space and Time they would designate themselves as its protectors. From that Moment on, their knowledge grew exponentially. Soon enough they weren't just regulating Space and Time… they learned how under certain circumstances, they could bend it to their will. Fortunately for the rest of The Wholeverse, they remain guided by the Sanctity of Continuance; vowing to only meddle when necessary to preserve the natural flow of The Wholeverse.

One should never dwell on the good without also mentioning the bad. Although the Masters' work gained definition it had come at the expense of their only documented mistake; forever serving as a constant reminder to protect the Sanctity of Continuance.

The mistake in question was with regard to The Mirror of Eternal Blissfullessness[100]. From what they surmised, The Mirror allows those who gaze into it the chance to experience glimpses of Space and Time. There was a randomness to the images shown that made the Masters believe a certain level of providence was involved. Although they weren't able to interpret what was experienced, it was ruled The Mirror would only be utilized by the Masters and even then, only in order to advance their understanding of its purpose.

For a long time the Masters had tried to interpret communications from The Mirror as pieces of a giant puzzle. Interactions experienced by viewers were hugely diverse and quite often contradictory, leaving the Masters lost in their ponderings. This was until

---

[99] The scientist in question was never able to fully articulate how exactly the future was being told… he was very convincing though!
[100] Even with the combined knowledge of The Masters of The 2nd Floor, The Mirror still remains a great mystery.

Jerome speculated experiences were unique to each viewer and consequently should be interpreted in isolation.

While the Masters had so fantastically named it The Mirror of Eternal Blissfullessness, I would hate for your mind to conjure some sort of ornate, full body, oval shaped, literal mirror… if I know the human mind at all, I've no doubt you likely now have that picture in your head… please dispense of that image… it is not literally a mirror. It is in fact an incredibly bewildering effect that one can observe after a great climb.

The Mirror stands at the climax of a tall and narrow mountain. Ascending to its peak is truly dangerous and wards off those who are unaware of the treasure it protects. At the top of the mountain the privileged few have an opportunity to stare out into the beautiful orange sky. At this point I'd ask you to conjure up a picture or perhaps even a memory of the 'Aurora Borealis' from your world. The Mirror's appearance is a relatively similar sight. Red paintbrush strokes scrawl their way across the orange sky; diffusing and dispersing in the most wonderful of ways.

To describe the experience of looking into The Mirror in terms of receiving a simple vision would be to greatly devalue and grossly undersell it. In an egotistical attempt to describe the event that occurs while gazing into The Mirror, the Masters coined the term 'Soulsions[101]'. Try and imagine the colors speaking to your soul, reaching out and embracing your very being; imbuing your essence with the most personal and abstract of messages. A trance-like meditation; it is undoubtedly an ethereal experience that is impossible to articulate in a way that truly respects its divine nature. I can only hope I've provided enough of a push to allow your mind to ruminate on the origin and spirituality of existence!

Jerome did his best; generally allowing James to accompany him while he worked. His son, now three Cycles old, was adventurous but would often just sit and watch as his father went about his 'Mastering'.

---

[101] Not bad I hear you say… be glad they didn't go with their second or third options… Mind Grabs and Soul Shakes!

On one specific occasion when Jerome was sent to study The Mirror in greater detail, James' curiosity would get the better of him.

Upon reaching the mountain's peak, Jerome set his son down and looked into The Mirror once again; his Soulsion remaining unchanged[102]. He stepped back and began unpacking; his gaze momentarily taken from his son. Jerome looked up to find James staring into the Mirror. He quickly ran over and grabbed him up into his arms. As he held James it was clear something had changed. There was a distant look in the boy's eyes; the comfort of his father's touch seemed to be gone. Jerome set him down and for the next few Moments tried desperately to get through to James without success. The boy's mind was somewhere else; his eyes completely glazed over.

Jerome's own mind was still very much present and panicking. He started racing back and forth, searching for the right thing to do. It was then that in the corner of his eye he noticed something odd. His focus moved back to The Mirror. Somehow his Soulsion had changed… similar in context to those previously experienced but it was evidently skewed; as if subjected to a stranger's interpretation.

In the Passings that followed, Master after Master looked into The Mirror to find their Soulsions were irrevocably altered. Concern quickly grew amongst all on The 2nd Floor and soon enough a meeting was called to discuss this most troubling of developments.

All of the Masters were present as Jerome was called to explain his actions. Each Master took the opportunity to share how their unique experiences had somehow been altered. It was not yet obvious how grave the impact would be but it was all too evident what was once

---

[102] The Masters had discovered each individual's Soulsion was both unique and permanent. This was actually the cause of a fair amount of jealousy on The 2nd Floor. Those with more impressive Soulsions, including Jerome, were quite the envy of their peers. As a result Jerome didn't receive a single Birthpassing card for three consecutive Cycles! He did however receive the obligatory gift card for use at 'Everything But The Kitchen Sink'; a marvelous store that sells everything you could wish for. Ironically due to market demands they have been forced to start stocking kitchen sinks!

meant to be, was no longer. The Masters were in agreement that by looking into the Mirror, Jerome's son had somehow affected the flow of the universe… thus laying the groundwork for their understanding of The Sanctity of Continuance.

A few Passings later, James' mind remained lost; his father a stranger to him. With a heavy heart the Masters decided it was in the best interest of the boy to no longer be subject to the dangers of The 2nd Floor or the mysteries of Space and Time. It killed him to let James go but Jerome was racked with guilt and felt he'd never be able to make amends for the unknown fate he'd brought upon his son.

With their lesson learned, the importance of the Sanctity of Continuance was forever engrained into the Masters' actions. Moreover they would begin to discover exactly how much Space and Time had been distorted…

A KARTILL'S DELIGHT

As Ruby departed the MHW her focus moved towards the mission at hand. It was easy enough to create a dangerous situation; she knew plenty of ruffians that could assist her with that. To be successful though she would need to understand this 'Chester', what made him tick and what exactly would set off this inner-drive he was supposed to possess? It also wouldn't hurt, she thought to herself, to add some context to the story the Elder of Eshua had shared with her. The mission seemed reasonable enough but having previously witnessed the fall of Jarko personally she was only too aware that appearances could be deceiving.

The Elder had informed Ruby that Chester was running a Pub called The Carpenter's Moons. From what she'd heard of this establishment there were already a number of criminals who chose to drink there. If that was true then she knew Chester wouldn't be a stranger to handling volatile and precarious situations. Ruby would definitely need to carry out some reconnaissance first.

Ruby's luck it seemed, had escaped her. With The Keliptar System coming into view, The Peculiar began to live up to its name[103]. The ship jolted ferociously and then came to a complete stop. Ruby screamed a number of expletives that I shall refrain from repeating... let's just say she wasn't happy. A couple of deep breaths… and several thrown items later, Ruby decided to approach the issue more rationally. She looked at the monitor and realized Andros was not as far away as she would have guessed. If she could land The Peculiar there it shouldn't be too much of an issue to get it repaired… but making it that far was going to be a challenge.

Ruby searched the cabin for something that would magically solve her most recent crisis. The futility of this notion became clear a Moment into playing with a laser rifle; motioning as if it could somehow be used to thrust the ship forward… maybe by holding it out of a side window she'd briefly wondered[104]. It occurred to Ruby that she may have captained this vessel for many Cycles but she really didn't have a clue as to how to repair it. She could only think of one option… wait 10 Moments and try and start the engine again!

Fortunately for Ruby her 'plan' worked… marginally. The engine jolted back up, shuddered forward slightly and then died once again; moving fractionally closer to her destination. Repeating this process another fifteen times, she finally reached Andros[105].

---

[103] The naming of The Peculiar! I can't believe I haven't told you this story yet! It's quite cute really and probably the reason Ruby had such an affinity for the ship in question… but you probably don't want to hear it… oh you do? OK then! You don't have to ask me twice! The ship had just arrived at Planet Tours. It was their most advanced vessel at the time so a heavily pregnant Mrs. Flare insisted on being present for its delivery inspection, leaving Mr. Flare to look over the contracts. A Moment or so later the loudspeaker burst into life. "Reginald! Come quick… I feel really quiTE PECULIAR!." By the time he arrived Bethany had already given birth to their first and only child… with that 'The Peculiar' was born… and Ruby of course.

[104] I kid you not! For a Moment or so this plan seemed very logical to Ruby!

[105] For those of you who aren't experienced with interstellar craft… this is NOT a good idea! Yes, she didn't really have a choice… but still… it's really not

The town she landed in seemed capable enough. A variety of stores were intermingled amongst the town's housing. As fortune would have it she found a shop that could help. Entering 'Scott & Son, Ship Repair' she was greeted by Mr. Scott senior who very graciously offered to tow the ship and call when it was ready to be collected. From what Ruby described, he felt a Passing would be sufficient but she would nonetheless be kept appraised as they investigated further. Mr. Scott proceeded to welcome her formerly to Verton; the town that greeted residents and travelers alike… and of course in such a friendly town there was a perfect hotel within walking distance!

The Hungry Kartill[106] was pleasant enough. Relatively small, it could only accommodate twelve guests at a time. As the only hotel in town it benefited from heavy foot traffic and a severe lack of competition! It would be wrong to say those were the only reasons for its success though. I'd probably most accurately describe the building as 'charming'. White awnings sat atop the windows of the three upper levels. On the ground floor two bay windows arched out from the red-brick structure; allowing patrons to sit in the onsite bar and people-watch as the town's residents walked by.

After a quick snooze, Ruby made her way down and pulled up a pew at the fairly crowded bar. All the booths and tables appeared to be occupied; constant chatter necessitating raised voices all around.

"Welcome. What can I get for you tonight?" The Zimplaxion barman asked.

---

surprising she'd have to buy a whole new engine a Cycle later… it's only surprising it lasted that long!

[106] If you're questioning whether this is a derogatory name for a hotel, question no longer… it is indeed highly disrespectful. How would you feel as a guest at the Smelly Human Being? Verton had previously given residents the opportunity to vote on the matter and only 90% agreed it was disrespectful…for some reason 95% was needed for the vote to pass… don't even get me started!

"Whatever's good... surprise me," Ruby responded. "Do you know much about Scott & Son?"

The barman chuckled. "They do good work... just don't expect it to be ready anytime soon... especially if the 'Son' is working on it!"

Ruby made a mental note to check in on The Peculiar after a few drinks. The first drink however was just about to be served.

"There you go... my specialty. One Kartill's Delight[107]," the barman offered, smiling from ear to ear.

The drink in question was a weird looking cocktail; blues, reds and yellows partially intermingling. The smell was hiding no secrets... if there was anything but alcohol in the glass it would be a major surprise[108]. His choice of drink alone made the barman's perceptions abundantly clear. Ruby was used to people presuming more than they should about her. She may not wear dresses every Passing but she doesn't go out of her way to cover up either. Tank tops and jeans made up the bulk of her wardrobe. Her style is what she refers to as 'Practical Sexy'. As a result it was all too often that strangers would make the general sexist assumptions that blight and sully males of all species. Ruby wasn't fazed by this behavior though. Her legend quite often preceded her; stranger's preconceptions being set aside shortly after a formal introduction. This was a convenient benefit but she almost resented the need for it. Long before she left home she'd decided what kind of woman she wanted to be. She wouldn't fit in the narrow boxes created by society. She was strong and independent but that didn't mean she couldn't have some femininity about her as well. What's more she wouldn't let other's hang-ups define her. The world is what it is. She was sure of herself and people were free to think what they wanted.

---

[107] Kartill's Delight - An off-menu order, made by this barman alone... furthermore made differently each time. It was essentially his rarely successful way to hit on women.

[108] It was all alcohol... literally 100%... even the ice cubes were made of frozen liquor!

"Thank you" she said, doing her best to hide her amusement at the presentation of this alcoholic abomination. "How about The Carpenter's Moons? Have you heard of it?"

"Well aren't you full of questions. As it goes I have. It's on our smallest Moon. Since they named it not too long ago it's been competing with us a little more. Our regulars have stayed but I know some of the town goes there to escape their mundane lives down here," he explained.

"Do you know the owner?" Ruby questioned.

"Not personally, but everyone knows of him. Hard to blend in when you're a Montar!" He responded with a now noticeably judgmental tone in his voice. "I guess it's probably not too dangerous with him there but I would still recommend you stay away."

With that Ruby picked up her drink and started making her way across the bar. She gave people allowances but that didn't mean she needed to stick around to be condescended. Besides, she was pretty sure she'd received all the 'Intel' he had to give.

Ruby spent the rest of the night talking with the patrons of The Hungry Kartill. It was clear there wasn't much more to be learned. No one had any more to share about Chester than merely his race. Seemingly those who drank at The Carpenter's Moons and those who drank at The Hungry Kartill were two totally distinct groups.

Just when she was about to concede, she received a sign that well and truly confirmed it was time to retire for the night.

"Ruby," the barman shouted across the noisy room. "Just got a call from the shop… they need another Passing."

That was as good a sign as any. It was time to head to bed!

She awoke pretty late the next Passing. It had been longer than she could remember since the opportunity to sleep in had presented itself. Why not make the most of it? After a quick shower she made her way down to the front desk; hoping for some positive news.

"Yes, we do have a message for you actually… they need another Passing."

Ruby's instinct was to head straight to the shop but she held herself back. She'd been paid ludicrously well for this job; so why not relax while progress eluded her. She spent the rest of the Passing meandering around town, asking about The Carpenter's Moons when she felt it appropriate. Oddly enough she had far more success than when talking to the guests at her hotel's bar. The consensus from those who'd met Chester was how happy he seemed to be. They all seemed to find this humorous; commenting on how bizarre it was for a Montar to have such an ordinary job. This didn't seem to mesh with what the Elder of Eshua had told Ruby but she was keeping an open mind. She'd been told the world around him was responsible for diluting his true nature after all.

Returning to the front desk, Ruby wasn't met with the answer she was hoping for.

"I'm sorry. They called again. They want another Passing."

Enough was enough, Ruby thought to herself as she headed back to the shop.

Scott & Son was probably one of the smallest repair shops in the System. The building was large enough to fit a regular ship… but just the one. The front office formed part of the shop itself; giant metal shutters descending from the height of the building at closing time. Upon arrival she was met by the Son of Scott & Son, Johnny.

"Oh, hey there, you must be Ruby," Johnny said in a warm, welcoming voice; surprised to have such an attractive lady visiting the shop.
"Yes I'm Ruby. I assume you're the Scott Son I've been told about," she responded, not impressed with the Zimplaxion she saw before her.

Johnny was struck by both her beauty and her brashness but as always wasn't prepared for how to deal with it. "All good things I hope!"

"No, not good things… and given I've received three messages asking for more time they seem to have been right on the mark!" Ruby added, annoyed at Johnny's jovial response.

Johnny wasn't the quickest on the uptake but his unique charm often came to his rescue in situations like this.

"I'm sorry, I really am. What it was… is… well… I wanted to make sure it was done right of course… so I thought it best to check everything… and then there was this Kartill that came by… and apparently they needed assistance… because they'd been mugged… and I couldn't not help them. So I did, by which time it was too late to be finished in time. Then when I went to check on your ship again I found there was another issue, so I went to fix that and then the Kartill came back and wanted to thank me… I couldn't say no… would you say no? So we had lunch and"

At this point I think it's fair to save you from the drivel spewing from Johnny's mouth. Rather than expend further effort let's just take it as read this went on awhile longer… until Ruby interrupted him.

"Look… just get it finished today. You can buy me a drink this evening and I'll forget about the delays."

"Absolutely" Johnny said, thankful for the interruption.

"Do you know The Carpenter's Moons?" Ruby asked.

"Of course, I'm a regular," Johnny responded confidently.

"Perfect. Finish up and we'll head over," Ruby concluded, happy at the fortunate coincidence.

This might work out better than she had hoped…

WHERE THE IMPOSSIBLE BECOMES NECESSARY, A SOLUTION AWAITS DISCOVERY

The Carpenter's Moons was relatively quiet that night. Johnny and Ruby sat at a table in one corner of the room. A couple of other tables welcomed customers and a solitary Kartill was sat by the bar[109]. A constant hum of laughter between friends and acquaintances echoed

---

[109] The Kartill in question had sought out the solace of The Moons to drown his sorrows. It had been a trying Passing… well relatively speaking anyway. Having purchased a Lottery ticket, the Kartill had spent a couple of Passings fantasizing all of the many ways his life would improve. Sadly the ticket hadn't been a winner… more depressingly the Kartill hadn't realized his ticket didn't guarantee him the jackpot… hence the vast quantities of alcohol he would consume that night!

around the room, loud, but not enough to cause anyone to shout to be heard. Johnny was thankful for this lucky turn, he was very keen after all to make the most of the circumstances he'd found himself in. It was very rare to find Johnny on a date with a beautiful woman… and this woman was a knockout. She'd appeared quite bolshie to start with but was warming up in the more relaxed atmosphere of 'The Moons'.

Over the course of the night the pair shared stories from their lives. While Ruby's involved inter-planetary travel and danger, Johnny's tended to involve anecdotes from his nights spent at The Moons. He mentioned Chester a few times; Ruby being careful to absorb the information without making it obvious she was trawling for information. In spite of the 'Intel' being thrown her way, Ruby was finding it hard to concentrate on her mission.

It could have been the normality of Johnny's life but there was something she found very magnetic about him. He provided a perfect balance to her wild and risky way of life. As the subjects became more personal, Ruby explained the early age she'd left her parents to strike out by herself. Johnny listened intently before meeting her display of vulnerability with his own. His upbringing had been relatively mundane. As an only child his parents doted on him meticulously. At times, he'd told her, it was almost suffocating but it was all he'd ever known. He knew their love for him was unconditional. It was an odd thing to complain about… not that he was really complaining… but he seemingly could do no wrong. It was as if they were scared of losing him; scared their love alone wasn't quite enough… worried the slightest reprimand or punishment could tip the scales and cause him to leave. He laughed as he spoke about it… it really did feel ridiculous voicing it, thereby awarding it any credibility… but it was important enough that it played on his mind. There was a freedom in baring his soul to Ruby; a therapeutic release.

I'm sure the alcohol didn't hurt but the two seemed to hit it off instantly; the conversation flowing without any need to break down the usual barriers found in fledgling relationships. They'd discovered a level of trust and safety that put them both at ease. By the time Chester made it over to formerly introduce himself the pair had become very affectionate and were almost oblivious to his presence.

"You not gonna introduce me to your friend then?" Chester asked with a suggestive wink towards Johnny.

"Of course… I was just giving you some time. I know how you are around people," Johnny responded playfully.

Chester smirked as he pretended to ignore Johnny's response and turned towards Ruby. "I apologize my establishment hasn't been able to provide better company for you this evening. I'd be happy to throw this one out if you need."

Ruby smiled back. "You might need to shortly. He can't seem to keep his hands to himself."

Chester and Ruby shared a laugh together… Johnny meanwhile didn't seem too impressed.

"It's quieting down now, do you mind if I join you?" Chester asked.

What followed was the first, but most certainly not the last time the three would play Farmer, Scientist, Smuggler[110]. As the last of the Pub's patrons left, the game was becoming progressively more rowdy. An empty Pub provided the ideal motivation to encourage the three even further. For the rest of the night, alcohol flowed freely and two of the three became quite enamored with each other… and no, Chester wasn't one of the aforementioned two.

---

[110] The trio's passion for FSS is really quite incredible… especially given they still haven't finished a single game with a clear winner being crowned! Apparently the sheer joy of playing is enough to negate the frustration and arguments that break up each and every round. Chester is generally the first to boil over. It is fundamentally difficult for a Montar to consider not winning… especially against a couple of Zimplaxions! If you're interested, my personal favorite round involved Ruby arguing her Scientist was able to disprove the existence of all Farmers and Smugglers… it's fair to say the arguments broke out a little earlier than usual!

Looking back, the only thing Ruby slightly regretted was not focusing on grilling Chester a little more. She was partly sidetracked by the surprise romance but more unnervingly she couldn't figure Chester out. Everything she witnessed seemed to directly conflict with the Elder's version of the circumstances; leading her to question her acceptance of this assignment. Chester was relaxed, laid back and entirely stress-free. It didn't appear he was deluded or depressed; rather he seemed at peace with himself and content with the path he'd chosen.

The next morning Ruby awoke and in the cold light of Passing the fog surrounding her mission began to clear. The night before had cast doubt into her mind for one of the first times in her life. It was true Ruby had been guilty of some acts she wasn't proud of but now free from Jarko, she wasn't a criminal and nor did she feel it right to force someone against their will.

Taking a step back, Ruby started to question what she stood for. Since escaping Jarko she'd made a concerted effort to stand and be counted. Yes she took some missions for the money but never when they betrayed her conscience.

Had she been taken in by a very convincing lie? Just because the Montars weren't vocally protesting, was that really tantamount to acceptance? Even if it was a form of acceptance, did that make it right? In a hundred Cycles would society look back and wonder how this was ever permitted to continue? This train of thought only amplified the migraine that was already threatening to claim her from the excesses of the prior night[111]. At the same time those questions excited her. It was a nice change to find herself concerned with something more meaningful than how best to capture the next mark… or maybe she was just overanalyzing the night before in order to avoid focusing on other events… either way she concluded this mission was more complicated than she'd originally thought.

---

[111] Yep. The consequences of excessive alcohol consumption are just as notorious in The Wholeverse.

Meeting Johnny had been another surprise. Ruby's independent nature often stood in the way of relationships. Maybe men were intimidated by her or maybe she was scared to harmonize her softer side with her strength. Either way she always found a level of difficulty in lowering her defenses[112]. Leaving Johnny had felt weird; like leaving home without your keys… feeling something is missing but not sure what. Nervous to open up too much, she'd waited to see if Johnny was interested in spending more time together. The excitement of hearing Johnny suggest they should see more of each other would prove to be addictive.

Finding a way to return Chester while also dating Johnny were two precariously balanced ideals… fortunately where the impossible becomes necessary, a solution awaits discovery… and this case was no different. In reflecting on the dilemma a solution screamed from the recesses of her mind. There was a place she'd heard of that would potentially kill two Devil Hawks with one stone… but finding a way to convince Johnny and Chester to join her might not be the easiest of missions…

---

[112] In fairness ten Cycles of Ruby's life had essentially been in captivity. It's hardly the best base from where to start a relationship. "Would you like to come back to mine?", "No, I'm sorry… I literally can't… unless you'd like to speak to Rapture that is." Surprisingly that rarely received a positive response!

PERSONALIZED PATTERNS FOR PILGRIMS

It's not really accurate to say Jerome said goodbye to his son… his love hadn't faltered. Every Moment stood as a constant reminder of the mistake that had stolen both his son and the only remaining connection to his wife, away from him. Submersing himself in his work was the only way Jerome was able to live with his guilt. He realized he would likely never fully comprehend the true nature of The Mirror but understanding how it had affected his son was all the motivation he needed.

The Passing James looked into The Mirror became so pivotal to The 2nd Floor's work they began referring to it as 'Zero Passing'[113]. The Master who coined the term was particularly proud of himself; never

---

[113] Yep, you've guessed it. Of course The Masters had other options! They turned down Broken Mirror Passing, Mirror Soul Thief and Jerome's Mistake… fortunately the majority voted down all three before Jerome could hear them!

missing an opportunity to bring the subject up in conversation. Counting the time since Zero Passing becomes obnoxious pretty quickly… especially when Jerome is in earshot!

On his first trip back, Jerome found his Soulsion had changed once again. He couldn't explain why, but he felt The Mirror was trying to communicate with him. It may well have been the grief clouding his mind but Jerome couldn't understand the message… the only way he knew how to approach the conundrum was in the way he always had… as a scientist. He called for a handful of Masters to relive their Soulsions and was surprised to find that while they had changed from before Zero Passing, they remained intact since. His methodology proved successful and troublesome in equal measures. It was clear Zero Passing had somehow affected Space and Time, resulting in each Master's Soulsion being permanently and radically altered… but why was it that only his Soulsions morphed each time… what made him so unique? His presence at Zero Passing was most likely responsible but even that was just a theory.

Each Passing Jerome returned to the Mirror, doing everything he could to interpret the messages. As with many things in life, experience would hold the key to discovery. After a couple of Cycles, trends and patterns became apparent. At first Jerome had been confused by the randomness of the scenarios; each one focusing on a distinct set of parameters and characters. He tried fruitlessly to analyze what seemed to be the psychedelic dreams of madmen. It was only when he simplified his scientific approach he realized they might actually be snapshots from time… more accurately the Soulsions were highlighting the fractures in Space and Time.

It was as if The Mirror needed him to be ready before it would communicate intelligibly with him. Jerome related it to learning a language… until he understood the grammatical requisites and logic for constructing a sentence, the words themselves were meaningless. With this realization, his Soulsions were suddenly translated perfectly for his joyful comprehension. Explaining exactly what Jerome experienced really is quite impossible… it's most unfortunate that Jerome can't explain it to you himself… and if I was to share the specifics as to why he is unable to… well… I've said too much already!

Imagine a dream so real your nerves twitch with every imaginary touch. Reality however, pales in comparison to Jerome's Soulsions; every sense and emotion exaggerated to the extreme. Whispers become screams, pastels become neon and contentment becomes jubilation. It's probably worth mentioning these experiences have the potential to prove quite addictive. All too quickly Jerome was hooked… presenting quite the dilemma for the Masters… which should they place as the highest priority; the safety of one of their own[114], or the Sanctity of Continuance? Let's go ahead and agree we can safely assume which the Masters chose… it was the safety of The Wholeverse at stake after all.

Every time Jerome experienced a new Soulsion he recorded as much detail as possible in the 'Journal of Soulsions'[115]. The JoS became the most sacred of documents to the Masters. With so many disturbances in Space and Time occurring, it was imperative they fully understood the implications upon the Continuance. It would however also make the entire 2nd Floor a whole lot busier! The Masters began investigating each disturbance and the full ramifications of Zero Passing became clear. The ripples through Space and Time were exponential… and when the fabric holding Space and Time starts to crumble, the Sanctity of Continuance itself is at risk!

It was while investigating one specific Soulsion something truly miraculous was discovered. Two Masters were sent to the smallest moon of Andros to investigate the death of an elderly Zimplaxion. Jerome had

---

[114] It is pleasing The Masters cared enough to even consider this question. In fairness the Space Ideology organization offers a marvelous health plan. Addiction is included under the basic plan and oddly even includes the cost of a Cycle's worth of the associated addictive substance… which some might argue is slightly counter-intuitive…

[115] Only available at the library within The 2nd Floor of Space Ideology; the Journals have thousands of volumes. Even with the unique security The 2nd Floor presents, the Journals can only be read within the library itself. Masters may however take lunch in to accompany their reading.

seen the male in question leave his home and not two Moments later be swallowed whole by the ground. Now don't get me wrong… earthquakes, sinkholes and the like are of course possible in The Wholeverse. It is however quite unheard of for the ground to swallow someone without leaving even the tiniest of traces.

The two Masters landed their ship next to a lake nestled between two fields and made their way to the two-storey building Jerome had described. Following his instructions they walked twenty paces forward into the pristinely kept field. Sure enough there was absolutely no evidence of the incident. Nonetheless, The 2nd Floor demanded the most stringent of testing; requiring the pair to take all manner of readings and soil samples. They followed their protocols and after concluding the investigation, labored back to their ship; disappointed at their lack of success.

As they neared the ship they heard a bang from behind them. Looking back to where the noise had emanated they identified the source… the front door to the home they'd just left had been slammed. Moving their gaze forward they could see an elderly man… just as Jerome had written. He was pretty short for a Zimplaxion; a beard extending down to his chest, blue coveralls partially hiding a white shirt.

The two Masters stared at each other, the elderly man and then each other again. Their shared look of confusion provided little comfort as they searched for an explanation to this sight. How could this man still be alive? Was he a relative? Perhaps the ground had spat him back out? The pair watched intently as the man proceeded to walk across the perfectly manicured lawn. Suddenly, a loud bang rang out; a thunderclap seemingly produced from thin air. The man stopped and looked up for a source… and just like that it happened… the ground seemed to ripple as it collapsed and sprang back up almost quicker than could be seen, leaving no evidence of the elderly man.

The Masters were stunned. Sprinting towards the same area they'd so recently investigated; confusion turned to all out bewilderment. Once again they searched the area for evidence but just as before there was nothing to be found. It was as if the incident had never happened. They quickly ran their tests a second time and rushed back to The 2nd Floor. What did this mean?

Upon the two Masters return, a meeting was called for all on The 2nd Floor to attend. So important was the event, even Jerome was called back from the Mirror. The pair relived the sequence of events to an awestruck room. At the end of their story the room was abuzz with whispers and wonder… it should not be surprising that Jerome was the first to speak up.

"Masters… I thank you all for the kindness and understanding you have shown me since Zero Passing. The consequences of my actions that Passing are a constant reminder of both my loss and the still unquantified effects of my carelessness."

His audience all remained quiet and attentive as he continued.

"I am beginning to wonder if there is a treasure to be found within this disaster. My Soulsions are unique and troubling in their frequency… but as soon as I understood them, they became crystal clear. One puzzle remained however. Some of my Soulsions are quite distinct. While still clear they seem to shimmer… an audible echo if you will. Hearing your story has, I believe, provided the final puzzle piece needed to complete my cipher."

The Masters eagerly awaited Jerome's every word; excited by the direction he was headed.

"Your experiences at the smallest Moon of Andros may have finally answered why some Soulsions appear to shimmer. These Soulsions can only be construed as a window to the future. Space and Time has become fractured by Zero Passing. What we have discovered today is the disruption has only just begun. With foresight of the future fractures, it's only too clear how grave the consequences of Zero Passing are. This has most certainly solidified our dire need to catalogue each disruption… but it has also given us a unique opportunity. We now have the gift of foresight. With this gift we can preempt various fractures. Not only can we minimize and potentially avoid their effect… but with some luck… and a lot of study… it might be the key to uncovering the mystery of not only Zero Passing, but The Mirror itself!"

The Masters quite often look back at that speech as the dawn of The 2nd Floor as we know it today. That's not to say they were previously just twiddling their thumbs… The Wholeverse had been known to break its own rules every now and then. When these instances did occur, however, they tended to be rare and open to interpretation; a vision could have been a cosmic sign but it could have just as easily been the constructions of an open-mind wanting to find providence… after Zero Passing it was as if The Wholeverse had become a boisterous child clamoring for attention; fractures springing up faster than the Masters could track them. The Cliffs of Calamity were no longer just providing visitors an opportunity to spiritually discover themselves… they were doing far more… but we'll get to that soon enough. I'm sure you'll also remember The Dunes of Yandel had started playing by their own rules as well.

The Dunes had long been famous for providing personalized patterns for pilgrims to interpret their futures; an innocent prod for those who sought it. Following the incident at The Mirror however, a gentle nudge had turned into a forceful push. I would hazard a guess there is one prime example of this you may remember… given we're reminiscing we might as well pick back up right there.

Jerome had been at the Mirror all Passing. After many Soulsions he was positively giddy yet simultaneously ever so mellow. Even during his Soulsigh[116] he was driven by the memory of his son… just one more… maybe this one would help him understand how The Mirror had affected James…

As he stared into the Mirror, Jerome let his mind relax. The crimson tinged orange sky soothed his soul; sight giving way to mind. His breath slowed and his skin began to warm. It was an odd sensation

---

[116] A term coined by Jerome for the unique 'high' obtained from experiencing many consecutive Soulsions. As his were the only Soulsions that were vivid enough to establish this effect it only seems fair he was the one to name them.

but a pleasant one. Imagine light trying to escape; forcing its way out from within. Succumbing to something greater, yet accepting part of that greatness for your own. A shudder passed through his body; a cold shock echoing from fingertips to toes. The first images burst into his mind. He could see a Montar at The Dunes of Yandel. As his mind focused in on the images, so did the knowledge to accompany them. He inherently knew this was Chester. A Montar educated amongst his peers but unlike any other. Jerome observed as The Dunes communicated with Chester. While the colors resonated as with any other Soulsion, Chester's presence screamed at him. It wasn't obvious why at that point but it would soon begin to make sense. Jerome watched as The Dunes pushed Chester to a new path. Almost spontaneously the scene dissolved, giving birth to the briefest view of a new setting. Jerome breathed in deeply, soaking in both air and knowledge. Chester was stood behind a bar; The Carpenter's Moons… with him sat two Zimplaxions; Johnny and Ruby his mind informed him. Just as quickly the image disappeared again. Chester and Ruby were now stood in a field; the Pub in a haze in the background… a large Gorat standing at their side… and before them stood another Zimplaxion… WAIT… it was him… it was Jerome… his body, started to shiver, his chest felt like it was going to explode. He broke away from the experience, shocked by what he'd just seen.

While confusing at first, Jerome had become accustomed to his Soulsions expanding the more he meditated on them… and this case was no different. Soon enough not only did he know what he needed to do… but even more spectacularly, his unique Soulsions were beginning to make sense…

TRANSFORMING RAGE TO SILENCE

'The Cliffs of Calamity' stand as one of the greatest tourist attractions in all The Wholeverse. Many travel to see its beauty but few discover its wonder. The Cliffs themselves are the purest of whites and as tall as tall can be… how tall is that I hear you ask… well… imagine the tallest building you can. Now place that upon a copy of itself… then imagine the smallest building you can and place that atop the two buildings… finally add a cherry at the very peak. That should be a pretty rough approximation of their height!

The hordes that travel to see The Cliffs either gaze upon its majesty from the ocean or look down from its crest. Both views are truly astounding and are a just reward for those who make the journey. It is another viewpoint however that provided Ruby's inspiration for leading Chester and Johnny to Thundos[117]. The slimmest of shorelines is hidden

---

[117] A spectacular planet in The Keliptar System. Known primarily for The Cliffs of Calamity the planet also provides a third of The Wholeverse's Self-Help books. The Cliffs have inspired and at the same time over-amplified the planet's many authors sense of credibility; ranging from the egotistical - 'Your Life Has

at the base of The Cliffs. No deeper than a few paces, the sheer
enormity of The Cliffs camouflage the golden sand. At high tide water
thrashes against The Cliffs. For a couple of Periods each Passing, the
tiniest of beaches allows those lucky or foolish enough to venture in, an
opportunity like no other. Only accessible from the water, it is a secret
that feels more like a myth.

Lying on the narrowest of beaches, staring up at the never-
ending Cliffs stretching out above you, the gentle waves pulsating
behind, a sense of calm like no other embraces your soul. It is often
suggested the mighty scale of The Cliffs induce an introspection that
cannot be obtained elsewhere; an intoxicating meditation. For those who
know The Cliff's true secret this is merely the beginning. The Cliffs had
begun to provide far more to a fortunate few who sought guidance. It
was for this reason Ruby had chosen to visit The Cliffs with her two new
comrades.

Ruby and Johnny were growing ever closer; sharing most of
their Moments together at The Carpenter's Moons. Ruby could see
Johnny was very close to Chester which made her assignment even
harder. Her suggestion of visiting The Cliffs of Calamity had fortunately
been met with unanimous praise. Chester often heard of the legend and
following his encounter at The Dunes, was hugely excited to see what
other guidance he could find. Johnny meanwhile had his mind firmly
fixed on a distinctly less noble reason… a beach you see meant there
would be bathing suits… and for Johnny this made the trip most
definitely worthwhile[118]. Ruby also had her own motivations. Maybe The
Cliffs could help solve her ethical conundrum. Was it right to convince

---

Improved Just By Reading This Title: Now Buy This Book If You Want A Life
As Good As Mine!', to the self-deprecatingly droll – 'My Life Isn't Wonderful,
But It's Not Bad, If You're Interested I Have Some Ideas You Could Borrow…
If You Want To That Is'.

[118] This was of course completely innocent. Johnny merely liked wearing
bathing suits and playing in the water. It certainly didn't have anything at all to
do with wanting to see Ruby in a bathing suit. For the sake of completeness
Ruby did wear a bathing suit. A pure black two-piece bikini with gold clasps…
not that Johnny would remember if you asked him...

Chester to head back to the MHW, potentially putting his life in danger… and what of her feelings for Johnny? Could she fall for him but still stay true to herself?

The three friends stepped off a small wooden rowing boat they'd rented and onto the beach. They were fortunate, as far as eyes could see they were alone. The unblemished golden sand stretched out alongside The Cliffs; welcoming their adventurous spirits. Although they were excited, there was also a level of trepidation; the danger of The Cliffs evident. The tide could rise at any Moment… and what's more… without having previously experienced The Cliffs, it wasn't entirely clear what awaited them. The three decided the safest option was to take it in turns to stare into The Cliffs of Calamity.

As the originator of the idea Ruby was nominated both by the group and herself to go first. She lay down on the beach; feet towards The Cliffs, waves slowly breaking behind her. As she began to relax, the scale of The Cliffs was awe-inspiring. The world above seemed to expand and lower itself down towards her. She was already a tiny spec amongst the vast Cliffs but now she felt non-existent. She embraced the most serene calm as her mind started to wander. Memories of Eshua filled her mind. Reliving her conversation with the Elder there was suddenly an added perspective that hadn't been there before. It was as if she could hear his thoughts. The conversation continued with the Elder's mind taking an active role in this bizarre performance. His thoughts belied his speech and Ruby began to receive the answers she was looking for.

The Elder's plan still seemed honest enough. His intention really was to have Chester move back of his own accord; rediscovering the gifts that made him so adept at war. A deeper, more menacing subtext became clear as the two characters advanced through their lines. The Elder's emotions unlocked Ruby's understanding; Chester wasn't important to the Elder, none of the Montars were. The Eshuan Elder and The Council thought themselves Gods; the Montars providing a means to an end. The Elder's subconscious briefly peered into a time before the MTP, when Montars were free to choose their own destiny. His concern was obvious as his mind dwelled on the risk Chester presented to The Council's current way of life. With the conversation drawing to a close, the Elder's mind wandered once more. This time to shallow desires; money, excess and the women he used to satiate his misdirected passion…

With that, Ruby's mind returned to the beach. She sat up and saw Chester and Johnny laughing to her right.

"Hey. Here she is. How was it? What did you see?" Chester asked.

Ruby didn't know how to respond; an all consuming guilt encompassing her spirit. Lying seemed to be the best route for her.

"Nothing unfortunately… maybe I wasn't supposed to see anything."

Chester's Intuition told him otherwise but he liked Ruby and respected her enough not to push further. He looked towards Johnny. "Go on then fella, you're next up. See if you can do any better than your Mrs."

"OK then, but no funny business while I'm out!" Johnny responded with a cheeky grin.

Johnny gave Ruby a kiss on the cheek before stretching out on the sand. He absorbed The Cliffs and just as Ruby before him, his mind started to wander. Johnny's experience however was distinctly different. Darkness surrounded him before a flash lit up the horizon. He searched for meaning but found none. What was he supposed to interpret from this? All around him images swirled of Ruby. He couldn't recall these Moments. They didn't seem to be his memories. As the images advanced they became clearer and he could see Ruby wasn't alone… she was with someone. They seemed very intimate, as if they had known each other forever. One image exploded into view, stealing his entire focus… it was Johnny… the image shattered and suddenly all of the other pictures pulsed. It was him in all of them. The clarity unlocked memories he couldn't recall… yet somehow they felt more real than those he could. The memories sparked his emotions, his feelings for Ruby building exponentially. He'd spent a lifetime with Ruby even though he'd only met her a few Passings ago.

The realization shocked him out of his trance. Looking up he saw Chester kicking the sand as Ruby stared out towards the water.

"Welcome back. Please tell us you saw something." Chester questioned.

"I… I… yes I did, but… I'm not quite sure what I saw," Johnny responded, the full weight of his vision still sinking in.

"I guess it's up to me then! I'll show you both how it's done!" Chester offered as he lay down in the sand.

As Chester began to fall under The Cliff's power, Johnny and Ruby were left alone. Neither was quite ready to speak. Ruby felt a sense of relief. She'd finally seen the truth and knew she couldn't proceed with her mission. Her confidence protected her from fear of the Elders but she'd deceived Johnny and wasn't sure how to look him in the eyes. This was fortunate for Johnny. He too was trying to come to terms with his vision. Looking over towards Ruby he found it almost impossible not to run over and grab her. It was like losing your soul mate after a lifetime together, only for them to suddenly appear before you. He was sure Ruby would be scared by a display of such affection.

Chester's experience wasn't nearly as long as Ruby's and Johnny's… but when you have a Montar's Intuition I guess that's not surprising… especially when combined with the rage of a Montar. Chester's vision contained a montage of his Moments with Ruby. In recalling them it was as if his Intuition had been upgraded. His mind was no longer clouded by his trust and respect for Johnny… Ruby had a plan… she was there to try and return him to the MHW!

Chester bolted up, instantly waking from his trance. The quick movement caught Ruby's attention; guilt keeping her on edge.

"How did it go?" Ruby asked; desperately seeking a positive response.

Chester stood up and charged towards her. "What are you doing here? Tell him! Tell Johnny why you're really here!" He demanded.

Dread filled Ruby's face. Chester must have seen the truth. "It isn't… it's not what you think."

"Wait…" Johnny said, "What's going on? What have I missed?"

Chester stared through Ruby, making her feel insignificant. "Tell him!"

Ruby looked over to Johnny. "I was sent to bring Chester back to the Montar Home World… but it's not like it seems… I came here to find guidance, to find the truth. I wasn't going to do anything until I knew what was right."

Johnny's already confused mind couldn't figure out how to deal with this new information. He turned his back to Ruby and started to walk away. Ruby lunged towards him, her hand landing on his shoulder in an attempt to stop him.

A shudder trembled its way through Ruby's hand, growing stronger as it reverberated up her arm and through her entire body. She fell to the floor as her vision turned to black. Her heart started to beat faster; every breath feeling like an almighty challenge. Without warning the darkness made way for a stream of images; exploding into view faster than she could comprehend.

Johnny knelt over Ruby; desperately trying to rouse her. She'd been still for an entire Moment without any visible sign of response. A deep gasp sounded as she sprang back up. There was silence as she stared into Johnny's eyes; his gaze meeting hers right back. Chester watched on as the two seemed to stare for several Moments. Neither could bring themselves to speak. Upon waking and seeing Johnny, the images that had been incoherent suddenly made sense. The memories Johnny discovered had found their way to Ruby. As their eyes continued to linger it was as if they were seeing each other for the first time in many Cycles; their souls communicating without the need for words. Finally the silence was broken.

"You saw it… didn't you?" Johnny asked.

"Yes… I… I saw you… I remember you," Ruby responded; confused but comforted at the same time.

Johnny was lost for a response. He couldn't find any words to articulate his emotions. Instinct taking over, he embraced Ruby; two soul mates reunited in time.

While Johnny was understandably forgiving of Ruby's mission, Chester was not so easily convinced. Ruby attempted to explain her intentions behind the trip to The Cliffs but the best she could achieve was transforming his rage to silence. Johnny's unique vision sealed his fate with Ruby's, the two sharing a lifetime of memories and love… but that was not all… the full extent of Johnny's awakening would be instrumental in the fate that awaited his best friend…

AN EXQUISITE FAILURE

After nearly ten Passings without receiving any form of update, the Elder of Eshua had grown concerned. The Council wouldn't be happy if his plan failed. The consequences were so grave he didn't dare think about it. He needed a way to figure out if his plan was still going to work… and when you're an Elder with something, anything, needing to be done, who do you turn to? The Master Elder's secretary of course!

An elderly Montar, Erica retired to the MHW after many Cycles of service, but it wasn't long before she found a role within The Council. She had hoped to retire alongside a Montar she'd fallen for during her final Cycles of service. Unfortunately life doesn't always turn out the way we wish. The Montar of her affections had been offered the Master General role on the MTP, an opportunity he felt was too good to turn down. Realizing her foolishness for hiding her feelings, she found a way to be closer to him. As the Master Elder's secretary she was afforded certain privileges. The most meaningful being an ability to work with the Montar she'd fallen for. Even with this benefit the choice hadn't been an easy one. She would come to learn many things she'd prefer to forget while working for The Council. It was however, her role in the Master Elder's plan she would regret the most.

The Eshuan Elder's instructions were simple enough. Visit The Carpenter's Moon's and report back on Chester and Ruby. Fortunately for Erica, guidance on the acceptability of alcoholic consumption hadn't been provided… and given The Council reimbursed her expenses... she figured why not take advantage for once!

She kept to herself that night in the Pub. A Montar drinking wasn't unheard of; they were after all allowed some personal time during their various mercenary activities… there was however no point in senselessly bringing undue attention to herself. As she sipped her second drink of the night[119] her attention was suddenly grabbed by a commotion at the entrance of the Pub.

"It's not good enough," Chester yelled as he flung open the front door; Johnny and Ruby following quickly behind.
"She's explained what happened… why are you being so stubborn?" Johnny snapped back.
"Stubborn? You might not mind but I do! It wasn't you she was after!" Chester's usually calm demeanor had gone fishing. The patrons of the Pub were unused to seeing this side of him and were doing to their best to blend in.
"Buddy, come on. You're overreacting. She wasn't 'after you'," Johnny responded in a calmer tone; trying to rationalize with his Montar friend. "Ruby's already explained she wasn't sure who to believe. We're lucky it was her and not someone else."

---

[119] She'd gone for Chester's Homebrew. The Pefrin tending bar had offered to let her test some cocktails... having clumsily spilt the contents of his first two concoctions; Erica decided the Homebrew would be the easiest option for all involved!

"Lucky?" Chester said, interrupting Johnny's flow. "Yeah… lucky we met so she could make a profit from my hind!"

Johnny tried his best not to be flustered by his friend's inability to reason. "Look Chester. She's seen through them now… and she's apologized for not being upfront. Try and be reasonable."

Chester went to speak but bit his tongue as he labored over towards the bar, pulling up a pew with his back to Johnny.

Erica had been watching intently from her corner. She'd seen enough that it was obvious Ruby's mission had failed. The situation was far too precarious for her to remain. The pair would surely calm down enough to realize this wasn't a conversation they should be having in public… when they reached that point, it wouldn't be long before they'd notice her. Sipping the last of her Homebrew she waited for Ruby and Johnny to join Chester at the bar and then slipped out unnoticed.

Returning to the MHW and more specifically Eshua, Erica's news sent the Elder into a great panic. His plan had failed. If The Council discovered this by themselves he would be swiftly replaced… it was time to face The Council… and most likely suck up like his life depended on it!

The Elders were all sat around The Council table; rumors driving various conversations. Rarely was a meeting called by anyone other than the Master Elder. The purpose of this meeting unknown; every Elder had their own guess, each wilder and more fantastical than the last. The room turned to silence as the Master Elder walked in and took his position at the head of the table.

"Thank you all for joining us today. I am as curious as each of you to hear what the Elder of the Eshua has to share with us. I must say… of all your guesses… my favorite involved an impromptu cocktail party! I suggest we proceed with that option immediately after today's meeting!" the Master Elder began. Looking towards a shrinking Elder, he continued. "Elder, you have the table"

The Eshuan Elder stood, clearly afraid of what would follow.

"It is to my great dismay that I stand before you this Passing with news to share. I've just received word that the plan I set in place has failed. Chester remains on the smallest Moon of Andros," he almost whispered; scared of the response he would receive.

As it goes the Elder of Eshua shouldn't have been so worried. The Master Elder's ego, like every other Montar, drove his every action. There was only one thing he really wanted… to be proved right… his alternative plan for Chester was now the only remaining option… and that served him perfectly.

"Thank you Elder," the Master replied. "I'm sure I speak for everyone on this Council when I share my sadness at this outcome. Our awareness of his existence is no longer a secret. We must assume the risk he poses is now significantly greater. You may all remember two options were presented at our last meeting. With this news our focus should now return to the original plan. I fear I must decree Chester's debt to this Council will be paid with his life."

You may not know him intimately but I'm sure you can deduce the Master Elder wasn't sharing all his cards with the table. He'd been waiting for this outcome and had been planning accordingly. The Elders started voicing their agreement with this decree as the Master Elder once again drew their attention.

"Chester will not be an easy target. As part of the almighty race of Montars we are all aware of the difficulties inherent in tracking and killing any one of us."

The Elders were entranced by their leaders call for action, waiting with baited breath for his next words.

"Sending soldiers of our own is quite clearly out of the question. We need neither the extra bad publicity nor the risk of a potential uprising. Fear not my esteemed Elders; I have a plan. We cannot hope to silence Chester with any regular mercenary. His Intuition will ensure he preempts any attempts on his life. A true mercenary's intentions are singular and predictable… a sadistic and deranged killer meanwhile cannot be anticipated… irrationality hides them from our Intuition… that is just what we need… and I have the perfect candidate in mind."

The Master Elder turned and looked towards the Eshuan Elder. "My Secretary informs me the mercenary you chose, who failed so exquisitely, is quite the legendary combatant herself. I'm sure you'll be pleased to hear her execution will most certainly be included."

… and so another delusional meeting of The Council came to a close, leaving plenty of time for the Elders to relax with a cocktail, or two, or three! While they enjoyed their cavalier attitudes to life and death, the future of Chester and Ruby was to be left in an all too familiar foe's hands...

A FAR MORE FEARSOME FOE

Public humiliation has a funny way of transforming a person… the first reaction is of course, depression and despair. Under just the right circumstances those feelings have the potential to adapt; guided by the hosts underlying desires. Sometimes this can be a joyful thing. Learning to become a stronger person after an ex decides to break your heart for example… just an example of course… notice there wasn't any detail given… like the ex dumping you in the middle of a disappointingly lukewarm homemade lasagna… again, just an example!

Other times a quite different coping mechanism takes hold. When depression sets in there are those who use bitterness to build a foundation. In these instances the resulting power is all consuming; absorbing one's soul. Where a conscience previously ruled, nothing is left but a deep and dark hunger for vengeance. This was the path Jarko was destined to follow.

Watching everything he built instantly crumble at his feet produced a rather ironic twist for Jarko. In Rapture he'd created an incredibly detailed character. Method actors could only dream of producing such a convincing deceit. It shouldn't be surprising therefore that while it was Jarko that fell into unfathomable bleakness, it was Rapture who escaped.

In his solitude there was nothing for Jarko to do but dwell upon his hatred for Ruby. The insecurities that had for so many Cycles focused his mind on maintaining a false persona were the very same that received the full brunt of Ruby's angst. He kept replaying the moment over and over again; the eyes of each of his followers suddenly awake to his deception; a room full of disgust targeted solely at him. The image was stuck on replay; a never-ending monument of his failure. His inner monologue became the Director's commentary to this scene; adding extra weight to his self-pity. In the middle of this vicious downward spiral, Jarko's mind began to buckle under the pressure. The commentary that was already so self-deprecating took on a rather familiar tone. Rapture, the personality he had for so long depended on, decided to take the reins.

Rapture's condescension of Jarko became greater by the Moment. A war raging inside his mind, the personalities fractured and diffused. Jarko was losing the fight for his sanity to a fictional representation of his own creation. Rapture was no longer just a character, he'd become a fully developed personality seeking to control his host. The final break was brutal. Without the grounding of an anchor in reality, Jarko was cast aside by Rapture. Jarko taking his place as the work of fiction; Rapture the scribe who no longer cared for his own creation.

Insanity in this instance was to become a most delightfully ironic pleasure. Jarko had spent so many Cycles convincing The Wholeverse they should fear him, he could never have predicted Rapture's reality would be so much worse than his mind could create. The Wholeverse was equally in for quite the surprise. Legends of Rapture's power had become fallacies overnight. All who once feared him now laughed at the mention of his name; more likely to be embarrassed of admitting they had feared 'The Great Showman'. It wouldn't be long before news would travel of a new chapter in 'The Life and Times of Rapture'[120]…

Having fully consumed Jarko, Rapture couldn't bear to feel the taste of weakness in his mouth one Moment longer. For the first time in many Passings he showed his face at Rapture's Landing. The bar was almost empty; time moving on quicker than Jarko. The only patrons were those who hadn't experienced Jarko's ownership. Sadly they would get to know Rapture very quickly indeed. The rage fueling him was no longer contained by any semblance of a conscience. His mercy was non-existent while his need to expel any remnant of weakness was all consuming.

Rapture walked slowly and deliberately over to a quiet Zimplaxion sitting at the bar. The lack of fear displayed only accelerated his intentions. One hand came to rest on the unsuspecting patron's shoulder as the other reached into his mouth; fingers cupping behind his teeth. With one fatal and swift tug, Rapture tore the Zimplaxion's head clean off. The already quiet bar became both literally and figuratively deadly silent. Rapture looked around. There were three others left. He didn't need witnesses to share this story; the thought didn't even pass through his mind. This was about cleansing his muddied soul. Without hesitation Rapture finished the slaughter. Jarko's reputation would remain for the time being but Rapture would savor this first taste of vengeance.

In the Passings to come Rapture continued to ruthlessly slay any who dared breathe in his presence. The old tales of 'Rapturing' would have been a welcome punishment by comparison. The new Rapture had no desire to instill fear; his focus only extended to revenge; brutal and total. Every canvas of mutilation served as a calling card. This new untold savage was far more menacing than Jarko could have concocted.

---

[120] The Life & Times of Rapture would become one of The Wholeverse's best-sellers. While not endorsed by the man himself, many find it to be a most compelling narrative and strongly agree he is worthy of being the main character in his own Tale!

With no survivors left to share the gory details of Rapture's quest for destruction, the unknown became a far more fearsome foe.

The Wholeverse is no stranger to evil; quite the opposite in fact. Its vastness is met only too eagerly by its ability to produce depravity by the bucket load. The trail of death Rapture left in his wake was by all accounts something quite different. Even the depths of depravity being ravaged by Rapture could not vanquish every slice of evidence… soon enough the stories gained a face… not that of Jarko or Rapture but rather the 'Ghost of Rapture'. The fearful many surmised Jarko had sought an end to his suffering by taking his own life. It was thought no mere mortal could possibly be as callous and deadly as was necessary for this trail of devastation… in his otherworldly state he was seeking revenge against those who turned against him. For a while it was even said The Blue Lagoons of Tranjuri stopped causing blindness; fearing they would inadvertently steal the sight from the Ghost of Rapture and incur his wrath[121].

And so it was… Jarko had finally instilled the fear he had always wished for… what a shame he only had to lose his soul to achieve that goal.

Let's not forget Rapture's vengeance had a target… otherwise known as Ruby. Having relieved some pent-up tension with his initial murderous rampages; Rapture's attentions turned to locating Ruby. Everyone was only too ready to share details of Ruby's growing legend… especially when confronted with the very face of their fears. Her current whereabouts however remained a mystery for the time being.

It's at our very favorite Public House that a number of streams began to intersect. A rather inebriated Bashtak[122] had decided to share

---

[121] This is of course quite absurd. The Lagoons are inanimate… but I never promised you The Wholeverse was comprised purely of logic!

[122] This Bashtak has been a regular at The Carpenter's Moons for as long as I can remember. Although he never seems sober enough to recall his real name,

the tale of the Ghost of Rapture and his murderous quest for Ruby with a Montar he'd seen sitting by herself in the corner of the Pub… this Montar was of course Erica. Fortunately she wasn't nearly as intoxicated as the story-telling Bashtak. Shortly after hearing this tale Erica would watch the Zimplaxion in question walk through the front door… and I'm sure you can recall how that turned out. Sat, drinking her Homebrew, she began formulating a plan that the Master Elder would gladly, albeit sloppily, appropriate!

The Elders are not what you would refer to as hands-on leaders… Very much your high level strategy types, there is very little chance of their metaphorical sleeves being rolled up. Erica can most certainly attest to that. As a result, their plan to have the new and improved Rapture take care of unfinished business fell to luck far more than logic. True, they are Montars, but they are certainly not fighters. Consequently the Master Elder's… 'Master' plan, relied heavily on good ol' fashioned word of mouth… and who better to task with this than Erica herself.

Erica's task, although arduous, provided an opportunity for an all expenses paid tour of a number of Systems' watering holes. Simple enough, she merely needed to plant the crumbs for Rapture to stumble upon… Erica was of course sure to explain to the Master Elder that in order to be effective it was of the utmost importance for her to spread the word in at least three Pubs or Bars per planet… and obviously the word would spread quicker if she was to stay in swanky hotels[123] as

---

Chester and Johnny affectionately refer to him as 'Donnie'. Funnily enough at this time he'd not only seen Ruby at The Moons before… he'd actually been introduced to her twice! The first time she even posed for a photo with him… now if that isn't a warning of the adverse effects of alcohol on the brain I don't know what is! On the flip-side he has an unbelievable ability to recite entire passages from the Missile Force series… like I said… adverse effects on the brain!

[123] Erica most definitely took advantage of this opportunity. This is exemplified by her three nights stay at 'The Fate of The Dunes'. With everyone looking for signs of divinity in The Dunes there wasn't many guests to talk to… there was however plenty of food and on-demand entertainment to enjoy!

well… there was no use in ignoring the upper echelons of society after all!

I'd like to take a Moment to paint a finer picture of Erica. Her role in this scheme is perfectly transparent… without her involvement there wouldn't have even been a plan. I would however ask you to remember The Council's power. Having spent many Cycles serving at their pleasure Erica was well aware of the risks of not following their orders… so please, don't judge her too harshly!

Fortunately for the Elders, their back-up plan bore some Rapture-sized fruit! Rapture's thirst had been quenched to such an extent that his executions were upgraded to include a modicum of interrogation. In the midst of threatening a particularly cowardly Kartill he uncovered a rumor of Ruby's whereabouts… even just a rumor was sufficient for a determined Rapture… Ruby was about to have a most unwelcome reunion with a face from her past… but this time she would need more than just her confidence…

THE PURITY OF AN ALMIA TREE

Chester while stubborn isn't completely unreasonable. Having vented his outrage at Ruby's actions he eventually made peace with her. Please do take 'eventually', very literally… Ruby attempted begging, pleading and even groveling. Having worn him down enough, Chester finally started actually listening to what Ruby was trying to tell him.

Taking a seat he asked her to explain what she'd seen at The Cliffs. Ruby relived the thoughts she'd heard from the Elder of Eshua; his concern over the risk Chester presented and the times before the MTP, when Montars had the ability to make their own choices.

Chester had never deliberately sought to anger the Elders. He was only ever trying to live his own life. The Elder's innermost thoughts forced him to view his existence in a whole new light. He had no intention of conceding and serving at the Elders pleasure. He wasn't sure what this meant but he was hoping Ruby's decision to abandon her mission would allow him to leave the question unanswered. Another question did however find its way back into his mind. A question Johnny has once posed to him. It didn't seem like his issue to solve at the time but he began to wonder why he was the only one. Why hadn't other Montars attempted to break away from the MTP?

On a pretty regular evening at The Carpenter's Moons, Donnie was propping up his designated table in the corner of the Pub. His legs sprawled on the booth seat with his neck rested haphazardly against the table. A puddle of drool had collected around his hairy mouth; bubbles gurgling up with every breath. It was a really quite disgusting sight if I'm honest… but there was a reason Chester permitted this.

"I want you to bring me a new drink every fifteen Moments or so… It's been one of those Passings and I want to forget all about it," the Bashtak had commanded.

Chester wasn't one to argue with the wishes of his patrons. Especially when they provided payment up front for a whole evening's worth of drinks. It might seem somewhat unethical but in truth Chester had been supplying glasses of water instead of alcohol since Donnie's third drink of the night… Chester was safe in the knowledge his deception wouldn't be discovered. This sequence of events had become a ritual for many Passings. It appeared Donnie was such a lightweight that just two drinks would result in a temporary form of amnesia. Chester knew in a Period or so Donnie would stumble outside, only to wake up sometime later resting against the front of The Moons… Chester quite often thought to himself this image was all part of the Pub's charm.

In another corner sat a rowdy group of Valatars. Four in total, three female, one male; they were apparently competing for who could drink from their glass in the most inventive way. One of the group had just completed a pretty impressive feat. Sprawled on the floor, feet facing out, head below the table; she'd managed to balance the glass in such a way the liquid ran quite wonderfully down towards her awaiting mouth[124].

---

[124] I strongly advise against trying this at home. I can personally attest to its difficulty! A glass falling on your head means you've already tried this one too many times!

Valatars are known for traveling in packs; as much for the camaraderie as the increased time between having to buy a round of drinks![125] Their appearance is similar in size and stature to that of a Zimplaxion. Facially you'd most likely compare them to a Lion. Rather than covering the entire circumference of their face, their manes generally just run from their forehead back... of course some have been known to have manes grow elsewhere, but we don't need to go out of our way to embarrass anyone!

Chester stood behind the bar, serving up the latest round for Johnny and Ruby who were sat on stools before him. Their conversation that night had centered squarely around the trio's favorite Missile Force films. It had become pretty contentious following Ruby's suggestion the original would never be improved upon... it was never intended to be a series after all.

Fortunately for the three, there would be little opportunity for the argument to progress...

The front door to The Carpenter's Moons was distinctly heavy. Made from the wood of an Almia Tree[126], its six hinges held on for dear life. Like Chester, the door was sturdy and true. Anyone unlucky enough to have it slammed in their face receives the message loud and clear. I'm happy to say this very rarely occurs; Chester is a formidable barkeep. I

---

[125] Fun Valatar Fact - Valatars are known for being one of the most forward thinking races in The Wholeverse. So much so they recently even voted in their first *Male President!* If you should ever happen to cross paths with a Valatar, don't be surprised if they give you a funny look at the notion of discrimination. The word literally has no meaning to them... save as an issue other races have to endure.

[126] Almia trees produce the toughest wood in The Wholeverse. They are so dense it's not until they eventually die that they can be cut. Native to Tranjuri; they stand as the most prominent reason the planet's air is cleaner than pretty much anywhere else. The Royal Family of Tranjuri originally chose to live upon the planet for its amazingly fresh air... and even they still try to mow down the Almia Trees on a regular basis... well... they is perhaps wide of the mark... Price Trado is primarily the guilty party.

can barely remember a handful of times trouble has escalated to that degree. When it does however the loud smash of the heavy door slamming shut is always by the hands of Chester… it provided quite a shock for everyone in the Pub to hear such a unique bang with Chester clearly serving behind the bar.

The bar fell silent as everyone looked up. The door had been slammed shut by an intruder entering the Pub; desperate to garner its occupant's attention. The Gampo that stood in the doorway was full of confidence, a look of satisfaction on his face. His eyes were fixated on one person.

"Jarko! What did I say last time you saw me?" Ruby shouted across the room.

The words fell on deaf ears. Rapture began to walk across the room as a smile crept onto his foreboding face.

"What are you smiling about? I warned you what would happen." Ruby was unaffected by the being she'd formerly known as Jarko.

Still her words had no effect. He was close now and not looking to stop. Ruby began to wonder what had possessed her old captor as his right arm reached out; his hand meeting her neck.

"Pathetic little girl. You think you know who you are talking to? You've never met me before!" Rapture snarled.

Chester was slow to react, his mind trying to work out how his gut hadn't warned him of this. Slow yes, but this is Chester we are talking about. His slow is another man's ultrasonic. His left hand clamped around Rapture's wrist and with a locked fist, his right hoof smashed into his unsuspecting foe. Rapture was forced back a couple of steps; a smile once again highlighting his lack of fear.

"So, my renegade slave has found herself a protector I see," Rapture seethed as he turned to face Chester. "I'm surprised to see you here. Haven't you got some orders to follow? How sweet to see two slaves become friends."

By now Chester had pounced across the bar, taking a solid stance between Ruby and Rapture. He waited for that feeling he usually loathes. The tingling inside that warns and leads him to act… but nothing came… it was as if his Intuition was broken; his opponent unrecognized by the assumptions its power depended upon. This was a new experience for Chester. There was no script to follow, no plodding steps for him to anticipate. A regular Montar would've been able to fall back on their training in situations like this but Chester had become accustomed to a far more relaxed life. His intimidating stature had been enough to nullify any threat for many Cycles. He couldn't remember the last time his fighting talents had been called upon.

Rapture hadn't anticipated a fight as such but was almost gleeful at the opportunity. The crowd in the Pub couldn't take their eyes away from the scene escalating before them. This promised to be quite a battle. Even the heavily inebriated Donnie was sat up; attempting to absorb what he'd originally thought was a Passingdream.

The next move was Rapture's; his left wing rising up and catching Chester off guard. The impact was so forceful Chester was sent flying; a loud thud sounding as he hit the far wall. The Pub's occupants all gasped at this sight and ran for the exits, leaving just Johnny, Ruby and a floored Chester to fight this battle. Rapture was unmoved by the evacuation. The only person he was interested in was stood before him.

He set upon Ruby once again; his fingers tightening around her neck as he lifted her clean off the ground. "Jarko's death was pleasing but yours is the one I will savor the most."

Ruby's face would have shown her confusion if only she wasn't struggling for breath. With Rapture's attention squarely focused on Ruby he hadn't noticed Johnny rushing up from behind. Johnny scrambled for a weapon but all he could find was a stool. With all the strength he could summon he smashed the stool against Rapture's back. The dark scales coating his skin offered enough protection to absorb the brunt of the force but the surprise was sufficient to force him to drop Ruby to the ground. Rapture spun around quickly to face his attacker.

"Another fool and more blood to be spilled today" Rapture screamed, staring at Johnny as if a Ramdil had just dared challenge him.

Chester had shaken off the shock, regained his composure and was racing towards Rapture. He grabbed a broken stool leg on his way and smashed it down into Rapture's wing. His scales once again mitigated the impact but Chester had earned his attention.

"OK Montar. We'll have to begin with you then."

Chester's Intuition wasn't providing any help but his skills with a Bo, or stool leg as it happened to be in this case, were flooding back to him with every swing. Rapture meanwhile was well and truly accustomed to the strengths of his body. The protection afforded by his reinforced scales was the perfect accompaniment to his powerful wings.

The two warriors exchanged blows, Rapture knocked to the ground with each swing that connected; Chester's power proving too much for Rapture's center of gravity. Each blow was a temporary setback for Rapture; regaining his stance as quickly as he was floored. Chester meanwhile was struggling to maintain his composure. This fight was completely alien to him. He'd never encountered anyone whose every attack wasn't signaled to his conscious mind.

There was another thud as Rapture's left wing connected with Chester's head… with his senses temporarily fazed he wasn't ready for the next attack. Pouncing on his stumbling prey Rapture followed up with his right wing, this time leading with its dense spike. A smirk enveloped the Gumpo's face as Chester collapsed to the ground; the wound proving too much for him to fight through.

Ruby and Johnny had been watching from behind. They'd felt confident Chester would triumph and were now reeling from the approaching Rapture. Johnny's protective nature overpowered his logic as he strode between Ruby and the advancing menace. There wasn't time for common sense to advise that his partner was the far more experienced combatant.

Rapture had lost patience by this time. Johnny was standing in the way and accordingly he was cast aside with another knock from Rapture's wing. This time his head collided with the wall, leaving him unconscious.

"Just the two of us now Ruby… I should really thank you for finally awaking me… but I have been looking forward to ending your life for far too long."

The confident look Ruby exuded at their last meeting was nowhere to be seen. The scared look of a child running from her parents had returned.

"Don't worry. Your death will not be swift. I want to enjoy watching you squirm." Rapture warned before striking a knockout blow.

Ruby couldn't put her finger on how long she'd been out. It could have been Moments or Periods; either would have been just as believable. As her faculties returned she began to feel the tightness of the rope restraining her arms behind her. Rapture had tied both Johnny and Ruby to chairs. Chester meanwhile was still sprawled out on the floor, clutching the wound on his chest that was bleeding profusely. Ruby looked around but couldn't see Rapture. A strong smell captured her attention. It was a propellant of some kind. Suddenly a voice came from behind her.

"Perfect timing Ruby… everything is ready. All that remains is to watch you burn with your friends."

Ruby couldn't understand what had become of the Jarko she knew. The ruthless maniac before her couldn't be the same being. She searched for an answer… the magical sequence of words that would save them all from this fate.

"Jarko… please… you kept me around for ten Cycles because you couldn't bring yourself to hurt me…. I know I'm responsible… but you left me no choice. I know who you really are and this isn't it," Ruby pleaded, the words finding themselves.

Rapture came to a threatening stop directly before Ruby. "Jarko is dead. You mean nothing to me."

He opened his right hand, displaying a familiar Necklace that shimmered in the flames. "I believe you might remember this delicate piece. It wasn't too long ago you left it to me. If I remember correctly, I believe you wanted it to remind me of my only real power." He smiled devilishly before continuing. "Well, my dear Ruby, I'm sure you'll agree we've put that misunderstanding to rest…" he leaned forward and clasped the shimmering jewel around her neck. "A little memento for you… I release you from its power. It is now yours to control. I want you to die wearing it… an eternal reminder of Rapture. In life and in death, my vengeance will be burnt to your flesh!" Rapture took a step back, his evil smile remaining. "All that's left is to watch you suffer."

There wasn't any doubt in Rapture's eyes as he lit a match, throwing it to the ground. The odious liquid spread throughout the Pub quickly caught light. Rapture had concentrated the fluid at the corners of the room to extend his viewing pleasure as long as possible. Smoke filled the Pub causing Ruby to choke and splutter. The heat was rapidly becoming unbearable; flames marching towards the three captives. The last image Ruby saw before passing out from the fumes was Rapture leering; an evil smile on his face, silently enjoying his vengeance.

Rapture kept watch over Ruby for as long as his threshold for pain would allow; delighting in his sweet revenge. The Legends of Rapture had once been mere fantasy. With the transformation of Rapture complete, The Wholeverse would finally experience those Legends for real…

JUMP, CHILL, THRILL, REPEAT

The Carpenter's Moons was creaking at the seams. Smoke surrounded the building and could be seen far beyond the property's fields. Thankfully the smoke was acting as a marker for our three would-be heroes.

A couple of hundred paces away a jet touched down. It was a small craft, capable of holding a maximum of two passengers. Built for maneuverability and combat, it wasn't intended for prolonged space travel. It's silver and blue exterior reflected the beams of sunlight struggling to break through the rising smoke. The pilot quickly descended down the ramp and onto the fields. The urgency of the situation struck him immediately. He hadn't been told Ruby was in trouble, just that he should seek out this Pub… a Pub that by the looks of it was just about to collapse!

He ran as fast as he could towards the building. The closer he got the more he could feel the temperature rising. If there was anyone left inside they would surely be dead by now.

Approaching the front door he summoned the remaining speed from his reserves and slammed right through. The room was filled with smoke, flames flickering throughout. The heat was unbearable.

"Ruby! RUBY! Are you in here?" He screamed.

No response came. Time was running out. Frantically he stumbled about in the bright but invisible space before him. As he rummaged about he heard a faint moan. He ran towards the sound and felt something connect with his foot. Dropping to the floor the sheer bulk of the body was evident. With no time to think he grabbed an arm and started dragging towards the exit.

He gasped for air as soon as he felt the light touch his skin. With a final tug, the body he'd been dragging was finally outside. He looked down and could finally see the beneficiary of his first rescue, a Montar.

Chester was barely lucid but could see his rescuer was trying to help. With the little energy he had left, he pointed back towards the building and out came the quietest of whispers. "Johnny… Ruby."

That was all the motivation this stranger needed. He rushed back into the burning building; his skin still searing from his first attempt to locate Ruby. Running towards the back of the building he again connected with something in the smoke. Whatever it was sent him crashing to the ground. There were two distinct sets of choking noises. Reaching out he felt a chair. It was heavy, heavy enough to confirm there was someone attached. As he pulled it forward he knocked into another. Grabbing both he headed once again towards the exit.

Reaching the relative cool of the outside he collapsed to the ground; the two chairs safely beside him. Five deep breaths followed until he could finally breathe naturally once again. He snapped back up hoping to find Ruby attached to one of the chairs. He didn't recognize the male Zimplaxion but the female… yes… it was her… Ruby!

"Ruby, Ruby" he screamed, shaking the lifeless body.

There was no response. He reached for a knife in his belt and cut the ropes. Ruby's body fell free from the chair. Leaning over he could feel air escaping from Ruby's mouth; her chest was definitely moving. With this discovery he relaxed a little.

A whisper escaped Ruby's lips, "Heethal!"

"I owed you one. Now we're even!" Heethal replied with a smile.

As Johnny and Chester followed Ruby back into the realms of consciousness, the fire behind them was dying down. Smoke was still seeping from windows and doors but there was little left for the flames to feast upon. The structure was intact but even from Heethal's uneducated eyes it was clear everything else had been destroyed.

Chester began to moan again, the blood from his wound still seeping out. Ruby rushed over and applied pressure to the deep gash.

"Heethal... quickly... untie Johnny. We're gonna need some help here."

As Johnny's senses awoke to the scene around him he could see Chester squirming on the floor; Ruby struggling to help him.

"Ruby," Johnny shouted as his memory returned. "We need to get him to the lake."

Ruby looked around. Her face made it obvious this was no time for jokes. Johnny knew what that face meant. He'd seen it many times in his memories... let alone several times recently.

"Don't give me that look. It will save him!"

The three grabbed a limb each and raced towards a large lake separating two of the fields[127]. Chester had lost consciousness, his body almost lifeless.

---

[127] Chester is always musing over the lakes potential. Most recently he was stuck between either hosting an Annual Regatta or creating a Water-Yoga 'studio'.

"Now what?" Ruby said with a worried expression taking up residence on her face.

"I guess we just throw him in. He never really explained it to me… just said that water helped Montars heal. He could've been messing with my head for all I know, but we're out of options," Johnny replied, beginning to panic.

Don't worry; I can hear what you're thinking. How could throwing an unconscious Montar into a lake possibly be a good idea? Well in reality it simply isn't! Water does indeed heal Montars. The Elders have never felt it important to study this principle; as it isn't a direct money earner… so it became an old wives tale more than anything else. The wound itself just needs to be submerged for the water to rapidly speed up the healing process… in fairness, I guess the three had accomplished this task very well… unfortunately their actions had a fairly high chance of drowning Chester… and he isn't fond of water at the best of times!

Fortunately the water worked as intended and it wasn't long before the wound healed up completely… Chester was rudely awoken by water rushing into his lungs. As Johnny paced up and down the water's edge looking for signs of life, Chester burst through the surface of the water. Gasping for air he soaked up the view before him.

"OK… whose bright idea was it to drown me!" Chester said in a convincingly unimpressed tone.

Frankly neither was a great idea… but for quite different reasons. Firstly Chester despises boats. He does however love the idea of rubbing shoulders with the rich and famous! As for the Water-Yoga possibility there had already been multiple successful lawsuits brought against the inventor of Water-Yoga. The original 'studio', appropriately named 'Breathe in Water, Breathe out Life', had tragically been responsible for ten separate deaths in its first and only Cycle of operation. Although death is always terrible, the real tragedy is that anyone felt this was a good enough idea to try it out… let alone the nine people that persevered in the face of "deathversity!" (Shout out to the Verton Sentinel!)

What followed was a sequence of blame, excuses, further blame, yet more excuses and a rather in-depth lecture as to the appropriate amount of water necessary to heal Montar wounds. It seems you can lead a Montar to water but you definitely shouldn't throw him in!

On their return to The Carpenter's Moons, the damage from the fire was abundantly clear. Sure, the building was still standing but everything that made it unique had been destroyed. Chester slouched to the floor, the full weight of events catching up with him.

With the situation somewhat under control, a question rose to the top of Ruby's mind. "Heethal… how did you know where we were? How did you know we needed to be saved?"

"I didn't" came his reply. "I was just told to come find you… that you'd want to see me. I didn't think you'd be in danger… it had been a while, so I figured why not come and check you out. Pretty lucky I did though."

"That seems like more than just luck," a confused Ruby replied. "What do you mean you were told? Who told you?"

Ruby felt like a toddler with her endless questioning but none of this made any sense.

"It was a guy. I guess at the time it didn't seem odd for some reason. It just felt like a good idea. His name was… damn… I can't think of it… something beginning with a J… maybe James… yes… that's right. James! That was it. A Zimplaxion like you two," Heethal said, pointing towards Ruby and Johnny.

Johnny didn't like the implication that accompanied being pointed at. "Hey! Leave me out of this! I'm not James!"

The weirdness became more evident as Heethal reminisced. "I was drinking in my regular bar[128] and he ended up sitting beside me… we got to talking and I happened to mention your name."

---

[128] I wonder if you'll be surprised to hear Heethal's regular bar is actually a Karaoke bar! Not only does he love to hear others sing, he quite often attempts a classic himself. His 'go-to' is 'Jump, Chill, Thrill, Repeat', recognizable as the

"Are you sure? Are you sure it wasn't the other way round?" She responded, both confused and intrigued.

"I'm sure. It was definitely me. I was telling him I knew you before you were famous. That's when he suggested I should go and visit you. He said you'd want to see me. Given he knew this was where you'd be, it seemed to make sense at the time."

All four had no idea what to make of this story. Having been so close to death they were exhausted enough as it was. Trying to understand how this 'James' could have possibly known they would need Heethal's help was beyond their tired minds.

Little did they know he was on his way to meet them…

---

title track to the Missile Force sequel of the same name. It produced the fabulously memorable line - 'I can't see myself when you look like you're not liking looking at the way I see"… I know… delightful!

THE RATHER PERTURBING SMELL OF HOOSH BLANDEL

It may not have solved the mystery of The Mirror but taking his first step in beginning to understand it had given Jerome a new lease on life. His Soulsion of Chester spoke to him, the message concise and intelligible. Jerome's previous mistake at the hands of The Mirror had taught him a lesson; he wasn't going to do anything without first consulting the other Masters[129]... they're forgiving but they're not silly. One calamitous mistake is OK, two and you'll be looking for a new job... especially when the Sanctity of the Continuance is involved!

It was with a great deal of excitement that Jerome called for the Masters' attention. He was hopeful his news would go some way to redeeming him in their eyes.

---

[129] I'm pretty sure we can agree that irreparably altering Space and Time, even just the once, will force a person to learn their lesson!

Forgive me if I've failed so far to mention the setting for 2nd Floor meetings. I'm positive you've gathered by now how busy the Masters are and furthermore the importance of the work they do… their fully-booked schedules provide no space for general meetings and town halls… as such a conference room per se doesn't exist. They do however have a marvelous cafeteria[130] which doubles as a 'room' to gather all of the Masters in sufficiently well. The only drawback really is the smell. Unfortunately even after a series of informative posters, a few unnamed Masters insisted on microwaving the most obnoxious of foods for lunch. Imagine for a Moment how hard it is to concentrate on the fundamentals of Space and Time disruption with the rather perturbing smell of Hoosh Blandel[131] wafting aggressively by.

With all the Masters sat, cake sliced and apportioned appropriately, their meeting could begin.

"Thank you all for joining me today… and Happy Birthpassing to Jalandra! We all appreciate the cake!" Jerome began. "The contents of my Soulsions have arguably allowed our work to take on more meaning than it ever has before. I would however be naïve not to realize our efforts have been necessitated by the fractures in Space and Time caused by the carelessness of my own actions."

---

[130] Cafeteria is probably the wrong word to use. Don't get me wrong, it is sensational, fully featured with the most modern appliances… The 2nd Floor being The 2nd Floor however means only Masters are permitted. Without staff the only appliances used are really just the microwaves… and occasionally the ice-cream machine.

[131] Hoosh Blandel can be found in The Blue Lagoons of Tranjuri; similar to a fish on your world yet simultaneously quite radically different; about the same size as a Cod but far denser. The three suns of Tranjuri do more than just create the neon colors radiating from their bodies… they are also responsible for the hellacious smell that these fascinating creatures exude... they are rather tasty though!

There was still a fair amount of hustle and bustle in the room. Jalandra's cake was going down splendidly and… well… Jerome was not known for getting to the point with any real urgency.

"For many Cycles I have been searching for redemption; answers to explain what happened that Passing to my son and I. While I may not be any closer to solving the mystery, I believe I'm learning to understand it."

The Masters were now listening a little more intently. There seemed to be a promise of progress in Jerome's words and that was definitely worth paying attention for.

"My latest Soulsion was unlike all others. Not only did I see the fracture occur but I witnessed its consequences… and more than that I saw the future… a future involving myself."

Jerome's audience was now almost silent. His unique Soulsions had long been the envy of his peers and this one seemed to promise even more than usual.

The beauty of Jerome's Soulsions was not just found within the initial experience. The more he meditated on his Soulsions, the more detail he uncovered and the greater his understanding would become. Snapshots of scenes evolved and sprang to life, detailed conversations flooding his mind with every word and nuance. The Soulsion of Chester had shown him a significant amount. As soon as the details all took hold, both the meaning and the message were all too obvious.

"I saw The Dunes of Yandel alter the timeline… push a Montar to the path he is now on." Jerome continued but was interrupted by a Master sat at the table nearest him.

"Wait! What do you mean alter the timeline?"

"That is just the question. This Soulsion was unique; illustrating both the cause and the consequence. It appears Space and Time are trying to course correct and redress what was once undone."

Jerome could see a mountain of questions waiting for answers and chose to face them head on. "It is my belief that the Moment my son stared into The Mirror, Space and Time were pushed off balance. We've seen fractures occurring almost quicker than we can track. The Dunes were vocal in their encouragement, steering the Montar to buy an abandoned Pub. The gift bestowed to me by The Mirror is an attempt to help rectify the imbalance through me. I am due to seek this Montar out. The information I share will help push the timeline back on track."

Jerome paused for a Moment and then continued. "Telling this Montar of the path he was destined for is not the only action that is being asked of me. Their lives will soon be at risk. There is a Gorat that can save them but only if I guide him to their location."

The enormity of Jerome's request was evident to the room. Weirdness had found a home on The 2nd Floor but this was on a whole new level.

"It is hard to deny the gravitas of the information I have been shown. There is still a lot to learn from The Mirror but I feel certain this is what I am supposed to do. I have come before you to ask for your blessing. The Sanctity of Continuance is sacred to every one of us. It is not my intention to harm it… my gut compels me to perform these actions in order to protect it."

His news delivered, Jerome was finished and took a seat, eagerly awaiting the Masters feedback. For at least a Period, the room was alive with debate; each Master wanting their opinion to be heard[132]. For all the back and forth, the Masters agreed Jerome's actions would affect the Sanctity… but if his Soulsion was to be believed they would also protect it. With some trepidation they allowed Jerome to continue on his path.

By now I hope you've pieced together that it was actually Jerome who guided Heethal to save Johnny, Ruby and Chester. The Masters made it clear he should keep his true identity secret and were

---

[132] On both Jerome's story… and Jalandra's cake.

eager to remind him of the importance of not sharing any details of The 2nd Floor. His son's name held nostalgic warmth, convincing Jerome it was the perfect alias to use.

One thing that you might not be aware of however is the guilt that stayed with Jerome as he left the cafeteria. He hadn't lied to the Masters… not a single word was out of place. It was in the absence of information that we find his deception. There was one person from his Soulsion he'd failed to mention… and in fairness the implications of that person's involvement were monumental...

ONE GENUINE CEREMONIAL MIRE FOLK HEADDRESS

It had been at least a Period and the four survivors were still laid in front of the remnants of The Carpenter's Moons. If there was an obvious next step it escaped them.

Ruby had tried to lift Chester's spirits but failed.

"The Elders gave me a small fortune to try and bring you back. We can use that to rebuild. I didn't earn it and they don't deserve to have it returned."

As nice as the offer was, Chester wasn't ready to think about rebuilding. The Pub stood as a reminder of the journey he'd taken to find his place in the world; his serenity away from the constraints of his upbringing. He'd failed to protect it… and his friends… even with his Intuition. His mind began to wander… in an odd way maybe the Elders were right. If he'd been living the life intended for his kind maybe he would've been a match for Rapture.

Johnny meanwhile, knew Chester needed time. He wondered if there was anything left in The Moons that could lift his spirits. It couldn't hurt to look and it would save him from the awkward silence that was holding the group captive. Walking through the entrance, he quickly understood why Chester hadn't approached the building. The entire room was black; everything reduced to ash. Somewhere below the ash were Chester's sturdier selections; jagged edges littering the scene. It could have been worse Johnny told himself. The building was still standing; a stubborn reflection of its owner. He walked across the room towards the stairs, his shoes leaving imprints in the ash. It wasn't logical but perhaps the upper floor had fared better.

Outside Ruby, Chester and Heethal remained. Johnny had been wise to venture inside… the silence wasn't just awkward… it was painfully awkward! Fortunately a noise in the distance called for their attention.

Behind them a craft had descended slowly and landed. It was unpainted and unmarked but appeared to be top of the line, almost as if its navigator was hiding something. A Zimplaxion exited the craft and began the short walk towards them.

As Jerome crossed the field an echo of his Soulsion reverberated inside his mind. It was a bizarre feeling, like the exuberant offspring of déjà vu and a lucid dream. He asked himself how much was he in control? Was he merely a slave to The Mirror?

"James? Is that you?" Heethal asked as Jerome approached.

"Yes… it is me…" Jerome responded, trying his best to look as 'Jamesy' as possible.

Ruby and Chester looked towards Heethal, over to Jerome and then back; stunned by the response.

"I've no doubt you have questions," he continued.

He was correct; Ruby quickly proceeded to unload. "If you knew what was going to happen why didn't you come yourself? Why didn't you send Heethal quicker? Why didn't you try and stop Rapture? How did you even know? Are you with him? Did Rapture send you?"

Chester gained his composure. Stomping over, he wrapped his stubby fingers tightly around Jerome's neck.

"She asked you a question! Are you responsible for this?" He shouted.

Jerome could barely breathe let alone speak. This part of the conversation hadn't been part of his Soulsion… that didn't seem particularly fair. He pointed inside the building in the direction of Johnny. It was enough to get Chester's attention, loosening his grip, enough to allow Jerome to answer anyway.

"I can't answer all of your questions and I can't tell you who I am… but I came to help. Yes, I did know about the fire."

Releasing Jerome, Chester clenched his fists, hooves ready to pounce.

"…but I couldn't do more than I did. Anything more would have changed the outcome. I couldn't risk that… believe me… I have too much to lose."

"What do you mean?" Ruby queried; confused by his words. "What do you have to lose? We're the ones who nearly died!"

"I'm sorry I can't tell you everything. What I can share is Rapture was only a weapon. The Elders were the true masterminds behind this attack…" he turned to face Chester. "… I know what happened to you at The Dunes… why you came to this Moon… you were meant for more."

Chester took a step back, shocked by what he was hearing. "What… how do you know that? What do you mean meant for more? I was happy here… you've taken that from me."

"You weren't meant to be here Chester. You were meant to follow the path your Elders intended for you. You're departure from their teachings scares them," Jerome continued, trying his best to placate Chester with his tone.

This information angered Chester. If there was one thing in his life that made sense it was leaving the MTP in his past. "If you're trying to convince us you have some privileged knowledge, you're failing. Ruby hasn't known me that long and I guarantee she'll agree this is where I belong."

He looked over to Ruby as she gave him a reassuring nod.

"Forgive me. That's not exactly what I was getting at. You were supposed to follow the Elders path… but that was not your destination… it was just the start of your journey."

Chester looked back, as puzzled as he was curious. "What are you trying to say?!"

"I'm trying to explain you were supposed to inspire your people… you led the other Montars from within their ranks. As their peer, they listened to you; you were their champion, the voice that resonated to their very souls. It was your courage, your faith and your vision."

Nothing Jerome was saying made any sense to Chester or Ruby and especially not Heethal; his credibility was failing and he knew it. There was another tactic he could try; another glimpse his Soulsion had presented him. He paused and looked towards Ruby.

"Perhaps I can ask for your assistance."

Ruby's look was one of disbelief. She didn't feel this assertion deserved an audible response.

"You know this wasn't the plan. You've seen what should have been."

Ruby wasn't following but felt compelled to listen.

"You haven't been able to explain it… but you've wondered. How you were able to recall a whole life that you haven't yet lived…"

Ruby went to speak but could barely muster more than a word. "What are…"

"The life that you remember… it was the life that you were meant to live. Those memories now connect the two of you…"

Ruby found another word. "Johnny…"

"Yes. You know him as Johnny. He doesn't understand these memories either. Not yet, but he will soon. He has a unique gift."

"Wait… what do you mean I know him as Johnny?" Ruby interjected.

This wasn't a question Jerome could bring himself to answer. He turned back to Chester. "Your destiny hasn't changed, just the route you're taking. The Elders fear you. They fear your potential, the influence you hold. Word of your choice to break from Montar customs has already begun to spread amongst your kind. Rapture can wait; it is the Elders you should focus on. The Council will soon learn of your survival." He stopped and paused for a second, ensuring he had the stubborn Montar's attention. "You are meant to enlighten your people. You can show them a different way."

The conversation Chester once had with Johnny sprang to mind. He still wasn't motivated to take action but the friends he'd left behind began to come into focus. He wasn't ready to share his vulnerability, not before he could understand it himself. "You have the wrong Montar. That's someone else, not me."

Jerome knew he was running out of time. "Your friend can help you as he did Ruby. Once you lead a revolt at The Montar Training Planet, you will have returned to the path that was truly intended for you. You are meant to inspire them, to show them the freedom that was stolen so long ago."

Ruby spoke up again, beginning to feel Jerome wasn't telling them everything. "You keep mentioning Johnny… what are you not telling us?"

"I can't say much more" Jerome replied, scared he would share too much, more even than he had with his peers. "His destiny is greater than he knows. Take him with you. Once he helps you remember he will begin to understand the full extent of his gift… you will need him."

Jerome's time was up. Johnny was making his way back out to his friends. That wasn't a conversation Jerome could handle… it certainly wasn't a conversation he could trust himself to be part of.

"I'm sorry. I have to go now. It will take all of you to free the Montars, but you can succeed."

Just as Jerome had foreseen, Johnny was heading through the front door of The Carpenter's Moons.

"Hey! I found something you'll love Chester!" Johnny yelled excitedly.

The trio were surprised by his voice and all looked round. Johnny was carrying one of Chester's most prized possessions[133]; the grin on his face eager to greet Chester's response.

"Johnny! Stop messing about and come here. Maybe you can explain what this guy is talking about," Ruby ordered, her tone stomping on Johnny's attempted levity.

As she turned back, ready with a smart remark for Jerome, she realized he was gone. Her eyes searched the area and then the horizon. Even his craft had vanished[134].

"Sorry baby," Johnny offered, having made it to the group. "What did I miss?"

Jerome had spoken for The Mirror as he believed it intended. He'd played by the Masters rules and laid the tracks necessary to repair this fracture in Space and Time. He hadn't shared everything but in

---

[133] There in his hands, Johnny held one genuine Ceremonial Mire Folk Headdress! A little ashy but probably still wearable.

[134] I can hear you! "Oh, how convenient… suddenly he can disappear in a flash"… you simply have to remember the Space Ideology building has many floors and numerous secrets that are way too vast to explain in just one Tale!

reality he wasn't sure of the implications of what he knew. Keeping his distance from Johnny seemed like the safest option... for now at least...

WHAT THE FLORA FEARS, THE FAUNA THRIVES UPON!

Fortunately for the Elders, Erica was no stranger to fleshing out the finer points of a plan… and by finer, I mean the majority of a plan. Logistics were not The Council's strong suit… that was largely reserved for ideas that were generally theoretically inept and grandiose to the extreme!

In truth, as has always been the case, potentially the most powerful member of The Council is in fact the Master Elder's secretary! I believe I mentioned previously how the MTP was created… a simple four point Decree on a napkin. I'm sure you understand how absurdly complex it was to set up the MTP. The inner workings were certainly not contained within those four guidelines! The Secretary of the time earned her keep and so on and so forth down the ages until we finally arrive at Erica.

While laying 'Rapture bait' at the Falls of Tranjuri, Erica's mind started to wander. The Council's original plan had failed. She had seen the evidence of that herself. While the back-up plan of killing Chester hadn't been hers, the method of having Rapture carry out the dirty deed had. Having said that, nothing spoken to the Master Elder is ever received quite as intended… and this was no different.

Erica's idea had been reasonably different… reasonably in as far as she didn't feel comfortable merely hoping Rapture would take care of Chester as well as Ruby. There was some logic there, no doubt, but it was the kind of basic sketch that allowed the Master Elder to promptly return to his cocktail… wasting no time dwelling on the possibility of Rapture killing Ruby and then moving on, no thought of the potential that Chester would best Rapture… and most worryingly no thought of what would happen if Chester was to survive and seek retribution!

While she didn't want to be responsible for the death of a Montar, she was more than aware of the fate that awaited her if she was perceived to have failed the Elders. Cycles of service had dulled her senses to the more untoward tasks that were so often left to her. With the Elders relaxing in their lives of leisure, Erica would, as always, seek to instill a contingency!

While soaking up a massage from a very attentive, yet oddly polite young Pefrin[135], Erica considered what Chester would do if he survived the encounter. An attack on The Council would be very bold. The Council's Sanctum is heavily guarded and visible by all. Any attempt would be futile and a totally unrealistic setting for a climactic battle…

What would be the more sensible option, she asked herself. Any battle would leave Chester hideously outnumbered, but maybe he didn't need to use his Intuition… instead perhaps he would use the very thing The Council most feared, his independence. With his new awareness of The Council's desire for his return, he might seek to turn his fellow Montars against the Elders. If he was able to convince a large enough number to follow his lead they could oust the Elders from their position

---

[135] For a number of Cycles 'The Falls' had been extra cautious to uphold the highest standards of respect to any Montars who chose to check-in… I've no doubt you'll remember a certain incident that caused this! Hotel management could most definitely not afford another hefty payout!

of power and control. Continuing this line of thought she questioned how he could attempt such a feat. The MHW was an option… but any Montar he met would be very much set in their ways, living a life of relaxation. There would be few who would deliberately choose to risk their retirement after spending so many Cycles serving the Elders.

There was only one obvious choice… the MTP. Fresh soldiers have an entire life to lead. The Planet's intense training regime wouldn't have completely eradicated their innate yearning for independence yet… a hefty supply of young impressionably minds who might well listen to an upstart Graduate… Erica was sure this would be his play. That being the case she knew she needed to make her way to the MTP. It was either that or risk the Master Elder's skewed version of her plan failing and him placing the blame squarely on her![136]

Arriving on the MTP Erica made her way directly to the Generals' quarters. Meeting with the Master General would allow her to implement her contingency without rousing any suspicion from The Council… while she didn't wish to be blamed for their plans failure; she equally didn't want to be seen attempting to circumvent their authority. Fortunately, Erica had previously fought alongside the Master General… back when she knew him as Tramano.

Tramano and Erica had once been a fearsome duo. Their final mission together saw them rescue the hapless Prince Trado from The Jungles of Shradell[137]. Saving Trado proved exceptionally difficult…

---

[136] It is with a most sincere sadness I mention this fact to you. Almost every secretary to the Master Elder passes on their torch not upon retirement but execution… the Master's secretary is a position that unfortunately shoulders the blame for The Council's numerous mistakes.

[137] The Jungles of Shradell are generally cited as one of the weirdest sites in The Wholeverse. The most deadly and bizarre creatures around are enticed by the promise of easy hunting. The Jungle's danger is in direct conflict to its delicate appearance that welcomes visitors. By a quirk of nature, pathways wind their way throughout the jungle; not a single leaf daring to cross the non-existent barriers. The white soil of the jungle floor highlights these pathways. To the uneducated visitor the jungle appears very appealing… but what the flora fears,

mostly due to his insistence on wandering off... even after being rescued from the razor sharp claws of a Devil Hawk! It did however provide the two an opportunity to fall for each other... even if neither had realized the mutuality of their feelings.

Walking into Tramano's office Erica was met with a warm embrace... well... in honesty it was more of a risqué squeeze.

"Well, well, well... it's been far too many Cycles my dear! When are you going to hurry up and retire so we can finally go on that long overdue vacation you promised me?" Tramano said with a beaming smile.

"Still the same old Tramano," Erica responded, as always, misunderstanding his sincerity for playfulness.

He met her quip with another smile. "Not really. You should really refer to me as Master General now... and unless I've heard incorrectly you're the Master Elder's secretary."

"For once you've heard correctly," Erica offered.

Tramano could see through her superficial seriousness. "Come on now," he replied. "You don't need to be guarded here. It's just us. What can I do for you?"

Erica allowed herself to smile as she continued. "We have an issue. There is a Montar who presents a risk to The Council. They've ordered his execution."

Tramano interrupted, already guessing where this was headed. "... and let me guess... they've approached it in their typically lazy manner with little thought of the consequences?"

Erica looked shocked upon hearing this. The elevated positions they'd both earned gave them a great deal of insight to the inner workings of The Council. They were only too aware of the risks in being seen to cross The Council.

---

the fauna thrives upon! The pathways providing the most optimum of hunting grounds for The Jungle's assortment of beasts!

"Be careful," she warned. "You never know who might be listening."

"Don't worry Erray… I keep a close eye on my camp. Now tell me. What do we need to be worried about?"

With that Erica, or Erray as Tramano affectionately referred to her, proceeded to fill him in on the details of Chester, Ruby and her projection of where they may be headed.

"Don't worry Erray. I'll make sure the camp is aware. If Rapture fails, we'll capture Chester here. I'll make sure I present him to The Council myself. I won't let you come to any harm because of their ignorance," Tramano offered, his sincerity clear for Erica to see.

"You don't think he could succeed do you?" Erica asked.

"I told you. Don't worry. I run a tight camp. These soldiers aren't easily fazed… you don't want him to… do you?" Tramano asked back, beginning to see there was more to her question than he'd first thought.

"Of course not," she shot back, a little too quickly. "He'd need to encourage the majority of your soldiers… more than would be possible… can you imagine how The Council would react and what they'd do to us? It would be all out war."

It was clear to him Erica's privileged position in The Council had become more of a prison. "You and I both know sometimes war is necessary. We've seen that many times. If he pulled it off… we could…"

Erica regained her serious demeanor, interrupting him mid-sentence and making it clear this line of discussion should go no further. "I need you to ensure he's stopped before this goes too far."

Her work done, Erica left and headed back to The Council's Sanctum. Tramano meanwhile had a job to do. He commanded his Generals to make the camp aware of Chester and Ruby's potential arrival; instructing them to bring the two to him should they arrive. Anymore than that could risk Erica's safety… and she'd been clear of what she wanted… even if she didn't know exactly what that was herself…

BELIEF BY ITSELF CAN OPEN WINDOWS

The group was still in a state of shock. An oblivious Johnny was met by anxious and impatient glares from Chester and Ruby. He felt uneasy in a way he hadn't for a very long time.

"Come on guys… what did I miss?"

Ruby walked over to her partner and stared deep into his eyes, searching for the truth. "Did you know? The memories you gave me… did you know it was the life we were supposed to have?"

Johnny could almost feel his heart stop. It seemed like an obvious explanation now Ruby had vocalized it… but for some reason it hadn't previously occurred to him… the puzzle had been too large to see past its pieces… but those words, that answer… it resonated, it somehow felt right. His face couldn't hide the realization he was experiencing.

Ruby saw his expression, she thought she knew what it meant. "You did know... didn't you?"

"No... I promise. Not until just now... you saying it... it suddenly makes sense... but... what does it mean... and how did you figure that out?"

Johnny's realization had caused Chester's already curious mind to want more. "The Zimplaxion that Heethal saw... the one that sent him to save us... we just met him... he seems to think I'm supposed to save my people... and apparently you know more than you're letting on."

Johnny sensed Chester's frustrations but didn't have the answers he was looking for. "I'm sorry. I'm really not hiding anything... I don't know who James is... I can't be that important if he didn't even hang around to see me!"

Generally Chester would have taken Johnny on his word but this was different. Barely escaping with his life had put Chester on edge... even before being told the fate of his race rested primarily on his shoulders. That wasn't the kind of pressure he needed... it might be selfish, but he had more than enough issues of his own to deal with.

"Johnny... you have to tell us what you know," Chester demanded. "What reason would he have to save us, but lie about you?"

Johnny didn't know what to say, his friend was clearly upset but he didn't have the answers. His silence seemed to frustrate Chester further.

Chester needed to know what this all meant. Johnny was supposed to help but was denying he knew anything. He stepped towards Johnny, grabbing him by the arms. "Just tell me!"

The emotion rising within Chester was beginning to take over... at least he presumed it was the emotion. A fire was burning inside. Suddenly the anger felt like weakness; his strength draining from his body as he collapsed.

...the next Moments were vivid, more than a fabulously modest writer can capture. The alternative timeline forced its way into the deepest crevices of Chester's mind... his return to the MTP as a General... displacing the Elder's teachings with his own and the eventual collapse of The Montars Golden Goose[138]. His new memories were a gift but a painful one! Chester's brain was rattled and bruised from the ordeal; the trauma enough to rouse him back to consciousness. Chester searched to center himself with this newly discovered knowledge.

Let's take a Moment and I'll see if I can describe his sensations in such a way that will assist you in comprehending this bizarre feeling. Our perceptions... I'm trusting yours are similar to everyone else's, are very much a result of our experiences. Feelings of love and hate are influenced by the memories of interactions. Imagine a person from work you barely know. You see them every day but have little knowledge of them with which to define your view of them as a person. You're lucky enough to receive a visit from a Master who brings with them a highlight reel of your colleague's life; a screening of their thoughtful and sensitive actions. Suddenly your perception of them is changed. Ambivalence has been replaced with feelings of warmth and a fondness that previously did not exist.

...and so, this was true of Chester as well. It would be unfair to say he didn't have the potential to see beyond himself... the seed had been planted; water and light was all it needed... well... that and probably some time away from alcohol and the distractions of the impulse driven world around him... in the unlikely absence of this

---

[138] 'The Montars Golden Goose' is also funnily enough the name of a perfectly wonderful Ballet! Now I don't class myself as an expert but my modest summary of the performance is as follows - The goose is stolen and lays a golden egg, which hatches and a monster is born... which then turns on its captors by way of dance... there is a struggle... or perhaps a serenade... it was hard to tell... and then everyone dances a lot more... until they hold up another egg... which is supposed to represent the completion of the circle I guess? Who am I kidding... I've no idea what was going on! Why can't they just speak for crying out loud! The things we do to impress a lady!

combination, a vision of what was supposed to be, turned out to be precisely what he needed. Funny how people wait to be confronted with their spurned opportunities before truly feeling the call to action… but let's face it… we're all guilty of that.

As Chester rose to his feet, he felt like a new Montar. The story 'James' had told didn't seem so unrealistic anymore; the fantasy now felt plausible. Previously, it was just his own life that had been restricted… quite spontaneously he felt a duty to an entire race… the guilt for his selfish actions thus far pulsed through his veins.

While Ruby and Heethal were anxious to ensure Chester was OK, Johnny was experiencing another level of awakening himself. For the second time Johnny had shared a vision of the alternate timeline. This time however, he lived through the vision alongside his recipient. It was a strange experience. These were memories that held no relation to him. Similar to gazing into The Mirror of Eternal Blissfullessness, it was as if they were his own memories; the feelings and sensations combining with his consciousness. With this second vision a canvas had presented itself to him. The picture was yet to be painted but two strokes had been indelibly scratched in. Johnny couldn't decipher the image but awareness had most certainly taken hold. There's no doubt his ability to share glimpses into an alternative timeline stroked his ego, but it was more than that… it had opened his mind to the potential for more… and belief by itself can open windows you never knew existed.

Chester looked over towards Johnny. "You know what you showed me don't you?"

"No… not until now… but yes… I saw it." Johnny replied, hoping Chester's temperament had cooled.

At this point Heethal took a step back. He'd been listening and watching intently since saving their lives and was thoroughly sure of one thing… he'd seen more than enough craziness for one Passing! The notion hadn't been suggested, but he felt compelled to voice his pre-emptive refusal.

"Do not touch me. I don't want to see anything!"

Being privy to the weirdness of that Passing had made Heethal feel connected to this trio in a way he couldn't explain… that didn't mean he wanted to see a different life he was sure existed… he didn't need the disappointment of finding he'd missed out on the opportunity of being a successful lounge singer![139]

While Ruby and Chester were surprised by his outburst, Johnny looked a little hurt. It hadn't dawned upon him that his new ability could be a curse as well as a gift. Just presenting what once was didn't mean it couldn't still be.

Ruby broke the awkward silence. "So… come on then… what did you both just see?"

The two looked towards each other, Chester taking command of the answer. "James was right… I was supposed to set my people free."

Even having already experienced the alternative timeline this response shocked Ruby. Her rational mind looked for an appropriate continuation. "OK… so… what does that mean then? We know the Elders will come after us as soon as they figure out we're still alive…"

Chester nodded. His body language was becoming more confident as his new memories settled in. "It means we go to the MTP. If we can encourage enough Montars to leave, the Elders will be too preoccupied to be concerned with us... and perhaps for once, I'll have helped someone other than myself."

As the monumental task standing before them came into focus, the group realized just how difficult it was going to be! Convincing his people that the Elders had actually enslaved them was not going to be an easy task. The soldiers had become accustomed to the reality painted for

---

[139] Heethal is quite confident in his singing ability you see; steadfast in his belief that one Passing he will be discovered and his life will change completely… and why ever not! Everyone's gotta have a dream!

them… some even loved the hand they were dealt. A portion of society always tends towards war… for that portion of the Montar society they were effectively living the dream… their inaction might benefit the Elders but it wasn't affecting them negatively in any way they could realistically comprehend.

Fortunately the insight gained from the alternative timeline was there to guide them. Chester had seen success was achievable. It would have to be driven from a different angle but he had nonetheless seen his fellow Montars could be reasoned with; his enlightenment could be passed on. His vision also shared the obstacles they would face. The Generals; shepherds of the Nursery, would oppose any uprising. The only way to succeed would be to convince a majority. Without this, any attempt to dismantle the Nursery would fail.

Chester realized success would rely on his ability to persuade the soldiers of their camouflaged servitude. He'd somehow need to buy enough time to speak to them freely, without fear of the Generals influence. Effectively dismantling a soldier's perceptions of the world around them would not be an easy sell. As his mind wandered, a plan began to emerge. He was ready to take his first audacious steps on the intimidating new path that lay before him…

THE DEVIL HAWK OR THE EGG?

Upon sharing his Soulsion of Chester with The 2nd Floor, you may remember Jerome had deliberately omitted a certain person's presence. I'm sure you've furthermore figured that person was in fact Johnny… I've no doubt you'll understand why he didn't share this crucial information with the Masters. Now before we proceed any further, I think it's only right to take a step back and explain what led Jerome to get involved with Chester's destiny and potentially risk The Sanctity of Continuance.

Seeing his future self in his Soulsion had been strange for Jerome… but it was the knowledge his future self shared with Chester that Jerome found deeply puzzling… a twist in Space and Time perhaps. How could he have learned so much just by observing himself in the Soulsion? That was surely a paradox, no? A most splendid example of what came first… the Devil Hawk or the Egg?[140]? Learning something

---

[140] This is of course, a very similar saying to the 'Chicken or the egg?' of your world. It is however I guess slightly different. Logically Devil Hawks are born

from yourself doesn't make any sense… you need to learn something before you teach it… but to teach it you need to learn it… and on and on the illogical problem continues…

It was in the brief vision of Johnny and Ruby at The Carpenter's Moons that Jerome found his answer and so much more. A 'regular' person appeared as just that in Jerome's Soulsions. As the experience sunk in, their motivations, dreams and desires spoke to him. Johnny however was quite different. Initially he appeared blurry, more a name than a fully formed person. In meditating on his Soulsion, the vision of Johnny became infinitely more detailed; expanding exponentially. Jerome struggled to interpret what this meant… it was as if James didn't belong there, his presence a splash of color in a black and white photo. Jerome searched to find meaning and understanding but the more he tried, the more confused he became. As Jerome's mind relaxed further into his meditative state, this vision of Johnny started to look familiar… the level of incomprehensible detail was similar to… yes… The Mirror of Eternal Blissfullessness! The realization struck him to his core, the connection finally becoming blatantly apparent. The man he saw, Johnny… it was his son! The images he'd seen… Johnny's soul bore the signs of The Mirror. Suddenly the door to Jerome's understanding was wide open. He could see the alternative timeline Johnny had merely glimpsed into… a Soulsion within a Soulsion. While Johnny was still piecing together this alternate view, Jerome could see the skewed timeline in all of its glory… the unabridged volumes of this parallel existence were his to marvel at. His knowledge had come from seeing his son in this Soulsion… Johnny was his teacher!

---

by way of an egg. Did the Devil Hawk evolve to give birth by egg or did an egg produce the first Devil Hawk? That is the simplest of definitions but over time it has become quite a lot more complicated. The Devil Hawk's feathers that refract light appeared over time you see… was this as a result of the Devil Hawk evolving or some significant change in the incubation properties of the egg… and whichever of these was responsible, how do they tie in with the original conundrum? It hurts one's brain just to comprehend the depth of this equation… essentially it's The Wholeverse's way of saying, "The implications of this issue are too vast and complex. They hurt my head, so I'm out!"

From what Jerome could tell, his son wasn't aware of his ability or his potential importance. Jerome could tell Johnny had a part to play in Chester's future… his visions of Chester's alternate life couldn't just be coincidence. Something more important suddenly occurred to Jerome… Johnny's life would soon be in danger… if Jerome didn't act quickly The Carpenter's Moons would burn down with Johnny and his friends still inside. Jerome had no choice… he needed to do something. With this crucial revelation, Jerome made the brave decision to request permission to act from the Masters of The 2nd Floor.

Having shared the knowledge as best he could with Chester, Jerome knew he had to leave quickly. He couldn't risk interacting with his son… for both his own sake and that of The Sanctity. Departing the smallest moon of Andros, he headed straight for The Mirror. He knew it was the only way he could tell if he'd been correct to intervene.

As Jerome made his way up the mountainside towards The Mirror, a million thoughts ran through his mind. He'd felt compelled to speak to Chester… to act as his Soulsion had instructed… but what if his Soulsion was a warning… trying to keep him from those very actions. His last mistake at this same location had cost him his son… he was desperate to look into The Mirror again… he needed to know if he'd inadvertently made the situation worse.

The anxiety filling his busy mind was causing Jerome to rethink his life. Focusing on those last images of James, a realization dawned upon him that he'd never previously given thought to. It was bizarre; like looking for your wallet only to find it in the fridge… you must have put it there but what was occupying your thoughts at the time? What had made him decide to leave James with Mr. and Mrs. Scott? Why couldn't he remember the logic that had led him to this destination? Of course Jerome had been stressed at the time but that was no excuse… why had this never occurred to him?

It wasn't as if the memories had vanished. They were still there… he could clearly remember the pain of leaving his son with Tom and Lily. They appeared to be the perfect couple; desperate to share the love they had for each other with a child… but even that seemed curious in retrospect. He couldn't remember any conversation about where this child had come from or how he knew of their desire to be parents. Replaying the Moments in his mind, it was almost as if he was there once again.

"His name… it's J… it's J… it's Johnny."

He recalled the Moment perfectly… how he'd been forced to sever all ties with James. It was so painful he needed something… he needed a way to always feel a part of his son's life. That 'J' seemed so little, it was nothing… but for Jerome it meant the world. It was his untraceable sign… his way of closing the door but choosing not to lock it.

The more he looked for answers, the more he began to question his actions all those Cycles ago. He hadn't conducted research, hadn't hunted for suitable parents. He'd flown straight to Andros… directly to Verton… and the Scott's had been ready, waiting to receive their new son. Why hadn't the absurdity of this screamed out to him before? The more he reflected, the more the haze lifted. He could remember the certainty of his actions. The feeling of comfort and safety in leaving James with the Scotts had been reassuring; knowing instinctively he was supposed to give his only child to this couple. He'd been walking through the motions, saying his lines… but it was someone else's script… someone else was directing… and there was only one answer that made sense… The Mirror… but if it had driven him to this end… it meant The Mirror was much more than just a window. Jerome came to a complete stop, the weight of this realization sinking in. He needed to look into The Mirror again… he needed answers.

As Jerome approached the peak of the mountain, his mind was filled with questions. If he was correct in postulating The Mirror had some level of sentience, then did that mean Johnny was supposed to look into The Mirror all of those Cycles ago? Were Johnny's abilities bestowed upon him deliberately by The Mirror? Was all of this part of some bigger plan?

The endless line of incessant questions raced through his mind until he reached his destination… with The Mirror before him, it was time to see if his actions had been foolhardy or divine. He looked down at his feet and said a prayer… not to a God but to his wife. Whenever he felt alone, he asked for her guidance. He found this brought him a level of peace… even just the Moment of picturing her face, her smile and warmth, helped him feel a little less lost in this world by himself. He asked for her help to find the strength he needed… the courage to look into The Mirror once more.

Gazing into The Mirror, he was relieved by what he saw. A Soulsion began appearing to him; bringing with it some comfort… The Mirror was still displaying the fractures of Space and Time… his actions hadn't made things worse… and that was most definitely a good start. His mind turned to look for answers to the plethora of questions that filled his mind.

Jerome allowed his mind to relax and be taken by this newest Soulsion. Falling away from his body, his soul embraced the experience… with his consciousness firmly focused on The Mirror; he was stunned by what he began to experience. His body froze; his mind grasping for an anchor in reality… the harder he tried, the more lost he felt. Scrambling for reason and logic a shock rose through his motionless body and cast his soul from The Mirror. His mind free once again, Jerome sat staring at the floor, not daring to look back into The Mirror… he was scared… not through fear but through hope…

A MIDNIGHT MARSH WALK

Ruby was very protective of The Peculiar. She had grown a… 'peculiar' attachment to it over the Cycles, seeing it as an extension of herself. As a rule, she didn't let others pilot her sacred ship, but in this instance it made sense… and in any event she knew Heethal had seen her maneuver it so many times she had no doubt it was in safe hands[141].

The group had decided to land on the outskirts of the encampment on the MTP. From there, they could safely make their way in unnoticed and unannounced. As The Peculiar touched down, the scope of the task before them came into sharp focus. They were descending onto a planet populated by the most efficient soldiers in The Wholeverse. If the mission was to fail, it would fail spectacularly.

---

[141] That didn't stop Ruby spending a whole Period instructing Heethal how to correctly pilot her prized possession. I probably shouldn't share that he was bafflingly made to take a written test, but I'm sure you will avoid judging her too much.

Stepping into the muddy marshes, they watched as The Peculiar departed and with it any chance of a quick escape. They'd been successful so far. The only noises to speak of were bird calls from deep within the far off jungles. There didn't seem to be any telltale signs of their presence being discovered. Perhaps they'd been lucky… or more than likely, there was just little need for security on the MTP… surely nobody would be stupid enough to attack a planet full of soldiers?

Foliage reached up to Johnny's hip. The pools of water were deeper in some areas than others, but no deeper than the top of Ruby's dark leather boots. The light of the MTP's green moon only amplified the eerie feeling from their midnight marsh walk. I don't mind sharing that the smell rising from the muddy puddles told more than they wished to know about the wildlife living within! Infiltrating the camp at night was working nicely; the moonlight just enough to guide their way without signaling their presence.

Chester turned to Ruby and Johnny. "You sure you don't want to call Heethal back down and go get a drink first?"

They were thankful for the joke even if it did incite a taste for a good Homebrew. Chester too regretted his words… getting drunk sounded far more appealing right now.

Climbing the fence surrounding the camp was deceptively simple; it was barely taller than Chester himself. The fence stood as a marker more than a security defense… that didn't however stand in the way of Johnny's declaration of triumph having successfully navigated this initial obstacle[142]. A cabin stood before them… their first challenge.

Their plan wasn't really scientific but then again the mission itself seemed pretty far-fetched. They needed access to the Montar soldiers without the presence of any Generals. Approaching by night afforded them this luxury as the Generals slept away from the soldiers… so long as they didn't enter the Generals' cabin they would be fine…

---

[142] "Oh yeah! Made it over!" he'd yelled; cupping his mouth as the words escaped. Ruby was equally unimpressed by his over eagerness to celebrate the smallest of achievements as she was by his carelessness in courting attention.

Fortunately that wasn't a concern they needed to worry too much about. The Generals' quarters were quite unlike the soldiers… set right smack dab in the middle of the compound their cabin was a three storey palace by comparison. Even the wooden siding was far more robust. A darker, denser wood compared to the flimsy thick cardboard that did little to protect the soldiers' cabin from the outside noise and weather. The cabin awaiting them was clearly the latter. As they approached the front door, Chester looked back to his friends. Opening the door, he tried his best to look confident.

The room was fairly dark, only the moonlight creeping through the windows provided any guidance of the number of Montars sleeping. It occurred to Chester he'd only contemplated making it into a cabin. He hadn't given any time to what he would say, let alone how he'd wake the soldiers without causing alarm. Quite frankly, this would have been a waste of time… he couldn't possibly have anticipated Johnny clumsily knocking into one of the beds, rousing its sleeping occupant. Even more fortunate was the cabin they had stumbled upon. The group in question had nicknamed themselves 'The Colts'. A collection of particularly egotistical Montars; calling for the Generals wouldn't be their first move.

Before Johnny could think to warn Chester and Ruby the room was filled with light; Montar soldiers springing out of their beds to attention. At least there was no time to come up with a plan, Chester thought. Whatever he was going to do, he'd have to do it now.

The waking soldiers had forced our three heroes into the middle of the room. With the exits covered and the group's focus gathered, Chester began.

"Before anyone freaks out too much… we're here to help."

Ramziel was the self-appointed leader of 'The Colts' and accordingly stepped forward. It was only by virtue of Chester's race he felt obliged to speak before commanding an all out attack. "…creeping in here with your friends in the middle of the night… I don't think you're here to clean our cabin! What possible help could we need from you?"

"I used to be a soldier here. I'm here because I want you to know there is another way. You don't have to train to be a warrior… I made a choice to follow my own path. I want you all to have that same option," Chester offered, looking around the room; attempting to meet with every set of Montar eyes.

Ramziel had no time for the nonsense spewing from this invading Montar's mouth. He laughed before speaking. "What makes you think there is anything wrong with this life? We are training to become the deadliest weapons in the universe. What are you… a failed soldier? That's a first… are you scared to use your Intuition?"

Chester had always been sure of himself. The realization of the beauty of life outside of the Elder's rule had been such a breakthrough for him… he hadn't contemplated any difficulty in communicating this message to others.

"If this is the life you want then you should be free to choose it. You have no choice… none of you do," Chester said, casting his gaze wider around the room. "I may not have met you before, but I know you. I know each one of you aspires for more than you are born into. The Elders have you all believing they have your interests at heart… they don't. They only serve their own agendas."

Chester knew he wasn't getting through to Ramziel. All he could see was a room of drones. He wondered if his words had made any impact at all. Even those who might have truly listened were clearly afraid to speak up.

"OK, we've heard enough. Listening to you, I've been realizing a few things. I see this Zimplaxion female alongside you… a Montar trying to overthrow the Elders… traveling with… Ruby I presume," Ramziel replied, his eyes staring down at Ruby.

Chester and Ruby's eyes met; they knew this identification didn't bode well.

Ramziel continued. "Just as I thought… the Generals have been on the lookout for you two… a perfect opportunity for 'The Colts' to illustrate our value!" He turned to look towards Johnny. "Alastill, Mendar. Drop the male Zimplaxion in the marshes outside the perimeter fences. I'm sure he'll enjoy a nature walk by himself[143]." Ruby and Chester went to speak but Ramziel cut them off. "As for you two… let's see what you're worth to the Generals."

Alastill and Mendar grabbed Johnny and shoved him towards the front door. As Johnny looked back he could see soldiers surrounding Ruby and Chester, restraining them from any attempts to help. This hadn't gone as they'd hoped… and at this point things looked like they were only getting worse…

---

[143] Just in case you were wondering… this was most definitely sarcasm!

A SILHOUETTE IN THE DARKNESS

The marshes seemed a lot more threatening to Johnny without the company of his friend and partner. Quiet shadows suddenly came to life; fear rising from the obscurity held within. If that wasn't enough, his concern for the two left behind was steadily increasing.

Johnny commanded his fear to subside, looking desperately for some inspiration; as if the foliage would magically scream out what his next move should be... understandably he received no answer, leaving him as lost as ever. Alone in the marshes, he wasn't sure there was realistically anything he could do to help. Heading straight back in would no doubt end in his immediate capture. The rest of the camp would surely be aware of their presence by now and extra vigilant as a result. He couldn't just leave them... he needed a genius idea... some way to not only reach them but help them as well.

With his mind searching for assistance he hadn't noticed a shadow quietly creeping towards him. Water ripples drew his attention just in time... his eyes quickly darted from left to right, looking for the source of this disturbance. Spinning around, the moonlight hid the face towering above him; a silhouette in the darkness… there was no denying the outline of a Montar.

Johnny's optimism won a fierce battle against logic. "Chester?" He whispered, hoping the response would be in the affirmative.

The silhouette before him lacked detail but it was clear enough as its owner shook their head in disbelief. Then from the darkness it spoke. "That isn't a great start. I'm putting a lot of faith in you by coming here."

The Montar stepped forward into the dim light of the moon. Johnny should have conceded to logic, it was clearly not Chester. Dressed in standard Nursery attire[144], the Montar before him was bulky but exuded a certain femininity.

Introducing herself as Amy, the Montar explained she was part of The Colts and had heard Chester's speech. Amy was as egotistical as her fellow Colt members but didn't share their closed minds. Being the only female in The Colts, she'd been offended by the name they'd chosen. This wasn't helped by their insinuation she should feel blessed they deemed her worthy of being part of an all male group. She'd suggested a couple of different, more encompassing ideas as alternatives but was struck down at each attempt[145]. Amy was skilled enough to

---

[144] The notion of Nursery attire conjures up a rather different image than is accurate. There are certainly not Montars running around in diapers if that's where your mind was headed. The reality is sadly quite mundane. Attire for both males and females is identical. Each soldier is supplied with a navy blue jumpsuit; stripes denoting how many Cycles they've spent at the camp… and yes… HydrateFive is emblazoned on their backs…

[145] She'd started with 'The Fillies'. When this was met with disgust she'd try to explain the hypocrisy… but of course that fell on deaf ears… shock, horror hey! Failing to successfully make her point she retreated to compromise with 'The Yearlings'. Unfortunately her insecure fellow members clearly needed the constant stroke to their egos that 'The Colts' represented. The joke of course is The Generals didn't permit group names at all! The Colts members were the only ones who ever knew of their secret… and yes… that has always amused me on many levels. I hope you're right there with me!

match the rest of The Colts but her open mind gave her a critical advantage… keeping her ego under control as much as possible, she remained open to perspectives different than her own.

"You know Chester, yes?" She asked.

Johnny's initial caution had faded a little; the Montar's calm demeanor helped him relax. "Yes, we're good friends."

"Good. I need to know more. Why does he think we don't have a choice? The Elders always look after us. We are raised to be the fiercest soldiers and after a life of service we retire without a care in the world. Why does he think we need saving?"

Johnny felt completely out of his depth. He'd been happy to ride shotgun but this was really Chester's mission. Providing moral support is one thing… convincing a Montar their existence is tantamount to servitude is another thing entirely. He was sure it wasn't his place, especially as a Zimplaxion, to have this conversation. Choices, however, were hardly competing for his attention right now.

He began to mutter his response, lacking the conviction or desire to speak confidently. "Chester… he wants you all to have the same opportunity he had."

"What does that even mean? We're not prisoners here. We're being trained by the best. Why would we want anything else?" Amy responded, no more convinced than before.

Johnny shook his head, not sure how to get through. "You've been conditioned to believe this is what you want. If you tried to do anything else you'd see how little freedom you really have."

Johnny's words were doing little more than frustrating Amy. If anything she was offended.

"Do you really think this is the place to be talking to me about freedom? You're lucky I even sought you out… but don't worry I'm regretting that already. I'm not sure what I thought you could tell me. He's living proof of our freedom… the Elders clearly didn't try and stop him… and his act of gratitude is to rebel!"

It felt like the wrong thing to be worried about but Johnny couldn't help but focus on his annoyance at this conversation being led by him rather than Chester.

"They did try and stop him! They tried to kill him… and Ruby… and me! Just because he chose to run a Pub for a living! We all made the choice to try and help you out!" He replied, before dropping to a whisper, "… great choice that was."

Amy was yet to be convinced but this information at least opened her mind to the possibility there was some truth in his words.

"…even if everything you're saying is true… you're having trouble convincing me. How are you going to convince a whole planet?"

"To be fair the convincing part of this mission was really going to be down to Chester… I'm not actually sure what my role is supposed to be."

Johnny felt some level of relief from voicing his frustration. More importantly he began to question why he joined Ruby and Chester. Ruby could help with the fight but what use was he… his mind pondered the question as the alternative timeline came into focus. Chester's drive to free his people once again became clear. There was reason and logic for their mission… his own significance suddenly fell into place. Before seeing what he was capable of, Chester hadn't been able to see past himself… Johnny was responsible for that revelation and it hadn't even been intentional.

Johnny looked at the Montar standing before him. If he could open her mind to what could've been, maybe others would listen as well. It was worth a shot he thought to himself. Stretching his arm out, he placed his hand on Amy's and waited for the transference.

Amy stared at the strange look on Johnny's face; his eyes closed and lips raised at one side.

"What are you doing?" She asked.

"You'll see," he responded. "This should put everything into perspective."

"How is touching me going to do that?" She responded, swatting his hand away.

The move had been a bold one. Johnny was beginning to accept his unique gift, even if he didn't fully understand it. Unfortunately his attempt at gaining control failed quite miserably; leaving Johnny looking foolish and dare I say a little lecherous. There had apparently been no transference at all… unless you can count offense that is!

"What a waste this has been. Good luck surviving the night," Amy offered with disappointment.

Johnny was almost glad she was leaving but his friends were still in danger… he needed to get something from Amy. As she walked away he bravely grabbed her arm.

"Wait… at least tell me where my friends are."
Amy glanced back; still annoyed she'd taken the time to listen. "… Sure… maybe you can watch. They've been taken to the Generals' cabin in the middle of the camp… probably…"

Before she could finish the sentence, Amy felt a surge of heat make its way through her arm as the alternative timeline began to take hold.

A montage developed at the front of her mind. She could see Chester, only in this reality he was a General. Over the course of many Cycles, he worked with the soldiers… helping them understand their role as pawns in the Elders regime. Slowly a group emerged that understood the restrictions they had been subjected to, until finally, their numbers were large enough to stand up and be counted. With Chester leading, the soldiers revolted; leaving the MTP with just the remaining Generals and a band of loyal soldiers.

Amy turned back towards Johnny and gave him a telling look. "Well that makes things a little clearer… why didn't you say?"

Johnny shot back an unimpressed look… at least he'd made some progress he thought to himself.

Amy brushed her fingers through her mane and twisted her lips. "So I guess we should find your friends together then… but maybe we should go and see some of my friends first… I'm pretty sure I know a few Montars who would be very interested to see who the Elders really are."

Johnny was happy to see some semblance of a plan was materializing… even if it did rest upon him being able to recreate a skill he hadn't yet mastered. The more he thought about it the more confidence replaced anxiety. His mind turned to focus on the three times he'd been capable of more than he expected. His visions began to meld together; a canvas desperate to share its secrets. The door was only slightly ajar, prohibiting his gift from fully surfacing… but… he could begin… in the most marginal of ways… to see something more than the sum of its parts… as if each view of the alternative timeline allowed him to see further than the scope of his individual visions.

Johnny felt an odd sense of déjà vu as he once again made his way into the camp. This time he seemed to have more of a plan… and although he was once again accompanied by a somewhat friendly Montar, he couldn't help but wonder if Ruby and Chester were faring as well…

BARRED FROM SUCCESS

Ruby and Chester had not been as fortunate as Johnny. Having cleaned Ruby of the weapons she had so intelligently decided to take on this mission, Ramziel and three of his trusted Colts were escorting the pair through the camp. Cabin after cabin passed by… a maze of the utmost complexity. Ruby had taken the opportunity to joke about this with Chester; speculating the camp itself was a test. Their captors hadn't taken kindly to their home being ridiculed… but then again they weren't really interested in hearing anything from their prisoners.

With umpteen identical cabins in their wake, Ruby decided to try and be heard once more. "You guys sure you know where you're heading? Seems like we're going in circles."

Ramziel halted where he stood and turned back towards Ruby. "I've heard you're quite the mercenary… I didn't believe it could be true… you're just a Zimplaxion after all… you're not even meeting the low expectations I had for you. Stop wasting my time and walk on."

Ruby had caught his attention and that was all she needed at this point. "Fair enough… just surprised you hadn't noticed we already passed the Generals' Cabin."

Ruby could see her plan was working; Ramziel's patience was being tested. She shot a look over to Chester who reciprocated with a telling glance. It seemed The Colts' egos were leading their untrained minds. On paper Ruby was far from a match for them; unfit to provide any sort of a challenge.

Ramziel took a step closer to Ruby. "You keep speaking to me like that; you won't make it to their cabin. There's still a long way to go before we reach the middle of the camp and it would be far simpler just to finish you here." He looked over to Chester. "We have him… I'm sure he'll be more than enough."

Ruby shared the briefest of smiles with Chester. She'd identified where they were headed but she still needed to know what The Colts were trying to accomplish.

"You're only going to kill us anyway," Ruby added. "Why wait?"
Ramziel's frustration was rising further. He stopped more abruptly this time. "We weren't going to kill you, but I'm very quickly changing my mind! The Generals may very well want that… but I'll leave that up to them. Delivering you should ensure we're fast tracked to be Generals… fortunately for you I'm more interested in that, than in killing you myself."

Ruby and Chester's eyes met once more. Chester knew what Ruby was planning; his Intuition, unlike The Colts', saw to that. He'd seen Ruby personally confront Rapture and Johnny had been more than vocal about her legends; she was capable of more than her relatively diminutive size suggested. Chester's lifestyle may have resulted in a lack of sharpness but he'd benefitted greatly in other ways… a Montar's Intuition is only as good as their perceptions. Chester had taken the time to understand and appreciate races from all over The Wholeverse. It would be a lie to say he'd hit it off with everyone but merely by interacting with them, he'd observed that strength can be found in all manner of places, faces and guises… when he looked at Ruby he saw vast potential. Accordingly his Intuition wasn't compromised by hollow assumptions… The Colts members were not so open-minded. When they looked at Ruby they just saw a weak Zimplaxion; no match for their skills and training… these prejudices stifled their Intuition in a way neither The Colts members, or the Elders, had been humble enough to appreciate.

"Oh… now I see, filly," Ruby began, seizing her opportunity. "You haven't got the guts to lead… you'd prefer to be told what to do. No wonder you need to travel in a pack!"

Ruby's scheme was working just as she intended. Ramziel's rage overpowered his already clouded Intuition. He saw red and lashed out; his right hoof locked into place and swung towards her head. Ruby ducked and flowed into a roll; opening the distance between them. Ramziel didn't even have time to bark orders before Ruby struck his right knee from behind; dropping him instantly to the floor.

Chester meanwhile had been ready to strike. The four Montars around him were stunned by witnessing a Zimplaxion outsmart their leader. Chester took advantage, shoulder barging the two on his left in quick succession. The remaining two raced over. Chester's advanced training and unconstrained Intuition literally kicked in, anticipating their move he fell forward, meeting the ground with his front hooves and kicking out with his back; knocking them down.

With Ramziel on the ground, Ruby dug her knee into his neck; quickly grabbing her weapons back before he could regain control.

Chester looked over to Ruby and motioned as if to offer his assistance.

Ruby smirked in response."Don't worry… I've got this!" She said, waving her Foeradicator™[146] for emphasis.

---

[146] The Foeradicator™, depending on your perspective, is either a terrifically efficient killing machine, or a horrific implement of death. Either way, Ruby had

Chester struggled to contain a laugh. He was surprised at her eagerness to handle this arrogant Montar by herself. I hope you've come to understand our heroine by now though. You don't live under Jarko's rule for ten Cycles without learning how to defend yourself… which should serve as a great lesson to all of us… it is those we underestimate that can teach us the most!

Ruby pointed her weapon towards Ramziel, leaving him with a taste of her own brand of education. "Next time, take a Moment to think before you act… you might learn something. Here's a perfect example… I'm not going to kill you, I'm just going to knock you out… you're welcome!"

Five blasts followed from Ruby's Foeradicator™; the Montars collapsing to the ground one after the other. The weapon wasn't intended for such a powerful enemy though. She knew they'd be awake and angry in no time.

She looked over to Chester. "Come on then… let's get out of here!"

Chester was still in awe of the scene he'd just witnessed. "OK, OK! I'm not going to argue with you!"

There was no time for celebration as they zigzagged through cabin after cabin. The enormity of the camp finally had a virtue… if they could distance themselves enough, the maze of cabins should hide them from Ramziel and company. Maintaining their pace, it wasn't long until they met their next obstacle.

---

the weapon to thank for her survival many times over the Cycles. In honesty she'd only ever used the setting to temporarily knockout her opponents. One of the reasons she'd grown so legendary was her ability to maintain complete control; rarely needing to resort to the use of her weapon. I almost forgot… Ruby had elected to go with the chrome version. As a limited time offer it came complete with an ever useful leather hip holster!

Chester reached across, bringing Ruby to a complete stop. "Wait!" he whispered.

Before them a group of Montars stood between two cabins. From his estimation there was about twelve of them. They were whispering amongst each other but their body language seemed more excited than their volume suggested.

"What's the plan now?" Ruby queried. "There's too many for us to take on."

Chester went to speak but stopped sharp as he saw one of the group turn and point them out. "...fancy talking us out of this as well?"

As the group approached, one of them called across the night, "Chester? Ruby?"

"Great" Chester said as he looked towards Ruby. "So now we're celebrities… and to think of all those TV offers I turned down[147]," he added to accentuate his point.

Little did our pessimistic friend realize this group was just as surprised but nonetheless happy to see them both. Running from behind the collection of Montars was Johnny. Upon seeing them he made a dash for Ruby and embraced her tightly.

"Sorry man… didn't mean to leave you out!" Johnny said, looking towards Chester. He jokingly went to hug Chester who brushed him off in response. "I'd offer for Ruby to give you a hug…"

Chester cut him off, not impressed with his sense of humor. "Not the time Johnny" he exclaimed swiftly.

As the rest of the group caught up, Chester and Ruby had a multitude of questions. They could see the Montars meant them no

---

[147] Chester has indeed received multiple offers to appear on "Barred from Success'. The premise of the show is simple. Every episode an industry expert attempts to turn around a failing bar. I'm sure you'll remember Chester wanted to avoid the limelight but in this case he quite simply didn't like the idea of someone telling him what to do!

harm but couldn't fathom how Johnny had managed it[148]. Their reaction wasn't a surprise to Johnny who was in fact quite looking forward to it. He'd impressed himself and was eager to share his contribution to the mission.

"Looks like you two could do with some help," Johnny said in an inappropriately obnoxious tone.

"We're impressed but let's not get carried away," Chester responded, aware of Johnny's propensity for exaggeration. "What happened?"

Johnny looked over to Amy. "Amy heard what you were saying to the group… she wanted to find out if there was anything to your story, so she came looking for me. We chatted and I guess my charm did the rest!"

Chester's look of disbelief was matched by Amy's, who was moved to add her side of the story.

"Your friend is lucky there's more to him than his mouth… whatever it is he can do, it's far more powerful than his words, that's for sure," she began. "I've seen what you're capable of… he showed me the true nature of the Elders. He showed all of us." She looked around as if to ask for agreement from the group and received a round of affirming nods. "You have our support… but you'll need more if you are to succeed."

Chester was shocked to hear this. Believing enough to attempt to free the planet was one thing… he was hoping this mission would be successful but seeing some level of progress made it feel like perhaps it actually was possible.

"She's right" Johnny said, his playful tone making way for a level of seriousness. "…we don't have time for me to go around showing everyone! Plus, it wasn't enough to convince every Montar we spoke

---

[148] Let's not dwell on this supreme lack of faith from both his best friend and his partner!

to[149]… we don't have time… there's thousands of Montars here!"

Ruby was equally puzzled by Johnny's sudden expertise. "I don't get it. When you were taken you had zero control over your 'power' and now suddenly you have disciples? I hope we didn't interrupt your sermon, Oh Holy one!"

Johnny was used to Ruby's humor and didn't mind the half question half statement… he was still coming to terms with it himself. "In honesty it was more luck than logic with Amy. She stayed long enough that it just kind of happened… each time it seems to get easier though. I think I'm getting a hold of it… sort of."

Amy had been listening and felt the need to speak up. "Whatever you do, you'll need to do it quickly. The Generals have called everyone to their cabin. As soon as all the soldiers are gathered, The Generals will order them to hunt you down. If that happens you won't stand a chance of convincing anyone."

"That serves us well then," Chester said with authority, to everyone's surprise. "If we're going to succeed then I'll need to have everyone's attention anyway. It sounds like The Colts have done the hard work for us."

In this Moment Chester was very sure of himself. He decided the task at hand seemed so impossible there was no reason not to be confident. If he was to fail why not fail with style?

Johnny turned to look at Chester. "If that's the plan then I think it's worth mentioning something else I saw. I keep seeing more each time I… do what I do. It took you a long time to get through to everyone before… but there was one thing that seemed to force everyone to stop and pay attention."

---

[149] There were two Montars who failed to see the benefit of an uprising. They were apparently more than happy with someone else making their crucial life decisions and were looking forward to stress-free retirements. Luckily for Johnny, the group numbered enough to knock these two out before they could cause any trouble.

...and so Johnny shared a memory he'd seen from the alternative timeline... the first link from the canvas that was developing in his mind... but it was far from a secret weapon... and whether the small group they had accumulated would be enough to persuade the rest of the Montars remained to be seen...

A CACOPHONY OF SIMULTANEOUS AND CONSECUTIVELY ASCENDING THUDS

Sure enough, the entire camp had collected outside the Generals' cabin. The light from the rising morning sun focused on the nearly six thousand Montars who were eagerly awaiting the reason for this impromptu gathering. A small stage strutted out from the front of the cabin, barely big enough for the twenty Generals to stand on. It was rare to gather all of the troops together; restricted mostly to Graduations and trivia sessions… which were usually limited to individual squadrons… thus avoiding the imminent warfare that commences when a thousand or so soldiers tie for first place!

The Master General stepped to the front of the stage and began speaking into the microphone.

"Soldiers! It took you entirely too much time to arrive! Tomorrow morning you will all rise a Period early and will run through the Serpent Waterfalls and back. Those who survive will be allowed back into camp."

The crowd of soldiers was less than impressed by these opening lines but knew better than to argue.

With Ramziel's news that Chester and Ruby had not only arrived but were now on the loose, Tramano knew he needed to address the camp. If his troops could find and return them before they caused any further disruption, then perhaps he could still keep this incident quiet. If not, the Elders would undoubtedly become aware of the situation and that would put Erica's safety at risk.

"Right now we have a bigger issue. We have an extremely dangerous Montar on the loose in our camp. The outside world has warped his mind. He presents a danger not only to himself but to everyone here. So twisted is his mind he depends on a pair of Zimplaxions for assistance. Your orders are to hunt them down and…"

Tramano was interrupted by a growing noise in the distance. He shaded his eyes, trying to find the source. A reckless soldier no doubt, looking to score points with his peers. Searching the crowd he couldn't see any guilty parties but the sound was rapidly growing louder.

"Whoever is responsible for that commotion I suggest you stop immediately… unless you want to be stuck on cleanup duty for the next ten Passings!"

The crowd looked around, not finding anyone to silence. As the distant roar continued to escalate the General began to see a cloud of dust rising in the distance. Relatively small at first, the dust expanded out higher and wider. The soldiers all turned to look.

The sound was now fuller and deeper. Instead of anonymous monotony it had gained clarity. A cacophony of simultaneous and consecutively ascending thuds deafened all extraneous sounds. The soldiers scanned each other's faces; looking for any clues as to the nature of this oncoming beast… none were to be found; only confusion was visible.

"Stay calm" he ordered over the microphone.

The cloud continued ever closer. The plume of dust hid the secrets that lay beneath. The Master General looked to his peers and was met only with shrugs. There was no point in sharing any further commands with the soldiers; his voice would be lost behind the almost deafening sounds heading directly for their position.

The General looked on as the monstrous dust approached the edge of the crowd. Its origin was still foreign to him but he could see soldiers jumping out of the way to clear a path; a deep cut widening in the crowd of soldiers before him. Closer and closer it came until finally it was close enough to see the oncoming threat. All twenty Generals gasped in succession, their eyes not believing the sight before them. With only half the crowd standing in the way the Generals could see a team of Montars stampeding towards them.

It was a sight that hadn't been observed for thousands of Cycles and never by any living Montar. A Montar galloping alone was a cue for embarrassment; this team thundering towards them however was enough to strike fear into each of the long serving Generals' hearts. I don't mind telling you it was a truly awesome and intimidating sight. It was as if the horizon itself had begun collapsing inwards; thirteen Montars forcing their way through the crowd… literally smashing the earth below so as to compel themselves onwards. The earth shaking with every hoof strike; the Montars sheer brute strength exemplified by the crescendo of deafening booms.

As the team of Montars came to a sudden halt on the stage, rearing up and sounding a memorable cry; the Generals jumped and fell hurriedly, desperately scrambling from the stage. The crowd, both soldiers and Generals alike were stunned; the shock of seeing their kin act in such a primitive way scaring away any reaction greater than resignation. The sudden silence was almost louder than the crescendo that preceded it.

The team of thirteen Montars stared out towards the crowd, Chester taking his place at its peak. Encouraging his new followers to break tradition and gallop together had electrified his senses. He was almost excited to address the crowd, any nervousness shattered by the emotion of the stampede. His fellow Montars gathered around him; setting up a defensive barrier and providing protection from any Generals that might seek to force back control.

The crowd before him was still silent, staring in awe as he began.

"...hello…" he began, the significance of the speech he was about to deliver, as yet still unwritten in his mind, started to sink in. "I'm not used to speaking to large crowds, so please, bear with me. This isn't really anything close to what I usually do. I own and run a Pub." Finding his way, he began to feel at ease. "I don't fight in wars or track criminals. I don't provide protection or fight for other's principles. I don't do any of these because I wanted to follow my own path… when I began speaking, you were all silent and I think I know why. You saw your brothers and sisters gallop in unison and feared the Elder's judgment."

Chester's selfish nature had all but disappeared. The mighty Montar stood before the thousands of soldiers had no fear, only belief in his convictions.

"I am not unlike you. I galloped only when I could be sure I was alone… but why? We should embrace our primitive instincts. I was once trained at this very camp. Taught we should fear no one, we have no equals and we shouldn't shy away from any challenge. So why do we fear being seen for who we are? Why are we being taught to hide our true selves from the world?"

The Generals behind the stage had started to regain their composure and were whispering amongst themselves. Amy attempted to warn Chester, but he was lost to the crowd.

"The Elders, our leaders who we have followed blindly for so many Cycles, have deceived and oppressed us. They tell us to master our gifts for the good of our race… but who really benefits from this? Who benefits from the sacrifices we make? The Elders profit from our service but what do we get in return? The last Cycles of our lives free to relax during our retirements? What if we want to forfeit our retirement to instead spend our lives making choices of our own? I've recently seen the result of independence and I'm fortunate to be alive and stood here before you all."

Chester's words were causing commotion; the crowd's dichotomous nature clear for all to see. While some were eager to absorb every word, others were outraged by the intrusion. The Generals standing behind the stage were very much part of the latter group. Tramano could see that the crowd was about to boil over. He'd been curious to see if Chester's words could really make a difference… the twelve Montars by his side had provided enough doubt that Tramano wondered if this courageous Montar actually stood a chance… but with the majority of the crowd voicing their dissent he couldn't let this go on. The fantasy of an exotic retirement with Erica faded away as he commanded his Generals to charge the stage; their numbers and experience overpowering Chester's guards. Amy was doing her best to defend Chester's position but was barreled over, narrowly missing him as she fell to the ground.

"WAIT!" Chester screamed at the top of his voice, trying his best to buy some extra time.

The Generals stopped their attack and stared furiously at Chester, daring him to speak again.

Chester looked off into the distance, hoping to find what he was looking for. His focus raced in and out and then he finally saw it. Just over the horizon, speeding into view was The Peculiar. A wonderful smile lit up Chester's face as he turned back to the microphone.

"Generals… if you'd kindly all look to the horizon I believe you'll find yourselves all too eager to leave the stage and sit quietly while I finish."

The Generals turned to face the horizon. Sure enough The Peculiar was screaming towards them. It quickly passed the crowd and came to a stop, hovering above the stage… close enough that Ruby, Johnny and Heethal could be seen inside. They shared Chester's smile and were pointing towards something below them. Each of the twenty Generals followed the hand signals down, their focus landing on the three large laser-barrels pointed directly at them.

Tramano realized they had reached an impasse and instructed his Generals to retreat. It seemed fate wanted to give Chester one more chance. Tramano had no choice for now. Needing to bide his time he might as well see if this Montar could achieve the implausible. Amy corralled the submissive Generals into a line against their cabin; The Peculiar's heavy artillery forcing their compliance.

The crowd had grown silent through the commotion but Chester had seen friction growing, he needed to make progress and quickly.

"OK… here goes," he started up once again. "I'm not a leader. I'm not here to ask you to follow me. Long ago I chose to find a path away from the one the Elders force upon us. It took me Cycles to finally find what I was looking for but I did. Just because it was difficult doesn't mean it wasn't worthwhile. Although I almost had to give my life, I recently realized how selfish I've been. While I had the opportunity to choose my own destiny I never stopped to realize I was the only one. Now that I've seen the true nature of our Elders; I can't remain quiet. I need your help so we can all be free from their tyranny."

Unrest was growing in the crowd. Two sides had clearly emerged and Chester was heartened to see at least some of the soldiers were listening to his message.

"I'm not standing before you today to command you to leave. I'm standing before you to let you know you have the option. Individually we stand no chance of freeing ourselves from the Elders control… but together we can forge a new path. Those who wish to stay, that is your right. By staying you're making the choice yourself… not because of me and not because of the Elders."

The crowd before him started jeering and cheering in almost equal measures. He needed to find a way to get through to more of them.

"By seeking my own path I have learned to appreciate others; their strengths and weaknesses, their emotions, their desires, their quirks and their curiosities. This has made me complete in a way I couldn't have previously understood. My Zimplaxion friend came here with me today to share the truth behind this planet. One of your best soldiers, Ramziel, was easily overpowered by failing to respect her potential."

The jeers fell quiet for a second upon the mention of Ramziel's name.

"Your abilities, your Intuition… they are meant for more than just war. We're taught through the training on this planet we'll be unstoppable, we'll be the mightiest warriors in existence… yet for all the Generals training, their brightest soldier was easily beaten by a Zimplaxion, a race we're taught to pity. Maybe it was a great lie, or maybe The Council is just too blind to see the truth. Whichever it is, I've seen the potential of our Intuition beyond the field of war… it's worth precious little without an appreciation for the world around you. Born into this captivity our minds are sheltered from the diversity that surrounds us… scripted preconceptions are force-fed to our subconscious minds… the Elders sculpting us in the image that best suits their needs. Our Intuition is not the perfectly polished weapon the Elders advertise… our prejudices limit our potential! If Ramziel had seen more than just a Zimplaxion, he wouldn't have underestimated Ruby's skill… his untainted Intuition would have been free to anticipate her actions. The First passed on a gift to each one of us. It's time to respect that gift. Before the Elders decided our lives were just a currency for them to trade, our possibilities were endless. You can excel anywhere you wish… whether you dream of being an artist, a teacher, a mathematician or an athlete… that choice should be yours to make! The Council has stunted our evolution… it's time to take back our future! In freedom we can thrive and finally allow our children to inherit more than just a predilection for violence. Don't be fooled into believing this planet or this Council of Elders know what's best for you. Only you alone know that. You are worth more than the price the Elders place upon your head. You deserve more and you can be much more than the restraints that shackle your potential."

While Chester had been speaking, the cheers from the crowd had overcome the jeers. Tramano had been listening intently; his emotions beginning to overpower his loyalty to The Council. Chester's progress had inspired his previously foolish fantasy to once again fill this Old Montar's mind. Tramano knew Erica didn't want the responsibility of Chester's death on her hands… neither did she want to continue working under the Elder's rule… not if there really was an alternative. Choosing to speak up now would risk both their lives… but this was a Moment that would never come again. He locked his hooves and braced as he stepped forward from the line.

Amy had been keeping an eye on the Generals and tried to usher Tramano back as she pointed up towards The Peculiar. Tramano refused to budge.

"Chester," Amy shouted, looking towards the stage. "The Master General has something to say."

The mention of the Master General caught Chester's attention. Maybe a sign of strength against the soldiers' commander would gain their respect. Chester signaled for Amy to allow Tramano up on stage.

Approaching Chester, he stopped and whispered something in his ear. Chester looked shocked but not as much as Amy as he stepped aside to let Tramano address the crowd.

"Soldiers… I'm going to give you a gift. Today you may make a decision for yourself. This is not a test. Your choice can be made free from any threat of repercussions under my command of the camp. This Montar has my support. If you wish to follow his example you must do so now. This is an opportunity like no other, the only one of its kind."

The look of shock on the faces of thousands of Montars before him was surreal. Their Master General had just given them the OK to revolt! Upon hearing his words the crowd began filtering itself; those who jeered doing no more than highlighting their dissenting opinion. Slowly they were forced to one side, towards the front and then finally taking their place alongside the fallen Generals. Tramano took a step back. Regaining the attention of the crowd, Chester could see his work was nearly done.

"Choosing to speak to you all today, I merely hoped I could start a chain of events. I want you all to have the freedom that I failed to fully appreciate for so long. I knew I couldn't change our fate alone. Your Master General, Tramano, just risked his own life to ensure you could all enjoy this choice. None of us can be sure how the Elders will react, but know this. They do not own you. They do not own our race or our future. Together we choose our own paths! Whatever you do, wherever your choices take you, be free, always be free!"

Chester looked around at the crowd still cheering before him. It was more than he expected and perhaps more than he knew how to handle.

THE BUDDY SYSTEM, FROM SUNRISE TO SUNSET

The Moments that followed his grand speech were quite a blur for Chester. You have to give it up to him, it really was quite moving. He spent a long time afterwards speaking to one Montar after the other; each with their own perspective to share. Many were scared by the uncertainty that now stood before them but all were grateful to have the opportunity to paint their own canvas.

Of course, there were many soldiers that remained with their Generals. Holding far inferior numbers they were careful not to object as their kin departed the planet. They'd heard Chester's speech but it may as well have been the ravings of a madman. They were soldiers through and through. The Elders remained their saviors; learned leaders who wanted only the best for them… training them to reach their potential and providing for them long after their service was complete.

The Council of Elders received a massive hit that Passing but their existence had survived knocks before… they had dictated the destiny of their race for hundreds of Cycles after all… and as you already know… this just marked the very beginning of the infamous War of the Montars…

As The Peculiar departed the MTP, Chester finally had a Moment to dwell upon the loss of his home. The Carpenter's Moons was no longer, literally a shell of its former self. Ruby's offer hadn't just been a method to cheer Chester up though. Sure, it aided in lessening her guilt, but it was more than that. She'd been without a home for many Cycles since leaving her parents. She was grateful her life was finally on track but there was something missing… a place to call home. Ruby was happy with the union of her old and new life. She loved the thrill only a mission could provide and equally loved the man she had fallen for… The Carpenter's Moons seemed to be the perfect next step.

Chester was fast to turn down her offer but that didn't stop Ruby. It wasn't long before the two agreed terms. Ruby became a full partner of the new Carpenter's Moons, obtaining a 45% ownership stake. Johnny meanwhile received an upgrade to his stake as a thank you for his assistance. His stake was doubled to a whole 5%! When Johnny queried the fairness of such a small number Chester was quick to refer him to his complete lack of financial contribution. His relationship with the other stakeholder was furthermore cited as a reason not to increase the number any higher… it seems Chester wasn't convinced he wouldn't be evicted as soon as the two decided it was time for kids!

The rebuild took almost a Quarter-Cycle. During this time Chester enjoyed the charming atmosphere of The Hungry Kartill. There was a strange comfort to be found in living at a hotel above a bar. The experience served Chester very well. His name had already gained notoriety around The Wholeverse for his actions on the MTP. Patrons of the Kartill would regularly join him for a drink and ask to hear his story. Chester became a central figure in the town and got to know many who would become regulars at 'The New Moons'[150].

If Ruby was to be part owner of a Pub she wanted to make sure it was a successful one. With the fame she'd earned and the legend Chester had created for himself, she was certain the Pub would attract attention. Chester was adamant the interior should be rebuilt just as it used to be. Ruby had a fondness for its original incarnation; it was the site of her first date with Johnny after all, so she didn't mind accepting his condition. She wanted to add a touch of her own style as well though. After racking her brain for a while she figured out just the way to make her mark without breaking Chester's rule.

As they approached the finished Carpenter's Moons for the first time, Ruby made sure Chester and Johnny had their eyes closed. She hoped her addition would be attention grabbing.

"OK. Stop here" she said, stretching her arms in front of the pair. "You can open them now."

Opening his eyes, Chester was drawn instantly to Ruby's 'flair'. Strutting out from the front of the building, a wooden beam held a brand new sign in place. Two chains descended from the beam allowing the sign to swing back and forth. Fashioned from a small but rare meteorite, Ruby had fallen in love with the idea of melding the small town feel of a Pub with the wonder of space travel. Emblazoned upon the fragment, etched in the most respectful of lettering, was the name of their new home and business, 'The Carpenter's Moons'.

Over the course of another Quarter-Cycle the three became accustomed to their joint living space. Johnny wasn't overly sure about sharing with his Mrs. and his best friend. He had nothing against Chester but there's some things a couple of Zimplaxions like to do that require a certain level of privacy. While Ruby didn't argue against this quite valid point, she did have a keen interest in her first joint business venture being successful. She respected Chester… a lot… but she'd seen him get

---

[150] Finally a nickname Chester actually liked. He would even occasionally use it himself!

drunk with Johnny far too many times. The thought of The New Moons regressing back to welcoming its former clientele presented too much of a risk for her to live elsewhere… especially when the Pub had started attracting patrons from all over The Wholeverse and was earning a tidy sum for all three. Even Johnny was seeing a nice level of income from his 5%! In fairness that wasn't the only reason Ruby didn't want to leave… she'd also invested heavily in renovations to the upstairs living area and had decorated the space exactly how she wanted it… I'm reliably informed a 'pot filler' is something to envy…

Living under the same roof as your best friend and partner wasn't all bad though. Ruby had insisted on continuing her regular job; accepting a multitude of missions near and far. Her role in freeing the MTP had done wonders for her original enterprise; demand for her services never slowing down. Quite often she would be far from home and although Johnny wouldn't admit it to Chester, he had a certain propensity for pining… having his friend around for company wasn't the worst thing in the world… and in honesty Chester had no complaints either.

With The Carpenter's Moons profiting from the attraction of its famous owners, our three protagonists were enjoying a refreshing new sense of peace and quiet. Many a night passed with a thrilling game of Farmer, Scientist, Smuggler. It's worth mentioning their inaugural Siesta-Soiree was a categorical hit! Ultimately a hideous idea, its inception was created with the best of intentions. Great fun would be had by all during an all-Passing party. Starting at Sunrise the Pub opened with drink specials that alternated by the Period. Buffet snacks were included with the entrance fee and games ran throughout the Passing, offering prizes that ran from the bizarre to the outrageous[151]… the 'Siesta' part was listed for legal reasons as well as the noble ideal that patrons would

---

[151] You want an example I see! OK, given you've been patiently reading… one winner was given the opportunity to bathe in what had become known as 'The Lake of Life'. Chester never felt it appropriate to correct people on their false assumption that it was the lake rather than his Montar genetics that healed him… especially as it attracted so many extra visitors to the Pub!

benefit from a well deserved nap if they were still actively participating at Sunset… unfortunately the reality was slightly different… those who desperately needed a break were either too drunk to want to slow down… or too drunk to wake up! The first anniversary of the event saw the implementation of the buddy system… upon entry each participant was assigned a 'buddy'… one member of each pair was obligated to undergo a lucidity test each Period. Failure to pass wouldn't lead to expulsion… but would ensure the Pub owners were released from any obligation to provide a duty of care.

There is one collection of Moments I feel moved to mention. On a night much like many that passed before it, Johnny and Chester were sat at the bar, deep into their fifth Homebrew. As Johnny got up to take a well deserved restroom break, he noticed a Zimplaxion in the corner of the crowded Pub that for some unknown reason caught his attention. He paused before feeling compelled to go over. As he walked past the tables of regulars laughing amongst themselves, he felt a strange sensation run across his face and down through his chest. His mind attempted to remember who this man was… he was sure the realization was within reach but the harder he fought, the farther away it seemed.

The Zimplaxion was sat at a small table with his back facing the wall. Approaching the table Johnny could see he was reading a book, he couldn't quite decipher what the picture was on the front but the title was clear enough, 'Space, Time & Other Fallacies'.

He came to a stop just before the table. That image, that feeling, just out of reach, suddenly sprang to the front of Johnny's mind. He didn't know how… but he could feel it… this man was his father. The ramifications of this revelation were more than he could absorb. He'd never had reason to question if Tom was anyone other than his real father. He wasn't ready to give voice to his thoughts but maybe this man could provide answers.

Johnny's presence had drawn the stranger's attention; seemingly startled, he quickly sat up straight.

A word escaped The Zimplaxion's lips before he could stop himself. "James…"

Johnny was suddenly even more confused. His face made it obvious.

Jerome immediately realized his mistake and composed himself. "Forgive me… my name is James. Would you like to join me?"

Johnny accepted his offer, as much from intrigue as desire. A million questions ran through his mind. He wasn't sure which to ask first. His instinct begged for acknowledgement of his realization… but he knew he wasn't ready for confirmation. He played it safe. "Do you know me?"

Johnny couldn't quite make out Jerome's reaction. It almost looked like guilt, maybe remorse.

Jerome tried to remember the reason he'd sought Johnny out. Seeing his son after all this time had thrown him off course. He wanted to tell him the truth but he knew the Master's logic had been sound. "Yes, Johnny, I've heard the stories."

Johnny could tell there was a longer answer to be heard. He braved a further question. "Are you here for me?"

Jerome could see the pain in his son's eyes; a lifetime of hurt he was desperate to find a way to make up for… but he'd summoned the courage to have this conversation for a reason and lessening his guilt was not it. "Yes I am. In honesty there is a lot I'd like to ask you… but I came to see you for a very specific reason."

As Jerome continued, the words resonated in Johnny's mind and he remembered why that name had felt so familiar. Was this the same Zimplaxion that appeared to Chester and Ruby? Before he could ask, he received his answer.

"Your recent actions at the MTP… you healed a fracture… but for every repair… there are consequences."

The answer spoke to Johnny. A blank envelope he knew was meant for him. His mind raced; his visions bursting into view. "The visions I have, that I can share…"

Jerome responded with a look of acknowledgment. "I would be lying if I said I had all of the answers for you… but it is fair to say I am aware of your visions. Since the events on the MTP… there is something I've discovered… something I have no choice but to tell you about… and I believe it affects you and I both… in ways I cannot begin to fathom."

Johnny's patience was growing thin. It was clear this man, who he somehow knew was his father, wasn't sharing everything. He wanted answers but a larger question needed to be answered first.

"Discovered… what do you mean… what have you discovered?"
Jerome took a deep breath. "You are not the only one who experiences visions… I have them too… they've helped me understand an answer to a question I didn't even know existed…"
"What are you trying to say?" Johnny said sternly, growing impatient for an answer.

"…your Mother, Johnny… it's about your Mother…"

EPILOGUE

So… how was it? I hope you enjoyed your first foray into The Wholeverse.

I'm sure you have many questions… as do I! In all my travels I have always marveled at the majesty of The Wholeverse but I must admit it is rather perplexing… but don't worry, I promise we've just begun our journey together… many more Tales are waiting.

Alas, I fear our time is nearly up… but bear with me… I do believe I can evade The Masters of The 2nd Floor for just a few Moments more… just enough to allow me to whet your appetites before next we meet.

Ruby's Necklace! Having been released from its power, Ruby wore it every Passing. Not only did she find it really did go with everything but it was also a wonderful reminder that Rapture was still out there.

…and given we've mentioned Rapture, I'm sure you're curious as to what became of him. It would most certainly be unfair of me to try and shorten his story to just a couple of sentences… I will however confirm that his tale really was just beginning!

What about Heethal!? You'll be delighted to hear he really did go on to live his dream. He wasn't signed to a glamorous recording label. Neither did he record a best-selling album. He did however land a job as a lounge singer at The Falls of Tranjuri! Which my friends, is not something to turn your nose up at! Having said that, Heethal does have to put up with being hunted in the hotel's grounds every now and then… but it is worth it to live his dream!

…oh come on. Did you really think I wouldn't realize you wanted to hear more about the Elders? I simply don't want to ruin it for you… I'll give you just a little more… I've mentioned the fall of the MTP was the inciting incident of the Great War of the Montars. Merely losing control of their Training Planet wouldn't be enough to dethrone their rule. The Montar Home World still housed a whole generation of Montars… having retired they wanted to take advantage of their Cycles away from service… and they were reproducing like crazy! With a whole new generation to mould in their image, The Council of Elders would soon be ready to begin a brand new era of control…

There is one part of our Tale however I think would be perfect to wrap up on… a loose end which we haven't quite tied yet… Erica and Tramano! When we last left him, Tramano had helped inspire the uprising on the MTP. He'd risked his life but was grateful it hadn't been in vain. Having witnessed a whole generation of soldiers receive an opportunity he'd never dreamt was possible, a grave realization swiftly brought him crashing back down… Erica! This revolt would distract the Elders but if he didn't get to her quickly it would be too late. She would surely be the first casualty of the uprising.

Arriving at the MHW, Tramano could see word of the uprising had raced quicker than he. Crowds were forming around The Shrine; excitement and speculation abundantly clear.

Erica should still be in her office at The Council's Sanctum. He could only hope the panic that was certain to be absorbing the Elders was enough to shift the focus away from her.

The usual guards standing in front of the Sanctum were nowhere to be seen. Maybe he still had a chance. Making his way past the gigantic Elder monuments he entered the building unnoticed. He knew he needed to act with the utmost stealth. As soon as The Council regained their composure they would undoubtedly realize he'd been part of the revolt.

Making his way down the hallway his luck was so far holding up. Any Montars he passed were wrapped up in the commotion; most likely fearing for their futures. Not much further and he'd make it to her office. He did his best to control his emotions. The potential of escaping with Erica was slowly creeping into his mind. It was too early in the mission though… he couldn't let his judgment become clouded.

The door to Erica's office was closed. He stopped and checked his surroundings. There was no one around. Now was his opportunity.

Opening the door, his future suddenly seemed brighter. Erica was there, sat behind her desk. Walking in, he began to see the fuller, less optimistic picture. Sensing the danger he closed the door behind him. That at least, would contain the issue.

In a corner of the room he could see the Master Elder. It was clear Tramano had broken something up. The Master Elder looked furious.

"Tramano… thank you for joining us. The Master Elder was just telling me how I was to blame for the soldiers uprising. Isn't that pleasant?" Erica said.

The Master Elder was seething. "I'm surprised to see you here Master General. I would have assumed you'd be hiding by now. You must know your part in this tragedy has been brought to our attention!"

Tramano couldn't quite read the situation. "I know what I've walked into… don't you worry. I couldn't leave without Erica though."

Erica looked stunned by this admission. Stunned but at the same time happy to hear her feelings were reciprocated. "Well I'm not gonna say no to that." She rose from her seat and started to walk towards Tramano, making it halfway across the room before the Master Elder spoke.

"Where do you think you're going? This is your fault! You will be standing trial for this treason!" The Master Elder screamed.

Tramano went to intervene but it was too late. Erica had already calmly walked over to the Master Elder.

While Tramano was confused, Erica knew exactly what she was doing. She'd worked with the Master Elder for many Cycles. She knew what made him tick. His threats came thick and fast but there was little power behind his words.

"Master Elder… Tramano and I will now be leaving. You have no choice in the matter. While we've both spent a lifetime mastering our Intuition, you've become lazy… accustomed to giving orders and never needing to act for yourself," she said, her words fueled by Cycles of pent-up fury.

The Elder maintained his stance and did his best to smirk. "Don't make me laugh Erica. You"

Erica cut him off before he could finish. Locking her right hoof into place, she pushed it into his chest; forcing him back against the wall. "No!" She growled. "You've underestimated me one too many times. Enjoy the ruins of your empire… good luck trying to get anything done without my help!"

With that she pulled away from the Elder and walked over to Tramano; linking her arm in his. "I believe you mentioned a vacation my dear."

www.ingramcontent.com/pod-product-compliance
Lightning Source LLC
Chambersburg PA
CBHW021009120726
47905CB00009B/2929